REVELATIONS IN BLACK

From acknowledged masters of the macabre, here are eighteen horror stories—in paperback for the first time—which bring a fellowship of fear, and a legacy of terror from the grave.

RAY BRADBURY's *At Midnight, in the Month of June*—The haunting, poetic story of a death, and a discovery, in a quiet midwestern village.

THOMAS M. DISCH's *Minnesota Gothic*—A childhood fairytale, told with relentless horror in a most shocking and sinister new context.

GAHAN WILSON's *Yesterday's Witch*—The bizarre tale of a band of prank-minded trick-or-treaters who discover that Halloween can bring an unexpected touch of sinister magic—even to little old ladies.

WALTER DE LA MARE's *A:B:O*—A shuddering fiction excursion into a prim, proper English back yard which contains a gruesome buried treasure.

H. P. LOVECRAFT's *Innsmouth Clay*—A gem of Lovecraftian horror, reconstructed from the master's notes by August Derleth, which reveals the fate of a sculptor whose creations take on frightening dimensions.

PLUS THIRTEEN MORE . . .
IF YOU DARE!

NIGHT CHILLS

Stories of Suspense and Horror

Edited with Notes by
Kirby McCauley

AVON
PUBLISHERS OF BARD, CAMELOT, DISCUS, EQUINOX AND FLARE BOOKS

AVON BOOKS
A division of
The Hearst Corporation
959 Eighth Avenue
New York, New York 10019

ISBN: 0-380-00397-X

First Avon printing, November, 1975

Printed in the U.S.A.

Contents

INTRODUCTION

This anthology was assembled with various things in mind but one primary: to publish quality stories of fantasy and supernatural horror not previously offered in a widely available book. I have endeavored to track down good stories that, at the time of this writing, have not appeared in a mass paperback edition in this country. I think that's important. The old chestnuts, presented over and over again—how many books has "The Monkey's Paw" appeared in?—become frustrating, by using up space that might make available less well-known works of merit.

Beyond that, simply, one man's taste. Doubtlessly my own preferences in the uncanny tale will be apparent to the discerning reader even more than they are to me. Stories of this kind have a way of sinking in very personally. In looking over the contents, I do note that only one story saw original publication before the First World War. Actually, the Victorian and Edwardian ages were high periods for works in this genre. The great names of the 19th and early 20th centuries are impressive: Poe, Bierce, Le Fanu, M.R. James, Machen, Blackwood, and so on. I tend to think the focus here on the post-1914 period relates to my belief that it too has been a rich one for this kind of story, too often charged off as anachronism. And nothing could be further from the truth: the form will be with us and vital as long as we fear and wonder about that fear.

I am also strong in believing the most satisfying appeal of the terror tale is not sadistic, though unfortunately sadism creeps in too often, especially in films. To be sure, unpleasant and terrible things do happen to people in these stories, but, whatever their fates, I have tried to deal in fright and strangeness rather than in the gruesome. I agree with Robert Aickman that the enduring appeal-effect of the supernatural story is akin to poetry, a poetry of wonder and uncertainty that leaves the reader reassured rather than upset. We read these stories hoping and looking to be scared but with the comforting knowledge that what we fear will not actually claim us permanently. Mr. Aickman writes eloquently on the subject of the ghostly tale in the forewords to his British Fontana anthologies and I urge all interested in exploring the subject further to acquire those books.

But enough said. If your setting and mood is right, as it should be for appreciating stories such as these, read on. I hope you enjoy yourself.

Kirby McCauley
New York City
March 23, 1975

Ray Bradbury has created so many unforgettable stories of science fiction and the supernatural that it is doubtless wise not to make up any kind of best list. Titles come to mind easily: Fahrenheit 451, "Uncle Einar," "Mars Is Heaven!," "The Emissary," "—And The Moon Be Still As Bright," "Homecoming," *and so forth. All remarkable, reading after reading. The most recurring setting in a Bradbury story is a small town in the American Midwest, most probably in the mind's past, richly evoked in moods, impressions and feelings about atmosphere and locale detail. There is a sensuous and haunting poetical magic in a Ray Bradbury story that somehow lights up a signal-response of common experience in nearly all who read him, a gift that has vaulted him into the ranks of the most widely read living authors. Herewith a fine, masterful Bradbury tale, out of print since its initial appearance in* Ellery Queen's Mystery Magazine *in 1954 and appropriately described as a terror-mood story by William F. Nolan, whose recommendation is responsible for its appearance here.*

AT MIDNIGHT, IN THE MONTH OF JUNE

by Ray Bradbury

HE HAD been waiting a long, long time in the summer night, as the darkness pressed warmer to the earth and the stars turned slowly over the sky. He sat in total darkness, his hands lying easily on the arms of the Morris chair. He heard the town clock strike 9 and 10 and 11, and then at last 12. The breeze from an open back window flowed through the midnight house in an unlit stream, that touched him like a dark rock where he sat silently watching the front door—silently watching.

At midnight, in the month of June . . . .

The cool night poem by Mr. Edgar Allan Poe slid over his mind like the waters of a shadowed creek.

> *The lady sleeps! Oh, may her sleep,*
> *Which is enduring, so be deep!*

He moved down the black shapeless halls of the house, stepped out of the back window, feeling the town locked away in bed, in dream, in night. He saw the shining snake of garden hose coiled resiliently in the grass. He turned on the water. Standing alone, watering the flower bed, he imagined himself a conductor leading an orchestra that only night-strolling dogs might hear, passing on their way to nowhere with strange white smiles. Very carefully he planted both feet and his tall weight into the mud beneath the window, making deep, well-outlined prints. He stepped inside again and walked, leaving mud, down the absolutely unseen hall, his hands seeing for him.

Through the front-porch window he made out the faint

2

outline of a lemonade glass, one-third full, sitting on the porch rail where *she* had left it. He trembled quietly.

Now, he could feel her coming home. He could feel her moving across town, far away, in the summer night. He shut his eyes and put his mind out to find her; and felt her moving along in the dark; he knew just where she stepped down from a curb and crossed a street, and up on a curb and tack-tacking, tack-tacking along under the June elms and the last of the lilacs, with a friend. Walking the empty desert of night, he *was* she. He felt a purse in his hands. He felt long hair prickle his neck, and his mouth turn greasy with lipstick. Sitting still, he was walking, walking, walking on home after midnight.

"Good night!"

He heard but did not hear the voices, and she was coming nearer, and now she was only a mile away and now only a matter of a thousand yards, and now she was sinking, like a beautiful white lantern on an invisible wire, down into the cricket and frog and water-sounding ravine. And he knew the texture of the wooden ravine stairs as if, a boy, he was rushing down them, feeling the rough grain and the dust and the leftover heat of the day . . .

He put his hands out on the air, open. The thumbs of his hands touched, and then the fingers, so that his hands made a circle, enclosing emptiness, there before him. Then, very slowly, he squeezed his hands tighter and tighter together, his mouth open, his eyes shut.

He stopped squeezing and put his hands, trembling, back on the arms of the chair. He kept his eyes shut.

Long ago, he had climbed, one night, to the top of the courthouse tower fire-escape, and looked out at the silver town, at the town of the moon, and the town of summer. And he had seen all the dark houses with two things in them, people and sleep, the two elements joined in bed and all their tiredness and terror breathed upon the still air, siphoned back quietly, and breathed out again, until that element was purified, the problems and hatreds and horrors of the previous day exorcised long before morning and done away with forever.

He had been enchanted with the hour, and the town, and he had felt very powerful, like the magic man with the marionettes who strung destinies across a stage on spider-threads. On the very top of the courthouse tower he could see the least flicker of leaf turning in the moonlight five miles away; the last light, like a pink pumpkin eye, wink out. The town did not escape his eye—it could do nothing without his knowing its every tremble and gesture.

And so it was tonight. He felt himself a tower with the clock in it pounding slow and announcing hours in a great bronze tone, and gazing upon a town where a woman, hurried or slowed by fitful gusts and breezes of now terror and now self-confidence, took the chalk-white midnight sidewalks home, fording solid avenues of tar and stone, drifting among fresh-cut lawns, and now running, running down the steps, through the ravine, up, up the hill, up the hill!

He heard her footsteps before he really heard them. He heard her gasping before there was a gasping. He fixed his gaze to the lemonade glass outside, on the banister. Then the real sound, the real running, the gasping, echoed wildly outside. He sat up. The footsteps raced across the street, the sidewalk, in a panic. There was a babble, a clumsy stumble up the porch steps, a key racheting the door, a voice yelling in a whisper, praying to itself. "Oh, God, dear God!" Whisper! Whisper! And the woman crashing in the door, slamming it, bolting it, talking, whispering, talking to herself in the dark room.

He felt, rather than saw, her hand move toward the light switch.

He cleared his throat.

She stood against the door in the dark. If moonlight could have struck in upon her, she would have shimmered like a small pool of water on a windy night. He felt the fine sapphire jewels come out upon her face, and her face all glittering with brine.

"Lavinia," he whispered.

Her arms were raised across the door like a crucifix. He heard her mouth open and her lungs push a warmness upon the air. She was a beautiful dim white moth; with the sharp needle point of terror he had her pinned against the wooden door. He could walk all around the specimen, if he wished, and look at her, look at her.

"Lavinia," he whispered.

He heard her heart beating. She did not move.

"It's me," he whispered.

4

"Who?" she said, so faint it was a small pulse-beat in her throat.

"I won't tell you," he whispered. He stood perfectly straight in the center of the room. God, but he felt *tall!* Tall and dark and very beautiful to himself, and the way his hands were out before him was as if he might play a piano at any moment, a lovely melody, a waltzing tune. The hands were wet, they felt as if he had dipped them into a bed of mint and cool menthol.

"If I told you who I am, you might not be afraid," he whispered. "I want you to be afraid. Are you afraid?"

She said nothing. She breathed out and in, out and in, a small bellows which, pumped steadily, blew upon her fear and kept it going, kept it alight.

"Why did you go to the show tonight?" he whispered. *"Why* did you go to the show?"

No answer.

He took a step forward, heard her breath take itself, like a sword hissing in its sheath.

"Why did you come back through the ravine, alone?" he whispered. "You *did* come back alone, didn't you? Did you think you'd meet me in the middle of the bridge? Did you hope you'd meet me in the middle of the bridge? Why did you go to the show tonight? Why did you come back through the ravine, alone?"

"I—" she gasped.

"You," he whispered.

"No—" she cried, in a whisper.

"Lavinia," he said. He took another step.

"Please," she said.

"Open the door. Get out. And run," he whispered.

She did not move.

"Lavinia, open the door."

She began to whimper in her throat.

"Run," he said.

In moving he felt something touch his knee. He pushed, something tilted in space and fell over, a table, a basket, and a half-dozen unseen balls of yarn tumbled like cats in the dark, rolling softly. In the one moonlit space on the floor beneath the window, like a metal sign pointing, lay the sewing shears. They were winter ice in his hand. He held them out to her suddenly, through the still air.

"Here," he whispered.

5

He touched them to her hand. She snatched her hand back.

"Here," he urged.

"Take this," he said, after a pause.

He opened her fingers that were already dead and cold to the touch, and stiff and strange to manage, and he pressed the scissors into them. "Now," he said.

He looked out at the moonlit sky for a long moment, and when he glanced back it was some time before he could see her in the dark.

"I waited," he said. "But that's the way it's always been. I waited for the others, too. But they all came looking for me, finally. It was that easy. Five lovely ladies in the last two years. I waited for them in the ravine, in the country, by the lake, everywhere I waited, and they came out to find me, and found me. It was always nice, the next day, reading the newspapers. And you went looking tonight, I know, or you wouldn't have come back alone through the ravine. Did you scare yourself there, and run? Did you think I was down there waiting for you? You should have *heard* yourself running up the walk! Through the door! And *locking* it! You thought you were safe inside, home at last, safe, safe, safe, didn't you?"

She held the scissors in one dead hand, and she began to cry. He saw the merest gleam, like water upon the wall of a dim cave. He heard the sounds she made.

"No," he whispered. "You have the scissors. Don't cry."

She cried. She did not move at all. She stood there, shivering, her head back against the door, beginning to slide down the length of the door toward the floor.

"Don't cry," he whispered.

"I don't like to hear you cry," he said. "I can't stand to hear that."

He held his hands out and moved them through the air until one of them touched her cheek. He felt the wetness of that cheek, he felt her warm breath touch his palm like a summer moth. Then he said only one more thing:

"Lavinia," he said, gently, "Lavinia."

How clearly he remembered the old nights in the old times, in the times when he was a boy and them all

running, and running, and hiding and hiding, and playing hide-and-seek. In the first spring nights and in the
warm summer nights and in the late summer evenings
and in those first sharp autumn nights when doors were
shutting early and porches were empty except for blowing leaves. The game of hide-and-seek went on as long
as there was sun to see by, or the rising snow-crusted
moon. Their feet upon the green lawns were like the
scattered throwing of soft peaches and crabapples, and
the counting of the Seeker with his arms cradling his
buried head, chanting to the night: five, ten, fifteen,
twenty, twenty-five, thirty, thirty-five, forty, forty-five,
fifty . . . And the sound of thrown apples fading, the
children all safely closeted in tree or bush-shade, under
the latticed porches with the clever dogs minding not to
wag their tails and give their secret away. And the counting done: eighty-five, ninety, ninety-five, a hundred!
Ready or not, here I come!
And the Seeker running out through the town wilderness to find the Hiders, and the Hiders keeping their
secret laughter in their mouths, like precious June straw-
berries, with the help of clasped hands. And the Seeker
seeking after the smallest heartbeat in the high elm tree
or the glint of a dog's eye in a bush, or a small water
sound of laughter which could not help but burst out as
the Seeker ran right on by and did not see the shadow
within the shadow . . .
He moved into the bathroom of the quiet house, thinking all this, enjoying the clear rush, the tumultuous gush-
ing of memories like a waterfalling of the mind over a
steep precipice, falling and falling toward the bottom of
his head.
God, how secret and tall they had felt, hidden away.
God, how the shadows mothered and kept them,
sheathed in their own triumph. Glowing with perspiration
how they crouched like idols and thought they might hide
forever! While the silly Seeker went pelting by on his way
to failure and inevitable frustration.
Sometimes the Seeker stopped right *at* your tree and
peered up at you crouched there in your invisible warm
wings, in your great colorless windowpane bat wings, and
said, "I *see* you there!" But you said nothing. "You're
up there all right." But you said nothing. "Come on
down!" But not a word, only a victorious Cheshire

smile. And doubt coming over the Seeker below. "It is *you*, isn't it?" The backing off and away. "Aw, I *know* you're up there!" No answer. Only the tree sitting in the night and shaking quietly, leaf upon leaf. And the Seeker, afraid of the dark within darkness, loping away to seek easier game, something to be named and certain of. "All right for *you!*"

He washed his hands in the bathroom, and thought, Why am I washing my hands? And then the grains of time sucked back up the flue of the hour-glass again and it was another year . . .

He remembered that sometimes when he played hide-and-seek they did not find him at all; he would not let them find him. He said not a word, he stayed so long in the apple tree that he was a white-fleshed apple; he lingered so long in the chestnut tree that he had the hardness and the brown brightness of the autumn nut. And God, how powerful to be undiscovered, how immense it made you, until your arms were branching, growing out in all directions, pulled by the stars and the tidal moon until your secretness enclosed the town and mothered it with your compassion and tolerance. You could do anything in the shadows, anything. If you chose to do it, you could do it. How powerful to sit above the sidewalk and see people pass under, never aware you were there and watching, and might put out an arm to brush their noses with the five-legged spider of your hand and brush their thinking minds with terror.

He finished washing his hands and wiped them on a towel.

But there was always an end to the game. When the Seeker had found all the other Hiders and these Hiders in turn were Seekers and they were all spreading out, calling your name, looking for you, how much more powerful and important *that* made you.

"Hey, hey! Where *are* you! Come in, the game's *over!*"

But you not moving or coming in. Even when they all collected under your tree and saw, or thought they saw you there at the very top, and called up at you. "Oh, come down! Stop fooling! Hey! we see you. We know you're there!"

Not answering even then—not until the final, the fatal thing happened. Far off, a block away, a silver whistle screaming, and the voice of your mother calling your name, and the whistle again. "Nine o'clock!" her voice wailed. "Nine o'clock! Home!"

But you waited until all the children were gone. Then, very carefully unfolding yourself and your warmth and secretness, and keeping out of the lantern light at corners, you ran home alone, alone in darkness and shadow, hardly breathing, keeping the sound of your heart quiet and in yourself, so if people heard anything at all they might think it was only the wind blowing a dry leaf by in the night. And your mother standing there, with the screen door wide . . .

He finished wiping his hands on the towel. He stood a moment thinking of how it had been the last two years here in town. The old game going on, by himself, playing it alone, the children gone, grown into settled middle-age, but now, as before, himself the final and last and only Hider, and the whole town seeking and seeing nothing and going on home to lock their doors.

But tonight, out of a time long past, and on many nights now, he had heard that old sound, the sound of the silver whistle, blowing and blowing. It was certainly not a night bird singing, for he knew each sound so well. But the whistle kept calling and calling and a voice said, *Home* and *Nine o'clock*, even though it was now long after midnight. He listened. There was the silver whistle. Even though his mother had died many years ago, after having put his father in an early grave with her temper and her tongue. "Do this, do that, do this, do that, do this, do that, do this, do that . . ." A phonograph record, broken, playing the same cracked tune again, again, again, her voice, her cadence, around, around, around, around, repeat, repeat, repeat.

And the clear silver whistle blowing and the game of hide-and-seek over. No more of walking in the town and standing behind trees and bushes and smiling a smile that burned through the thickest foliage. An automatic thing was happening. His feet were walking and his hands were doing and he knew everything that must be done now.

His hands did not belong to him.

He tore a button off his coat and let it drop into the deep dark well of the room. It never seemed to hit bottom. It floated down. He waited.

It seemed never to stop rolling. Finally, it stopped.

9

His hands did not belong to him.

He took his pipe and flung that into the depths of the room. Without waiting for it to strike emptiness, he walked quietly back through the kitchen and peered outside the open, blowing, white-curtained window at the footprints he had made there. He was the Seeker, seeking now, instead of the Hider hiding. He was the quiet searcher finding and sifting and putting away clues, and those footprints were now as alien to him as something from a prehistoric age. They had been made a million years ago by some other man on some other business; they were no part of him at all. He marveled at their precision and deepness and form in the moonlight. He put his hand down almost to touch them, like a great and beautiful archeological discovery! Then he was gone, back through the rooms, ripping a piece of material from his pants-cuff and blowing it off his open palm like a moth.

His hands were not his hands any more, or his body his body.

He opened the front door and went out and sat for a moment on the porch rail. He picked up the lemonade glass and drank what was left, made warm by an evening's waiting, and pressed his fingers tight to the glass, tight, tight, very tight. Then he put the glass down on the railing.

The silver whistle!

Yes, he thought. Coming, coming.

The silver whistle!

Yes, he thought. Nine o'clock. Home, home. Nine o'clock. Studies and milk and graham crackers and white cool bed, home, home; nine o'clock and the silver whistle.

He was off the porch in an instant, running softly, lightly, with hardly a breath or a heartbeat, as one barefooted runs, as one all leaf and green June grass and night can run, all shadow, forever running, away from the silent house and across the street, and down into the ravine . . .

He pushed the door wide and stepped into the owl diner, this long railroad car that, removed from its track, had been put to a solitary and unmoving destiny in the center of town. The place was empty. At the far end of the counter, the counterman glanced up as the door shut and the customer walked along the line of empty swivel

10

seats. The counterman took the toothpick from his mouth.

"Tom Dillon, you old so-and-so! What *you* doing up this time of night, Tom?"

Tom Dillon ordered without the menu. While the food was being prepared, he dropped a nickel in the wall-phone, got his number, and spoke quietly for a time. He hung up, came back, and sat, listening. Sixty seconds later, both he and the counterman heard the police siren wail by at 50 miles an hour. "Well—*hell!*" said the counterman. "Go get 'em, boys!"

He set out a tall glass of milk and a plate of six fresh graham crackers.

Tom Dillon sat there for a long while, looking secretly down at his ripped pants-cuff and muddied shoes. The light in the diner was raw and bright, and he felt like he was on a stage. He held the tall cool glass of milk in his hand, sipping it, eyes shut, chewing the good texture of the graham crackers, feeling it all through his mouth, coating his tongue.

"Would or would you not," he asked, quietly, "call this a hearty meal?"

"I'd call that very hearty indeed," said the counterman, smiling.

Tom Dillon chewed another graham cracker with great concentration, feeling all of it in his mouth. It's just a matter of time, he thought, waiting.

"More milk?"

"Yes," said Tom.

And he watched with steady interest, with the purest and most alert concentration in all of his life, as the white carton tilted and gleamed, and the snowy milk poured out, cool and quiet, like the sound of a running spring at night, and filled the glass up all the way, to the very brim, to the very brim, and over . . .

Walter de la Mare (1873–1956) was an English poet and author who began making his impact felt on the British literary scene in the 1890s and whose career zenithed in the 1920s, with such extraordinary books as The Riddle and Other Stories, On The Edge *and* The Connoisseur and Other Stories. *He also published numerous books for young readers and some very fine books of verse. But de la Mare seems destined to be remembered for his supernatural stories. "Seaton's Aunt," for example, has reached classic status and many more of de la Mare's tales deserve ranking with the best of their kind, elegantly written, with a poetical feeling for the inexplicable. This story originally appeared in* The Cornhill Magazine *before the turn of the century, under the pen name of Walter Ramal, and was revived in hardcover by August Derleth in 1971 in the Arkham House book* Eight Tales. *This is the first appearance in paperback of this hair-raising piece.*

A: B: O.

by Walter de la Mare

I LOOKED up over the top of my book at the portrait of my great-grandfather and listened in astonishment to the sudden peal of the bell, which clanged and clanged in straggling decisive strokes until, like a dog gone back to his kennel, it slowed, slackened and fell silent again. A bell has an unfriendly tongue; it is a router of wits, a messenger of alarms. Even in the quiet of twilight it may resemble a sour virago's din. At a late hour, when the world is snug in night-cap and snoring is the only harmony, it is the devil's own discordancy. I looked over my book at my placid ancestor, I say, and listened on even after the sound had been stilled.

To tell the truth, I was more than inclined to pay no heed to the summons, and, secure in the kind warmth and solitude of my room, to ignore so rude a remembrancer of the world. Before I could decide either way, yet again the metal tongue clattered, as icily as a martinet. It pulled me to my feet. Then, my tranquillity, my inertia destroyed, it was useless and profitless to take no heed. I vowed vengeance. I would pounce sourly upon my visitor, thought I. I would send him back double-quick into the darkness of the night, and, if this were some timid feminine body (which God forefend) an antic and a grimace would effectually put such an one to route.

I rose, opened the door, and slid cautiously in my slippers to the bolted door. There I paused to climb up on a chair in an endeavour to spy out on the late-comer from the fanlight, to take his size, to analyze his intentions, but standing there even on tiptoe I could see not so much as the crown of a hat. I clambered down and, after a dismal rattling of chain and shooting of bolts, flung open the door.

Upon my top step (eight steps run down from the door to the garden and two more into the street) stood a little boy. A little boy with a ready tongue in his head, I perceived by the smirk at the corner of his mouth; a little boy of spirit too, for the knees of his knickerbockers were patched. This I perceived by the light of a lamp-post which stands over against the doctor's house. Grimaces were wasted on this sturdy youngster in his red flannel neckerchief. I eyed him with pursed lips.

"Mr. Pelluther?" said the little boy, his fists deep in the pockets of his jacket.

"Who asks for Mr. Pelluther?" said I pedagogically.

"Me," said the little boy.

"What does me want with Mr. Pelluther at so untoward an hour, eh, my little man? What the gracious do you mean by making clangour with my bell and waking the stars when all the world's asleep, and fetching me out of the warmth to this windy doorstep? I have a mind to pull your ear."

Such sudden eloquence somewhat astonished the little boy. His "boyness" seemed, I fancied, to leave him in the lurch; he was at school out of season; he retrogressed a few steps.

"Please sir, I've got a letter for Mr. Pelluther, the gentleman said," he turned his back on me, "but as he ain't here I'll take it back." He skipped down the step and at the bottom lustily set to whistling the *Marseillaise*.

My dignity was hurt, and a coward. "Come, come, my little man," I called, "I myself am Mr. Pelluther."

"Le jour de gloire . . ." whistled the little boy.

"Give me the letter," said I peremptorily.

"I've got to give it into the gentleman's own hands," said the little boy.

"Come, give me the letter," said I persuasively.

"I've got to give it into the gentleman's own hands," said the little boy doggedly, "and you don't see a corner of the envelope."

"Come, my boy, here's a sixpence."

He eyed me suspiciously, "Chestnuts," said he, retiring a step or two.

"See, a silver sixpence for the honest messenger," said I.

"Honest be blowed!" said he. "Put it on the step and go

15

behind the door. I'll come up for the tanner and put the letter on the step. Catch a weasel?"

I wanted the letter; I trusted my boy; so I put the sixpence on the top step and retired behind the door. He was true to his word. With a wary eye and a whoop of triumph he made the exchange. He doubled his fist on the sixpence and retired into the garden. I came like a felon out of the stocks for my letter.

The letter was addressed simply "Pelluther," in uncommon careless handwriting, so careless indeed that I hardly recognized the scholarly penmanship of my friend Dugdale. Forgetful of the messenger, who yet lingered upon my garden path, I shut the door and bustled into my study. I was reminded of his presence and of my discourtesy by a rattling shower of stones upon the panels of my door and by the sound of the *Marseillaise* startling the distant trees of the quiet square.

"Dear, dear me," said I, perching my spectacles most unskilfully. Indeed, I was not a little perturbed by this untimely letter. For only a few hours ago I had walked and smoked with dear old Dugdale in his own pleasant garden, in his own gentle twilight. For twilight seems to soothe to sleep the flowers of my old friend's garden with gentler hands than she can have vouchsafed even to the gardens of Solomon.

I opened my letter in trepidation, only a little reassured of Dugdale's safety by the superscription written in his own handwriting. This is the burden of the letter— "Dear Friend Pell. I am writing, in a fever. Come at once—*Antiquities!*—the lumber—a mere scrawl—Come at once, or I begin without you. R. D."

"Antiquities" was the peak of the climax of this summons—the golden word. All else might be meaningless; as indeed it was. "Come at once. *Antiquities!*"

I bustled into my coat and was pelting at perilous speed down my eight steps, before the *Marseillaise* had ceased to echo from the adjacent houses. Isolated wayfarers no doubt imagined me to be a doctor, bent on enterprise of life or death. Truly an unvenerable appearance was mine, but Dugdale was itching to begin, and haste spelt glory.

His white house lay not a mile distant, and soon the squeal of his gate upon its hinges comforted my heart and gave my lungs pause. Dugdale himself, also, the noise brought flying down into his drive to greet me. He was without his coat. Under his arm was clumsily tucked a spade, his cheeks were flushed with excitement. Even his firm lips, children of science, were trembling, and his grey eyes, wives of the microscope, were agog behind the golden-rimmed spectacles set awry on his magnificent nose.

I squeezed his left hand and thus together we hurried up the steps. "Have you begun?" said I.

"Just on the move when you came round the corner," said he. "Who would believe it, Old Roman, or Druidical, God knows."

Excitement and panting made me totter and I was dismayed at the thought of my digestion. We hurried down the passage to his study, which was in great disorder and filled with a vexing dust, hardly reminiscent of his admirable housemaid, and with a most unpleasant mouldy odour, of damp paper I conjecture.

Dugdale seized a ragged piece of parchment which lay upon the table and pressed it into my hand. He sank back into his well-worn leather arm-chair, the spade resting against his knee, and energetically set to polishing his glasses.

I looked fixedly at him. He flourished his long forefinger at me fussily, shaking his head, eager for me to get on.

Rudely scrawled upon the chart was a diagram rectangular in shape with divers scrawls in red ink, and crazy figures. I drove my brains into the open, with vain threats and cudgelling; no, I could make nothing of it. A small chest or coffer upon the floor, of a curious workmanship, overflowing with dusty and stained papers and parchments, betrayed whence the chart had come.

I looked at Dugdale. "What does it mean?" said I, a little disappointed, for many a trick of the foolish and of the fradulent has sent me on an idle errand in search of "Antiquities."

"My garden," said Dugdale, sweeping his hand towards the window, then triumphantly pointing to the chart in my hand. "I have studied it. My uncle, the antiquarian; it *is* genuine. I have had suspicions, ah! yes, every one of yours; I'm not blind. It may be anything. I dig at once. Come and help or go to the——"

He shouldered his spade, in which action he shivered a

precious little porcelain cup upon a cabinet. He never so much as blinked at the calamity. He slackened not an inch his triumphant march to the door. Well, what is a five-pound note in one's pocket to a sixpence discovered in a gutter?

I caught up the pick and another shovel. "Bravo, Pelluther," said he, and we strutted off arm and arm into the pleasant and spacious garden which lay at the back of the house. I felt proud as a drummer-boy.

In the garden Dugdale whipped out of his pocket a yard measure, and having lighted a wax candle stuck it with its own grease in a recess of the wall. After which he knelt down upon the mould with transparent sedateness and studied the chart by the candle-light, very clear and conspicuous in the darkness.

"Yew tree ten yards N. by seven E. three—semicir—um—square. It's mere A.B.C., 'pon my word."

He darted away to the bottom of the garden. I followed in a canter by the path between the darkened roses. All was blackness except where the candle-light bleached the old bricks of Dugdale's wall and glittered upon the dewy trees. At the squat old yew tree he beckoned me. I had repeatedly beseeched him to fell the ugly thing—but he would not.

"Hold the reel," said he, with trembling fingers offering me the yard-measure. Away he went. "Ten yards by how much?"

"Five, I think," said I.

"Spellicans," said Dugdale, and bustled away to the house for the chart. His shirt-sleeves winked between the bushes. He fetched back with him the chart and another candle stick.

"Do wake up, Pelluther, wake up! Oh, 'seven,' wake up?"

I was shivering with excitement and my teeth sounded like a skeleton swaying in the wind. He measured the yards and marked the place on the soil with his spade.

"Now then to work," said he, and set the example by a savage slash at a pensive *Gloire de Dijon*.

Exceedingly solemn, yet gurgling with self-conscious laughter, I also began to pick and dig. The sweat was cold upon my forehead after a quarter of an hour's hard labour. I sat on the grass and panted.

"City dinners, orgies," muttered Dugdale, slaving away like a man in search of his soul.

"No wind, thank goodness. See that flint flash? Good exercise! Gentenarians and all the better for it. I am no chicken either. Phugh! the place is black as a tiger's throat. I'll swear someone's been here before. Thumb that time!—bless the blister!"

Even in my own abject condition I had time to be amazed at his sinewy strokes and his fanatical energy. He was sexton, and I the owl! Exquisitely, suddenly, Dugdale's pick struck heavily and hollowly.

"Oh God!" said he scrambling like a rat out of the hole. He leaned heavily on his pick and peered at me with round eyes. A great silence was over the place. I seemed to hear the metallic ring of the pick cleaving its way to the stars. Dugdale crept very cautiously and extinguished the candle with damp fingers.

"Eh, now," whispered he, "you and I, old boy, d'ye hear. In the hole—it's desecration, it's as glum a trade as body-snatching. Hush! who's that?"

His hand pounced on my shoulder. We craned our necks. A plaintive howl grew out of the silence and faded into the silence. A black cat leapt the fence and disappeared with a flutter of leaves.

"That black beast!" said I, gazing into the wormy hole. "I would like to wait—and think."

"No time," said Dugdale, doubtfully bold. "The hole must be filled up before dawn or Jenkinson will make enquiries. Tut, tut, what's that noise of thumping. Oh, yes, all right!" He clapped his hand on his chest, "Now, Rattie, like mice!"

Rattie had been my nickname a very long time ago.

We set to work again, each tap of pick or shovel chased a shiver down my spine. And after great labour we excavated a metallic chest.

"Pell, you're a brick—I told you so!" said Dugdale.

We continued to gaze at our earthly spoil. One strange and inexplicable discovery we made was this: a thickly rusted iron tube ran out from the top of the chest into the earth, and thence by surmise we traced it to the trunk of the dwarfed yew tree; and, with the light of our candles eventually discovered its termination imbedded in a boss between two gnarled encrusted branches a few

19

feet up. We were unable to drag out the chest without first disinterring the pipe.

I eyed it with perplexity.

"Come and get a saw," said Dugdale. "It's strange, eh?"

He turned a mottled face to me. The air seemed to be slightly phosphorescent. Whether he had suspicions that I should force open the lid in his absence I know not. At any rate, I willingly accompanied him to the tool-house. We brought back a handsaw, Dugdale greased it plentifully with the candle, and I held the pipe while he sawed. What the purpose or use of the pipe might be I puzzled my brains in vain to discover.

"Perhaps," said Dugdale, pausing, saw in hand, "perhaps it's delicate merchandise, eh, and needs fresh air."

"Perhaps it is not," said I, unaccountably vexed at his halting speech.

He seemed to expect no different answer and again set busily to work. The pipe vibrated at his vigour, dealing me little shocks and numbing my fingers. At last the chest was free, we tapped it with our fingers. We scraped off flakes of mould and rust with our nails. I knelt and put my eye to the end of the pipe. Dugdale pushed me aside and did likewise.

I am assured that passing in his brain was a sequence of ideas exactly similar to my own. We nursed our excitement, we conceived the wildest fantasies, we brought forth litters of surmises. Perhaps just the shadow of apprehension lurked about us. Possibly a familiar spirit may have tapped our shoulders.

Then, at the same instant we both began to pull and push vigorously at the chest; but, in such a confined space (for the hole was ragged and unequal) its weight was too great for our strength.

"A rope," said Dugdale, "let's go together again. Two 'old boys' in the plot." He laughed hypocritically.

"Certainly," said I, amused at his suspicions and wiles.

Again we stepped away to the tool-shed, and returned with a coil of rope. The pick being used as a lever, we were soon able to haul the chest out of its hole.

"Duty first," said Dugdale, shovelling the loose earth into the cavity. I imitated him. And over the place of the disturbance we planted the dying rose bush, already hanging drooping leaves.

"Jenkinson's eyes are not microscopes, but he's damned inquisitive."

Jenkinson, incidentally, was an old gentleman who lived in the house next to Dugdale. One who having no currants in his own bun must needs pick and steal his neighbours! But he is dumb in the grave now, and out of hearing of any cavilling tongue.

Dugdale swore, but a man would be a saint or a fool who could refrain from swearing under the circumstance. Even I displayed blasphemous knowledge and was not ashamed.

Dugdale took one end and I the other side of the chest. Together we carried it with immense difficulty (for the thing was prodigiously weighty) to the study. We cleared away all the furniture to the sides of the room. We placed the chest in the middle of the floor so that we might gloat upon it at our ease. With the fire-shovel, for we had neglected to bring the spade, Dugdale scraped away mould and rust and upon the top of the chest appeared three letters, initial to a word, I conjectured, which originally ran the whole width of the side, but the greater part of which had been rendered illegible by the action of the soil. "A–B–O" were the letters.

"I have no idea," said Dugdale peering at this barely perceptible record. "I have no idea," I echoed vaguely.

And would to God we had forthwith carried the chest unopened to the garden and buried it deeper than deep!

"Let us open it," said I, after arduous examination of the inscription.

The fire flames glittered upon dear old Dugdale's glasses. He was a chilly man and at a suggestion of east wind would have a fire set blazing. The room was snug and cozy. I remember the carved figure of a Chinese God grinning at me in a very palpable manner as I handed Dugdale his chisel. (May he forgive me!) The intense silence was ominous. In a cranny at the lid of the chest he inserted the tool. He looked at me queerly, at the second jerk the steel snapped.

"Dugdale," said I, eyeing the Chinese God, "let's leave well alone."

"Eh," said he in an unfamiliar voice.

"Have nought to do with the thing."

"What, eh?" said he sucking his finger, the nail of

which he had broken in his digging. He hesitated an instant. "We must get another chisel," said he, laughing.

But somehow I cared for the laugh not at all. It was not the fair bleak laugh of Dugdale. He took my arm in his and for the third time we made our way to the tool-shed.

"It's fresh and sweet," said I, sniffing the air of the garden. My eyes beseeched Dugdale.

"Ay, so it is, it is," said he.

When he again set to work upon the chest he prised open the lid at the first effort. The scrap of broken steel rang upon the metal of the chest. A faint and unpleasant odour became perceptible. Dugdale remained in the position the sudden lift of the lid had given his body, his head bent slightly forward, over the open chest. I put one hand upon the side of the chest. My fingers touched a little cake of hard stuff. I looked into the chest. I took a step forward and looked in. Yellow cotton wool lined the leaden sides and was thrust into the interstices of the limbs of the creature which sat within. I will speak without emotion. I saw a flat malformed skull and meagre arms and shoulders clad in coarse fawn hair. I saw a face thrown back a little, bearing hideous and ungodly resemblance to the human face, its lids heavy blue and closely shut with coarse lashes and tangled eyebrows. This I saw, this the monstrous antiquity hid in the chest which Dugdale and I dug out of the garden. Only one glimpse I took at the thing, then Dugdale had replaced the lid, had sat down on the floor and was rocking to and fro with hands clasped over his knees.

I made my way to the window feeling stiff and sore with unaccustomed toil; I threw open the window and leaned far out into the scented air. The sweetness of the flowers eddied into the room. The night was very quiet. For many minutes so I stood counting a row of poplars at the far end of the garden. Then I returned to Dugdale.

"It's the end of the business," said I. "My gorge rises with despair of life. Swear it! my dear old Dugdale. I implore you to swear that this shall be the end of the business. We will go bury it now."

"I swear it, Pelluther. Pell! Pell!" The bitterness of his childish cry is venomous even now. "But hear me old friend," he said. "I am too weak now. Come tomorrow at this time and we will bury it together."

22

The chest stood in front of the fire. The metal was green with verdigris.

We went out of the room leaving the glittering candles to their watch, and in my presence Dugdale turned the key in the lock of the door. He walked with me to the Church and there we parted company.

"A damnable thing," said Dugdale, shaking my hand.

I wagged my head woefully.

The next day, being Wednesday, the charwomen invaded my house, as was customary upon that day, and to be free of the steam and the stench of soap I took my way to Kew. Throughout the day I wandered through the gardens striving to enjoy the luxuriance and the flowers.

In the first coolness of evening I turned my back upon the gorgeous west and made my way home again. I met the women red and flustered leaving the house.

"Has any one called?" said I.

"The butcher, sir," said Mrs. Rodd.

"Thank you," said I and entered my house.

Now in the twilight as I sat down at my own fireside, my surroundings recalled most vividly the scene of the night. I leaned heavily in my chair feeling faint and sick, and in so doing was much inconvenienced by some hard thing in the pocket of my jacket pressed to my side by the arm of the chair. I rummaged in my pocket and brought out the little cake of hard green substance which had been in the mouth of the chest. I suppose that my fingers had clutched it when they had come in contact with it the night before and unknowingly I had deposited it in my pocket.

Deeming it prudent to have care in the matter, I rose and locked up the stuff in my little medicine chest, which is hanged above the mantelpiece in the room which looks out upon the garden. For to analyze or examine the stuff I feared. This done I came again to my chair and composed myself to reading.

Supper had been prepared by the women and was set upon the table for me in my study. It has been my custom since the death of my sister to dine at mid-day at my club.

True! I sat with the book upon my knee but all my thoughts were with Dugdale. A rectangular shape obtruded itself upon my retina and floated upon the white page. The hours dragged wearily. My head drooped and my chin tapped my chest. In fact I was dreaming, when I was awakened by a doubtful knock upon the front door. My senses were alert in an instant. The sound, just as though something were scraping the paint, was repeated.

I rose stealthily. A vague desire to flee out into the garden seized upon me.

The sound was repeated.

I went very slowly to the door. Again I climbed the chair (I loved the little boy now.) But I could see nothing. I peeped through the keyhole but something obscured the opening upon the other side. A faint odour—unpleasant—was in the house. With desperation of terror I flung open the door. I fancied I heard the sound of panting. I fancied something brushing my arm; then I found myself staring down the hallway listening to the echo of the click of the latch of the door of the room which overlooks my garden. In this unseemly rhythm and this succession of words I write with intent. Thus my thoughts ran then; thus then I write now. Many years ago when I was a young man I was nearly burnt alive. I felt then an honest fear. This was a dim skulking horror of soul and an inhuman depravity. It is impossible for me to tell of my horrid strivings of brain. I staggered into my room; I sat down in my chair; I took my book upon my knee; I put my spectacles upon my nose; but all the time all my senses were dead save that of hearing. Distinctly I felt my ears move and twitch, with the help of some ancient muscle, I conjecture, long disused by humanity. And as I sat, my brain cried out with fear.

For ten minutes (I slowly counted each sounding 'cluck' of my clock) I sat so. At last my limbs began to quake, solitude was driving me to perilous ravines of thought. I crept with guilty tread into the garden. I climbed the fence which separates the next house from mine. This house, No. 17, was inhabited by a caretaker, a rude uncouth fellow who used for his living room only the kitchen, and who had tied all the bells together so that he might not be disturbed. He was a cad of a man. But for companionship I cried out.

I went to the garden door keeping my eyes fixedly turned away from the window. I hammered at the garden door of the house. I hammered again. A sullen footstep

24

resounded in the empty place and the door was cautiously opened a few inches. A scared face looked out at me through the chink.

"For God's sake," said I, "come and sup with me. I have a leg of good meat, my dear fellow, come and sup with me."

The door opened wider. Curiosity took the place of apprehension. "Say, Master, what is moving in the house?" said the fellow. "Why is my 'ead all damp, and my 'ands a shiverin'. I tell you there's a thing gone wrong in the place. I sits with my back to the wall and somebody steps quick and quiet on the other side. Why am I sick like so? I ask yer why?"

The man almost wept.

"You silly fellow! May a sick man not pace his mansion. I will give you a five-pound note to come and sit with me," said I. "Be neighbourly, my good fellow. I fear that a fit will overtake me. I am weak—the heat—epileptical too. Rats crowd in the walls, I often hear their tumult. Come, sup with me."

The cad shook his villainous head sagely.

"A five-pound note—two," said I.

"I was chaffin'," said he, and returned into the house to fetch a poker.

We climbed the fence and crept like thieves towards the house. But not an inch beyond my door would the fellow come. I expostulated. He blasphemed. He stubbornly stuck to his purpose.

"I don't budge till I've 'glimpsed' through that window," said he.

I argued and entreated; I doubled my bribe; I tapped him upon the shoulder and twitted him of cowardice; I performed a pirouette about him; I entreated him to sit with me.

"I don't budge till I've glimpsed through that window."

I fetched a little ladder from the greenhouse which stands to the left of the house, and the caretaker carried it to the window, the ledge of which is about five feet from the ground. He climbed laboriously step by step, stretching his neck so as to see into the black room beyond, while I, simply to be near him, climbed behind him.

He had got halfway and was breathing loudly when suddenly a long arm, thin as its bone, clad in tawny hair, pallid in the dim starlight, pounced across the window and dragged the curtains together—an arm thin as its bone. The fellow above me groaned, threw up his hands and tumbled headlong off the ladder, bringing me to the ground in his fall.

For a moment I lay dazed; then, lifting my head from the soil and the sweet lilies I perceived him clambering over the fence in savage hurry. I remember that the dew glistened upon his boots as he flung his heels over the fence.

Presently I was upon my feet and pelting after him, but he was a younger man, and when I reached the door at the back of his house he had already bolted and barred it. To all my prayers and knockings he paid no attention. Notwithstanding, I feel certain that he sat listening upon the other side, for I discerned a hoarse breathing like the breathing of an asthmatic.

"You have left the poker. I bring you the poker," I bellowed, but he made no answer.

Again I climbed the fence, now determined to leave the house free for the thing to roam and to ravage, nor to return till daylight was come. I crept quietly through the haunted place. As I passed the room, I distinguished a sound—like the sound of a humming top—of incessant gabble. I ran and opened the front door and just then, as I peered out upon the street, a beggar clothed in rags shuffled past the garden gate. I leapt down the steps.

"Here my good man," said I speaking with difficulty for my tongue seemed stiff and glutinous.

He turned with an odd whine and shuffled towards me.

"Are you hungry?" said I. "Have you an appetite—just a stubborn yearning for a delicate snack of prime Welsh lamb?"

The scraggy wretch nodded and gesticulated with warty hands.

"Come in, come in," I screamed. "You shall eat a meal, poor man. How dire is civilization in rags—Evil fortune! Socialism! Millionaires! I'll be bound. Come in, come in."

I was weeping with delight. He squinted at me with suspicion and again waved his hands. By these movements and by his articulate cries, I fancied the man was dumb. (He was vexed with a serious impediment in his speech I now conjecture.) He was manifesting mistrust. He snuffled.

"No, no," said I. "Come in, my man and welcome. I am lonely—a Bohemian. Ancient books are musty company. Come sit and cheer me with an honest appetite. Take a glass of wine with me."

I patted the wretch on the back. I gripped his arm. In my tragic acting, moreover, I hummed a little song to prove my indifference. He tottered upon my steps in front of me—his shoes were mended with brown paper and the noise of his footsteps was like the rustle of a lady's silk dress. I blithely followed him into the house leaving the door wide open so that the clean night air might go through the house, so that the clatter of the railroad which lies behind the doctor's house might prove the reality of the world. I sat the beggar down in an arm-chair. I plied him with meat and drink. He luxuriated in the good fare, he guzzled my claret, he gnawed bones and crust like a bony beast, considering me the while, apprehensive of being reft of his meal. He snarled and he gobbled, he puffed, he mouthed and he chawed. He was a bird of prey, a cat, a wild beast, and a man. His belly was the only truth. He had chanced on heaven, and awaited the archangel's trump of banishment. Yet in the midst of his ravenous feeding, terror was netting him, too. Full of my own fear, in watching his hands shivering, and the pallor overspreading his grimy face, I took delight. Still he ate furiously, flouting his fears.

All the while I was thinking desperately of the horrid creature which was in my house. The while I sat grinning at my guest, the while I was inciting him to eat, drink, and be merry, the while I analyzed each deplorable action of the rude fellow and sickened at his beastliness, the vile consciousness of that thing on its secret errand prowling within scent, never left me—that abortion—A-B-O, abortion; I knew then.

On a sudden, just as the tramp, having lifted the lamb bone, had set his teeth to gnawing at the gristly knuckle, there came to my ears the sound of breaking glass and then a rustling, (no extraordinary sound), a rustling sound of a hand wandering upon the panel of a door. But the beggar had heard what speech cannot make intelligible. I felt younger on that day than I have since my childhood. I was drunken with terror.

My beggar, dropping his tumbler of wine but still clutching the lamb bone, scrambled to his feet and eyed me with pale grey pupils set in circles of white. His dirty bleached face was stained with his meal. Dirt seamed his skin. I took his hand in mine. I caught up the lamp and held it on high. The beggar and I stood in the doorway gazing into the darkness; the lamplight faintly lit the familiar passage. It gleamed on the door of the room whose window overlooks my garden. The handle of the door was silently turning. The door was opening—almost imperceptibly. The beggar's pulse throbbed furiously; my elbow was pressed against his arm. And a very thin abnormal thing—a fawn shadow—came out of the room and pattered past the beggar and me.

My jaws fell asunder, nor could I shut them so that I might speak. Tighter I clutched the beggar and we fled out together. Standing upon the topmost of the steps, we peered down the street; afar off with ponderous tread walked a policeman, playing the light of his lantern upon the windows of the houses and the doors. Presently he drew near to a lamp, to where flitted a monstrous shadow. I saw the policeman turn suddenly round about. With fluttering coat-tails he ran furiously down a little lane which leads to many bright shops.

The beggar and I spent the rest of the night upon the doorstep. Sometimes he made vain splutterings of speech and vexed gesticulations, but generally we waited speechless and motionless as two stuffed owls.

At the first faint ray of dawn, which leapt above the doctor's house opposite, the beggar flung away my hand, hopped blindly down the steps and, pausing not to open the gate, vaulted over it and was immediately gone. I scarcely felt surprise. The green-shaded lamp which stood upon the doorstep slowly burned itself out. The sun rose gladly, the sparrows made the morning noisy as they fluttered and fought in their busy foraging. I think my round eyes vaguely watched them.

Soon after eight the postman brought me a letter. And this was the letter—"God forgive me, friend, and help me to write sanely. A miserable curiosity has proved too strong for me. I went back to my house, now woefully strange to me. I could not sleep. Now pacing with me in my own bedroom, now wrapped in its unholy sleep, the thing as always with me. Each picture, indeed each chair, however severely I strove to discipline my thoughts, carried with it a pregnant suggestion. In the middle of the

28

night I took my way downstairs and opened the door of my study. My books seemed to me disconsolate friends offended. The case stood as we had left it—we, you and I, when we locked the door upon the tragedy. In fear and trembling I went a little farther into the room. Two steps had I taken when I discovered that the lid no longer shut the thing from the stars, that the lid was gaping open. Oh! Pelluther, how will you credit so astounding a statement. I saw (I say it solemnly though I have to labour vigorously to drive back a horde of thoughts) I saw the wretched creature, which you and I had raised from the belly of the earth, lying upon the floor; its meagre limbs were coiled in front of the fire. Had the heat roused him from his long sleep? I know not, I dare not think. He—he, Pelluther—lay upon the hearth-rug sunken in slumber soundlessly breathing. Oh, my friend, I stand eyeing insanity, face to face. My mind is mutinous. There lay the wretched abortion:—it seems to me that this thing is like a pestilent secret sin, which lies hid, festering, weaving snares, befouling the wholesome air, but which, some day, creeps out and goes stalking midst healthy men, a leprous child of the sinner. Ay, and like a sin perhaps of yours and of mine. Pelluther! But, being heavy with such a woesome burden it becomes us alone to bear it. I left the thing there in its sleep. Its history the world shall never know. I write this to warn you of the awful terror of the event which has come upon you and me. When you come,* we will make our plans to destroy utterly this horrid memory. And if this be not our lot we must exist but to hide our discovery from the eyes of the sane. If any suffer, it is you and I who must suffer. If murder can be just, the killing of this creature—neither man nor beast, this vile symbol—must be accounted to us a virtue. Fate has chosen her tools. Come, my old friend! I have sent away my servants and locked my door; and my prayer is that this thing may sleep until darkness comes down to cloak our horrid task from the eyes of the world. Science is slunk away shamefaced; religion is a withered flower. Oh, my friend, what shall I say! How shall I regain myself?"

From the slender record of this letter I leave you to

*I perceive that Dugdale omitted to post this letter in time to reach me on the second evening. I bitterly deplore the omission.

deduce whatever conclusions you may. I may suppose that at some time of the second day (perhaps, while I was rambling through the green places of Kew!) Dugdale had again visited the thing and had found it awake, alert, vigilant in his room. No man spied upon my friend in those hours. (Sometimes in the quietude, I fancy I hear an odd footfall upon my threshold!)

In the brilliant sunshine I drove in a four-wheeled cab to Dugdale's house, for my limbs were weak and would hardly bear my body. I limped up the garden path and the familiar steps with the help of two sticks. The door was ajar—I entered. I found Dugdale in his study. He was sitting in the chest with a Bible resting on one of the sides.

He looked at me. " 'For we are but of yesterday and know nothing because our days upon earth are a shadow.' What is life, Pelluther? A vain longing for death. What is beauty? A question of degree. And sin is in the air,—child of disease and death and springing-up and hatred of life. Fawn hair has beauty and as for bones; surely less for the worms. Worms! through lead? Pelluther, my dear old Pell. Through lead?"

He gazed at me like a child gazing at a bright light.

"Come!" said I, "the air is bland and the sun is fierce and warm. Come!" I could say no more.

"But the sunlight has no meaning to me now," said he. "That breeder of corruption, tall here and a monstrous being, walks under my skull strangling all the other beings, puny and sapless. I have one idea, conception, vivid faintness, a fierce red horrid idea—and a phenomenon, too. You see, it is when a deep abstract belief rots into loathing, when hope is eaten away by horrors of sleep and a mad longing for sleep—Mad! Yet fawn hair is not without beauty; provided, Pelluther, provided—through lead?" . . .

A vain idle report has been set about by the malicious. Oh, was there not reason and logical sequence in his conversation with me? I give it for demonstration's sake. I swear that he is not mad—a little eccentric (surely all clever men are eccentric), a little aged. I swear solemnly that my dear friend Dugdale was not mad. He was a just man. He wronged no one. He was a benevolent kindly gentleman and fine in intellect. Say you that he was eccentric—not mad. Tears ran down my cheeks as I looked at him.

"Minnesota Gothic," with its gentle, lyric cast might seem a surprising story coming from the author of 334, one of the most brilliantly hard and realistic projections of the future ever written. Or surprising coming from the author of the searing Camp Concentration, to say nothing of a small army of short stories of elegant black humor and stinging satire. Norman Spinrad has written that there is ". . . something of the wolf in pussycat's clothing in Disch, and the mask has a way of slipping at strategic moments." Where, then, does this story come from? Perhaps it's significant that it was published originally under the by-line Dobbin Thorpe. More certain is that Thomas Disch is that kind of consummate artist who has many faces behind many masks, all real and all impressive. Which is not to say that this return to Mr. Disch's Midwestern beginnings is without an element of the sinister.

MINNESOTA GOTHIC

by Thomas M. Disch

GRETEL was caught in the bright net of autumn—wandering vaguely in the golden, dying woods, vaguely uncertain where she was but not yet frightened, vaguely disobedient. Ripe gooseberries piled in her basket; the long grass drying. Autumn. She was seven years old.

The woods opened onto a vegetable garden. A scarecrow waved the raggedy stumps of his denim arms at the crows rustling in the cornstalk sheaves. Pumpkins and squash dotted the spent earth, as plump and self-sufficient as a convention of slum landlords. Further down the row, an old woman was rooting in the ground, mumbling to herself.

Gretel backed toward the wood. She was afraid. A strand of rusted barb-wire snagged at her dress. The crows took to the air with graceless to-do. The woman pushed herself up and brushed back a tangle of greasy white hair. She squinted at Gretel, who began to cry.

"Little girl?" Her voice crackled like sticks of dry wood burning. "Little girl, come here. I give you some water, eh? You get lost in the woods."

Gretel tore her dress loose from the barb and stepped nervously around the fat pumpkins, tripping on their vines. Her fear, as is often the way with fear, made her go to the old woman, to the thing she feared.

"Yes, I know you," the old woman grated. "You live two houses down the road. I know your mother when she is little." She winked, as though they had shared an amusing secret. "How old are you?"

Gretel opened her mouth but couldn't speak.

"You're only a *little* girl," the old woman went on, with a trace of contempt. "You know how old I am?

32

A hundred years old!" She nodded her head vigorously. "I'm Minnie Haeckel."

Gretel had known who the woman was, although she had never seen her before. Whenever Gretel was especially bad or muddied her Sunday frock or wouldn't eat dinner, her mother would tell her what terrible things Old Minnie Haeckel did to naughty piglets who didn't eat cauliflower. Mother always concluded these revelations with the same warning: "You do it *once more,* and I'm going to take you to live with that old Minnie. It's just what you deserve." Now too, Gretel recognized the clapboard house with the peeling paint and, around it, the sheds—omens of a more thorough disintegration. The house was not as formidable viewed across the vegetable garden as it had seemed in brief glimpses from the car window, the white hulk looming behind a veil of dusty lilacs. It looked rather like the other old farmhouses along the gravel road—the Brandts', the Andersons'.

Minnie took Gretel by the hand and led her to an iron pump. The pump groaned in time to the woman's slow heave and stagger and a trickle of water spilt over its gray lip, blackening it.

"Silly girl!" Minnie gasped. "Use the dipper."

Gretel put the enamel dipper under the lip of the pump to catch the first gush of cold water. She drank greedily.

From inside the house, there was the bellow of a mans' voice. "Minnie! Minnie, is that you?"

Minnie jerked the dipper out of Gretel's hand and bent over the little girl. "That's my brother," she whispered, her dry voice edged with fear. "You must go. First, I give you something." Minnie took Gretel to a sagging wooden platform at the back of the house, where there was a pile of heavy, dirt-crusted tubers the color of bacon grease. Minnie put one of these in Gretel's basket on top of the tiny green gooseberries.

"Minnie!" the voice roared.

"Yeah, yeah!" Minnie returned. "Now then, that's for you. You give it to your mother, understand? And walk home down the road. It's not far. You know how?"

Gretel nodded. She backed away from Minnie and, when she was far enough, turned and ran to the road, clutching the basket with its terrible vegetable to her chest.

33

Mother was outside the house, collapsed in a lawn chair. The radio was turned on full-volume. Mother flexed her polished toes to the slow, urban beat of the music.

"Did you bring in the mail, love?" Mother asked. Gretel shook her head and stood at a distance from her mother, waiting to recover her breath.

"I tore my dress," she brought out at last. But Mother was not in a mood to be upset by small things. It was a very old dress and it had been torn before.

"What's in your basket, love?" she asked. Gretel glanced down guiltily at the hard, ominous vegetable. She handed it to her mother.

"I was picking gooseberries."

"This isn't a gooseberry, though," Mother explained gently. "It's a rutabaga. Where did you get it."

Gretel told about Minnie.

"Isn't that nice of her. She's such a sweet old lady. We'll have the rutabaga for dinner. Did you thank her, I hope?"

Gretel blushed. "I was afraid."

"There was nothing to be afraid of, love. Minnie is a harmless old woman. She does the sweetest things sometimes, and she's had a hard time of it, living all alone in that firetrap of a house that really should be torn down. . . ."

"But she's not alone, Mommie. Her brother lives there with her."

"Nonsense, Gretel. Minnie doesn't have any brother, not anymore. Now, put the rutabaga and the gooseberries in the kitchen and go back and see if there's any mail."

At dinner Gretel ate everything on her plate but the diced rutabagas. She sat staring at the yellowish lumps morosely, while her mother cleared away the dishes.

"You're not to leave the table until you've eaten every one of them, so take all the time you need."

Finally, at eight o'clock, Gretel bolted down the cold, foul-tasting lumps of rutabaga, fighting against her reflex to gag. When she had quite finished, Mother brought in her desert, but Gretel couldn't eat it.

"Really, Gretel darling, there's no reason to *cry*."

The next day, Gretel was sick. Purely for spite, her mother was convinced. But, of course, that wasn't it at all. It was only the spell beginning its work.

Left to her own devices, Gretel would not have renewed her acquaintance with Minnie Haeckel. Unfortunately, late in October, Grandfather Bricks died; her mother's father, who had built the farmhouse they were living in. Mother was to meet Daddy in the city and then fly to California, where the Bricks had retired. Gretel, who was too young to attend a cremation, was deposited at Minnie Haeckel's doorstep with a canvas bag of playthings and a parting kiss. She watched her mother drive down the gravel road until there was nothing to be seen but a cloud of dust and a glint of chrome from the last hill of the horizon. Minnie was hunched over a swaybacked chair on the front stoop.

"Your old grandfather is dead, eh? He used to bring Minnie a fruitcake at Christmas." Minnie sucked in her cheeks and made a sound of regret. "People are always dying. What do you think of that?" Gretel noticed with distaste that the old woman's mouth contained, instead of proper teeth, brown stumps at irregular intervals that Gretel surmised were snuff. Her mother had told her once that Minnie chewed snuff.

"Come into the parlor, child. You can play there. Nobody uses the parlor nowadays."

The creaking pine floor was covered with a rag rug. There was a huge leather chair that rocked on hidden springs and a handsome mahogany table with a lace cloth. The bay window was hung with curtains that had once been feedbags, their red check now a sunbleached, dusty pink. On the walls, decades of calendars advertised the First Commerical Bank of Onamia. They pictured a perpetual *January* of wintry woods and snowy roads, ponds and icebound houses.

"Can you read?"

"A little."

Minnie opened a tin box that lay on the table and handed Gretel a small bundle of cards and envelopes. They smelled of decayed spices. Minnie shook the box. A gritty black ball rolled into Gretel's lap.

"You take an apple," Minnie explained, "and you stick it full of cloves and let it dry for a whole year. It shrinks up like this. Doesn't it smell nice?" Minnie picked up the black ball and held it under her nostrils, smelling it noisily. "You read the letters now, eh?"

The first was a postcard showing a ship. *"Dear All,"*

she read. *"I am in France. It gets cold at night, but I don't mind it. How is everyone? They say the war is almost over."* The signature, like the text, was printed in crude, black letters—*"Lew."*

"My daddy was in the war, too. He flew a plane."

"This is a different war, a long time ago."

The next postcard had no picture. GREETINGS FROM NEW YORK, it said in front. On the back there was only Lew's clumsy signature.

"Who is Lew?" Gretel asked. "Does he live upstairs?"

"Yes, but you can't see him. He can't walk now and he doesn't like little girls. Read some more, eh? The big one."

Gretel took the largest envelope and opened it. The letter was typewritten and crinkly with age. *"Dear Miss . . .* Is that how you spell *Haeckel?"* She giggled at the vagaries of spelling. *"We re—gret to inform you that your brother, Lew Haeckel, has been . . ."*

"Go on," Minnie prodded.

"The words are too hard."

"You can't read very well."

"I'm only in first grade. Read them yourself."

"This letter is from the hospital. He was there for weeks. Then they sent him home. It costs me a lot of money."

"What happened?" Gretel asked, although she was not terribly interested.

"He used to drink." Minnie looked at Gretel narrowly. "Your mother drinks too, eh?" Gretel thought so. "He was in a car accident. That's what happens to drinkers. You stay in here while I work outside, eh? Then we eat."

Gretel promised to be good. Minnie replaced the letter in the box carefully and went out through the kitchen. Gretel climbed into the largest leather rocker and pumped it with her body, like a swing, until she had filled the room comfortably with its creaking. The corners of the parlor sank into shadow and the deep colors of the room deepened with dusk. Gretel rocked the chair harder, but it was a poor defense against the encroaching darkness. And there was no light switch on the wall. She went to find Minnie.

The hall was even darker, and darker yet the staircase to the second floor. Piles of mail-order catalogues and old magazines formed a sort of bannister on the stairs.

"Hey—you!" He had a smooth, urgent voice. Gretel peeked up the stairs at him shyly. He was fat and he could hardly stand up. In the dark, Gretel could make out few details. He was leaning against the wall for support with one hand. With the other, he waved a cane at Gretel, as though he would catch her in its crook. "Come up here. I want to talk to you. Don't be afraid. C'mon, sugar."

"I'm not supposed to see you." Gretel liked to tease.

"Don't pay attention to Minnie. She's crazy, you know. I'll tell you a thing or two about *her*." Then his voice hushed so that Gretel couldn't understand his words. She advanced up two of the steps.

"That's right. C'mon into my room. In here." He vanished from the top of the stairs, and Gretel listened to him shuffle along the corridor. She followed him and was relieved to see a shaft of light in the corridor.

His room was a sty of cast-off clothes, out-of-date magazines, and tins full of cigar ashes and butts. These—and Lew—were all piled on the double-bed at the center of the room; there was no other furniture except a dresser without drawers upon which a kerosene lamp was burning. Lew, collapsed in the debris of the bed, was breathing heavily—pale cheeks billowed and slacked like a mechanical toy. His belly sagged out of a blue, navy-issue, knit sweater and his thighs had split through the seams of his trousers, which were fouled with weeks, months of use.

"She keeps me prisoner here. I can't get downstairs by myself. She won't let me go anywhere, see my friends."

Gretel stared in amazement—not at this confidence—at him.

"And she tries to starve me, too. C'mere, sugar. What's your name?"

"Gretel."

"Forty years! I've been a cripple in this leg for forty years. She doesn't let me out of her sight. Come over here and sit on the bed, why doncha? I don't bite."

Gretel didn't move from the doorway. Lew picked up his cane again and tried to hook her around the neck, playfully.

"You afraid of your Old Uncle Lew?"

Gretel pursed her lips at what she knew to be a lie.

"You know why she does all this? You wanna know? She's a witch. That's what it is, honest to God. When she

37

was a kid, she could take off warts. She's put her name down in the devil's book, and she'll never get any older now. And if she has a mind to, she can turn you into a mouse. You'll have to hop on her thumb and beg for crumbs of bread. You can hear her mumbling all the time, sorts of crazy things. Charms and such. And cursing, oh, she can curse." He stopped for breath again and struggled to his feet. Gretel backed further away.

"She hexed me. I was a thousand miles away, I was in New York. But that don't matter one iota to *her*. She made my leg go bum." He staggered forward angrily. *"It's all her fault!"* he shouted after Gretel as she clambered down the stairs and out of the house. Minnie was nowhere to be seen.

Gretel found her in one of the lean-to sheds shoveling corncobs into a tin bucket. "It's dark inside," she complained. She had decided not to mention Uncle Lew.

"There are rats in the sheds as big as you are," Minnie said between shovelsfull. "You only see them at night. Big rats."

"What are those?" Gretel pointed.

"Corncobs. I burn them up and they never get used. Every day I burn some more." She laughed, although Gretel did not recognize it as such. "Now we go inside. I turn on a lamp."

The kitchen table and the cupboards were stacked with unwashed dishes and pans. Minnie, apparently, had as little use for soap as Lew. Minnie lighted the kerosene lamp and made a fire in the stove. They ate dinner in silence: vegetables from Minnie's garden and canned meat from Mother's larder. Minnie ate with a spoon, but she offered Gretel a fork as well.

"Nibble, nibble, little mouse," Minnie chortled.

Gretel looked up at Minnie with delight, for she remembered the line. "Who is nibbling at my house?" she concluded. Minnie looked at her suspiciously. "Mommie read me that story lots of times. My name is in it—Gretel."

"What are you talking about? You want some cake, eh?"

The cake tasted nothing at all like the ones Mother took from boxes, but it wasn't bad. Gretel had two pieces.

"I take you home now. I come and get you in the morning. You can't sleep here."

Gretel kept close to Minnie on the gravel road, but she

wouldn't hold the old woman's hand. Even with a sweater, it was cold. Owls hooted in the dark woods, and there were other, less definite noises.

"You're afraid of the dark, eh?"

"It's scary at night."

"I like the night best of all. I build a fire in the stove and sit down and warm my old bones. When you go back to the city?"

"Daddy has to find a new apartment. I'm studying my lessons at home. I can read anyhow. Most first-graders can't read at all."

"Here you are. You want me to put you to bed?"

"No. We have electric lights, so I won't be afraid by myself. Minnie?"

"Eh?"

"Are you really a witch?"

Minnie choked on her phlegm and spat and choked again. This time Gretel knew her laughter for what it was. She went into the house angrily and locked the door behind her. Even upstairs in her chintz bedroom she could hear Minnie, as she walked back along the road, rasping with glee and mumbling—something—loudly.

The morning drizzled—cold, a clothes-damping mist that did not fall but hung, filmed the house and leafless trees but would not wet the earth. Gretel was wakened by a tattoo of pebbles on the clouded window. She dressed herself, sleepily, in the warmest clothes she could find and joined Minnie outside, wishing that her mother were there with the Buick. While they trudged down the road, Minnie interrupted her grumbling long enough to ask Gretel if she had been with her brother the day before.

"Yes. He told me to. And he said you were a witch. Can you take off warts?"

"I stop the toothache too—and measles. Once, I am at every laying-in but no more. They come to Old Minnie for a love-doll, for a sick horse. For everything."

Gretel considered this in silence. She did not quite dare to ask if Minnie could turn children into mice. She remembered, with grave suspicion, the rats in the corncrib that only came out at night—rats as big as she herself. She felt serious and wary but no longer afraid. And she felt, too, though she could not have said why, a touch of contempt for the old woman shuffling through the mist, bent under the oversized pea-jacket.

"Aren't we going to your house?" Gretel asked as they walked past the dripping lilac bushes.

"Not now. You are warm enough, eh?"

"Is it far?"

"Not far." Half a mile didn't seem far to Minnie. A dirt track led from the road to the Onamia Township Cemetery. Minnie paced in a circle about a small stone that rose bare inches above the clovered grass. There was an inscription on it which read simply:

HAECKEL
1898–1923.

Three times she circled it, crooning anxiously, and then three times again, but in the other direction.

"Who's inside?" Gretel asked, but Minnie wasn't listening to her ward. "My grandfather," she persisted, "is going to be burned. Mommie is bringing the ashes home in a jar. Is that your brother?"

Minnie finished her pacing and started back to the road, still oblivious of Gretel. Gretel was piqued. She considered hiding from her unresponsive guardian, as she had often hid from her mother when she (her mother) needed to be punished, but it was too cold and wet a day to go into the woods. Gretel would remember not to forget.

Minnie's stove was already crackling; the kitchen was soaked in a warmth that drew a history of odors from the cracks in the woodwork: smells of last year's apples and this summer's onions, of nutmeg and cinnamon, the scrapings of stews, the coffee burnt on the iron stove, the musk of drying wood in the orange crate by the stove, of snuff, and strangely, of cigars. There was a wooden sign above the porch door, painted in crude, black letters. Gretel sounded them out—CIGAR FACTORY NO. 4.

"Is this a cigar factory?"

"Not anymore. My brother makes cigars before he is too sick. It makes a little money. It is a good thing to make some money. I sell vegetables in town. And go to the sick people. It isn't much. He makes them just to smoke nowadays. I have to sell the land sometimes."

"Has your brother lived here a long time?"

"Oh, a long time. Can you cook?"

"Mommie won't let me. I'm too little."

"I teach you to make cookies, eh? Little cookies—just for you."

"Okay. Is he as old as you are?"

"We don't talk about him now. What is this, eh?"

Gretel shrugged at the handful of white powder Minnie had taken from a glass cannister.

"Silly girl. It's flour. Everyone knows flour." Minnie put three more handfuls of flour into a mixing bowl. "First, you put the sugar with the lard. Then, the flour."

"Ich."

Undaunted, Minnie detailed all the rest of the steps in making the dough. Without cups and measuring spoons, Gretel was doubtful if the results would be edible. "What *is* it?" she asked, losing all patience.

"It's gingerbread. You don't know anything."

Gretel gasped. Gingerbread. She stuck her finger into the magic, brown dough and tasted it. Like swan or mermaids, like nighttime or a candy cottage with panes of sugar. She gloated at the forbidden old sweetness.

"You don't eat it yet. We roll it out on the table and you can cut out the people. Little gingerbread girls, eh? then we bake it. *Then* we eat."

"Aren't *you* going to make anything?" Gretel asked cautiously.

"I have a cutter. I show you." Minnie dug through a drawer of unfamiliar-looking utensils and drew forth a cookie-cutter in triumph.

"What is it?"

"It's a rabbit."

Gretel examined it closely, first on the outside, then its cutting edge. *"It's a toad!"*

Minnie backed away from the little girl. She cocked her head to one side.

"Tell me about the rats," Gretel said anxiously. She came over to Minnie and took her hand. "Are they *very* big? As big as me? Are there a lot of them? *Tell me!"*

"I don't know what you're saying." Minnie began to cough. It was not a laughing cough.

"You don't want to tell me, do you?" The old woman lowered herself onto a stool, bent double with the pain that spread across her chest and into her stomach. Gretel put her hands on Minnie's shoulders and pushed her back up to stare intently into her rheumy eyes. "Why is he alive? How did you make him come alive again?"

41

"Devil's child!" Minnie screamed. "Leave me be!"

"He died. A long time ago. I know. You showed me the letter. It said he died. Killed—I read it."

Minnie pushed Gretel away from her and ran out the kitchen door. For a moment she stood, uncertain, in the mist, then walked at a quick hobble to the road, turned toward the cemetery.

It had happened months before, in spring, while she helped Mother in the flower garden. Squeezing the clods of earth between her hands until, sudden as the pop of a balloon, they broke between her fingers in a sift of loam —enjoyable. Then, one, as she squeezed, squished. Dried mud flaked from back and belly, and Gretel had found, locked tight in her two hands, the toad. Her fear was not of warts; she had not heard that a toad's touch bred warts. Gretel had been spared many of the old-wives' tales: her mother's unbane imagination fed on cancer, heart disease, and, more recently, thalidomide. Gretel's fear was greater and less definite—without specific remedy. Through the summer, it sank malignant roots in the country soil, hung like pollen in the air, infected the water in the pumps. She seeded the country-side with her fear, subdued but ready to spring to her pale blue eyes, like a rabbit started from its hole, at the slightest provocation. Diffuse, private, echoing the bedtime legends —the Grimms and Andersens—that then composited their several horrors in her own dreams: an enchantment.

Yet, she was not helpless. She had a natural talent for exorcism. She was thorough, and she could be ruthless. And if fear could not be circumvented, it could be joined.

Without haste or bravado then, Gretel climbed the stairs once more. She tiptoed through the hall and inched open the door to Lew Haeckel's room. He was there, sleeping. A thread of brown saliva rolled out the side of his mouth. Gretel raised the blind, and a hazy, gray light spilled into the room, across the double-bed, beneath his eyelids.

"Whadaya want?" He raised himself on one elbow, blinking. "Why, hello sugar."

"Minnie's making gingerbread," Gretel announced.

"Well, she's not making any for *me*." Lew looked at Gretel cannily. "What's wrong, kid?"

"Is she a witch, really?"

"You bet your life she is."

"And the mouse . . ."

Slowly, Lew began to understand. His fat lips curled into a smile, showing brown teeth like Minnie's. "Oh, she can do that, too. You think she's up to something?" He looked around nervously. "Where is she?"

"She went . . . outside." Gretel did not dare mention the cemetery. "She made dough, but she hasn't made the cookies yet. She's going to make a *toad*."

"With the gingerbread, huh? A gingerbread toad?"

Gretel nodded.

"And you're afraid. Well, you can beat her at witching. She's pretty dumb, you know. For a witch." He began to speak more softly. "You think she'll turn you into a toad? Is that it, honey?" Gretel crept closer to the bed to hear what he was whispering. "She can do that. A black toad hopping in the mud. You wouldn't like that, a pretty girl like you." A chuckle, soft and lewd. "You've got to watch out for that gingerbread. I'll tell you what . . ." His voice was a wisp of sound. Gretel stood at his bedside, frozen with attention. "You go downstairs and take that dough, and make a cookie like Minnie . . ." His hand snaked out to circle her waist. She was too horrified at his implications to notice.

"And eat it!" she exclaimed.

"That's right, sugar. Then you don't have to worry about any old gingerbread toad. You'll take the wind out of her sails, all right."

He held her firmly now, pulled her closer to him.

"You're a pretty little girl, you know that? How about a kiss for your old Uncle Lew, seeing as how he's helped you out?"

"Let go." She tried to pull his hand away. His face bent toward hers, smiling. "Let me go! I know about you. Stop it!"

"Whadaya know, huh?"

"You're *dead*," Gretel screamed. "They buried you. Minnie is there now. You were killed. Dead."

The man's hulk shook with something like laughter. His grip loosened. Gretel broke away and retreated to the doorway. He quieted suddenly, although his body continued to tremble like a tree in a light breeze. He pulled himself up in his bed and spat into one of the tin cans.

"You're great, kid. You'll be the greatest witch yet. No fooling." When Gretel was halfway down the stairs, he called out after her—"We'll get along, sugar. You and me. Just wait." A drop of blood fell from Gretel's lip where she had been biting it. It made a blot on her jumper, the size of a pea.

In the kitchen, she rolled out the dough, according to Minnie's instructions, and cut out a five-inch witch with a greasy knife. The gingerbread witch stuck to the table. She scraped it free with the knife and reassembled it on the cookie sheet, which Minnie had already prepared. She took three raisins from the bag on the table and gave the gingerbread figure eyes and a black mouth—like Minnie's. She put the cookie sheet in the oven and nibbled fingers of the raw dough while she waited.

She brought the cookie sheet out of the oven. The witch was a rich brown on top, but crisp and black underneath. She had still to wait for it to cool. She was afraid Minnie would return, and sat at the parlor window to watch the road. Upstairs, Gretel could hear Lew shuffling about.

And, then, in the kitchen. The gingerbread witch was warm but—Gretel touched her tongue to it—not too warm to eat, easier, too, if you closed your eyes. One bite beheaded her. The three raisins were cinders, too dry to chew. She rinsed down the rest of it with water.

Outside the window, Gretel could see a wind spring out of the wood, tearing through the corn sheaves, striking the sodden clothes of the scarecrow, tumbling his hat into a furrow, lifting it into the air. Higher.

Lew was standing in the doorway, holding to the frame. Except for a week's stubble of beard, his face was white as his shirt collar. He was wearing a suit that was moderately clean.

"You done it, sure as hell, sugar." He spoke in short bursts of breath. "As good as roast her on a spit and serve her up at a church supper with whipped potatoes and green peas."

"You told me to."

"I needed to get away from her, get some fresh blood. Run with the tide. Minnie was old-fashioned. She kept me prisoned here." He pointed out the window to the scarecrow. "But the spell's broke." He inhaled deeply; his belly lifted and fell. A spate of blood darkened his cheeks and ebbed away. "You and me, sugar, we're going places. You gonna kiss me *now*, for old time's?"

Gretel wrinkled her nose. "You're fat and ugly."

"That's how she wanted me. A witch always keeps something beside her—a cat, a mouse, a cricket maybe."

"Rats?"

"Rats too. Or a black toad." He grinned. Gretel shuddered. "But Minnie had to have something that looked like her brother—so she dug him up. I had to do all the work, dragging this hulk around."

"Go away."

"Not anymore, sugar. I'm yours now. You outwitched her, but you've still got a lot to learn . . . and a lot of time to learn it. You're stuck with me, like it or not. And I like it."

"I don't want you." He shrugged and sat beside her at the table. The chair creaked under his weight. He wrapped his paw about her forearm. "You're ugly. You stink!" It was the harshest word she knew, but since it was, in this case, accurate, it seemed, like coffee made from used grounds, to lack full strength.

"If you don't like me the way I am, just say the word."

Gretel's eyes widened. "You mean. . . ."

"Gary Cooper," he suggested. "Fabian."

"No."

He leered. "—Bobby Kennedy?"

"No," Gretel said. "I want . . ."

Gretel, for the sake of propriety, bundled into her warm clothes and set off for the cemetery to find Minnie. The clouds had cleared away but the sun they revealed was feeble, an invalid's sun.

"Come along, Hansel," she called to the lovely cocker spaniel pup. He ran to her with an obedient yip. A bead of saliva glistened on the tip of his distended black-pink tongue.

Gretel glanced back once at the clapboard house that a grateful Township would soon—and at long last—have an opportunity to raze. It seemed to take forever to get to the cemetery.

Minnie was there under the poplar, where Gretel had expected her to be. The used-up body was draped indecorously over the stone. The half-hour of sunlight had dried the grass, but Minnie's wool dress was still damp and clinging. Her fingernails were caked with mud and shredded grass from digging around the stone. Hansel began to whine.

"Oh, shut up!" Gretel commanded.

He sat back on his haunches and watched a powerful, slow smile spread across his mistress' face.

A Connecticut-born poet and short story writer, Joseph Payne Brennan has published in a number of magazines, ranging from Weird Tales *to* Esquire. *His verse, collected in several books, has slowly but surely gained him a wide respect as one of the outstanding contemporary American poets. His poems depict a variety of moods and concerns—spectral, regionalistic and life-reflective—with some recurring themes, all of which form a distinctive and highly personal viewpoint. Brennan's work in prose is no less interesting, filled with striking atmosphere and a keen feeling for things sub rosa. He has created some memorable uncanny tales, including the often reprinted "Slime" and "Levitation," and his most recent book,* Stories of Darkness and Dread (Arkham House), *is one that deserves a place on every haunted bookshelf. Not in any of his books to date, though, is this suspenseful tale, first published in* Alfred Hitchcock's Mystery Magazine.

THE JUGULAR MAN

by Joseph Payne Brennan

MARLISS didn't tell me the full story about the bizarre burglary-murder attempt until several years after it happened.

Late one evening he set down his glass of port and looked at me keenly. "Funny, in a way," he commented, "we get on so well together. I myself a confirmed materialist, you a believer in unknown forces, unseen entities."

He leaned back in his armchair. "Only once in my life," he went on reflectively, "was my skepticism shaken —and that one time it was shaken pretty badly."

He paused and I grinned at him. "Marliss, if you stop now, murder will be committed right here in this room!"

He glanced around his crowded library. "Well, as you know, in a conservative sort of way I go in for curios and antiquarian bits. Conflicts a bit, I suppose, with my materialistic viewpoint, but maybe at the same time it serves as a sort of balance.

"Anyway, a number of years ago I used to prowl around the local flea markets. Picked up some unusual items for nominal prices."

I nodded. "I've heard of some fabulous finds."

"One Saturday afternoon," he continued, "I was rummaging around one of those open-air bazaars where they have stuff strewn on tables. I spotted a small metal turtle with a high curved carapace and realistic appendages. The carapace—the upper shell, that is—was meticulously carved into little squares. The head was gold colored with tiny red eyes—garnets I guess.

"I picked it up and examined it. Aside from a few scratches, it appeared to be in good condition. I supposed it was brass or some other base metal, but nevertheless it intrigued me.

"As I recall, I felt the price was too high and I began haggling with the owner—an accepted practice at flea markets. Our haggling was good-humored; in the course of it, the merchant told me there was a quaint legend connected with the little turtle. He said that he had only just acquired it and that it came from 'an impoverished Southern family' who had been forced to auction off all their possessions.

"At one time, he revealed, it had been equipped with some sort of concealed bell mechanism. You pressed down on the carapace and a bell rang. It was used for many years to summon servants. Finally there was only one servant left, an ancient man named Shift, a faithful 'old retainer.' At length Shift became so knotted up with arthritis and other ailments that the turtle bell was used only in cases of actual emergency.

"Finally—from lack of use, most likely—the mechanism ceased to operate. At least, the merchant admitted, he had been unable to ring the bell, no matter how hard he pressed down on the carapace. But he assured me the curio was 'virtually unique' and 'a steal,' in spite of the fact that the bell had stopped working. He suggested, moreover, that any jeweler worth his carats could probably repair the bell mechanism.

"I bought the thing. Paid twenty dollars. I felt that was high and I had no intention of giving a jeweler more money to repair a bell for which I had no real use anyway."

He sipped his port meditatively. "You know how it is at those flea markets. Your haggling is usually interrupted by five or six other people bent on beating down the price on a pressed-glass vase, a pair of bookends or what-have-you. My case was no exception. I wanted to get more detailed information about the legend connected with the turtle, but once the sale was consummated, the merchant—understandably—turned most of his attention elsewhere and I had to be content with the sparse information I had acquired. I half-suspected, in any case, that the old rascal had made up the whole story simply to help sell the little ornament. I never got back to that particular flea market and consequently never saw the merchant again.

"I took the turtle home, polished it a bit and set it on the night stand next to my bed. I had no special reason for putting it there. Perhaps it was simply that the night-stand was less littered than any other surface I could find at that particular time. The carapace had a sort of sheen to it under the night stand lamp and I got used to seeing it there—so there it remained. I tried pressing the carapace a few times, but nothing ever happened—I never heard even the faintest click or whirr.

"Well, life hurried on and the turtle receded into the background. Once a friend of mine spotted it and offered to buy it for twice what I had paid. This immediately made me suspicious and I refused to sell.

"Then came that gory business with 'the midnight slasher' or 'the jugular man', as the local papers called him. You remember, of course?"

I filled my glass. "I could scarcely forget. Especially in view of the finale. He broke into homes around midnight. Never content merely to steal. Unless the house was un-occupied at the time of entry, he slashed his victims' throats. In most cases they never managed to get out of bed. He murdered five people as I recall."

"Those are the correct facts," Marliss resumed. "The whole city was in an uproar. Police patrols were doubled; people bought guns and watchdogs. Local hardware stores sold locks by the carton—all to no avail."

I looked at him curiously. "Until your turn came."

He frowned. "I never thought about the matter much. Just too busy I guess. And I wasn't known as a man of wealth. Small house in an area barely above middle-class. Not the sort of place the jugular man usually selected for his midnight caper.

"I'd gone to bed about ten-thirty. A tough day; I was bushed. I don't know what woke me up. The jugular man seldom made any noise. He walked like a cat and they said he could see in the dark. Possibly on this one occa-sion he did make a little noise. Or perhaps as you would probably prefer to believe, some kind of intuitive warn-ing touched my brain even through the tangled mists of sleep. No matter. I woke up. Abruptly. He was standing right inside the open window. The room was filled with moonlight. I could see his features clearly—high cheek-bones, modified Roman nose, thin lips, altogether neat and intelligent looking. Not what you'd expect. But his eyes had a peculiar glitter to them. *That* wasn't the glitter that froze me with fright however. It was the glitter of moonlight on the ten-inch knife blade in his right hand that turned me into a jellyfish.

"I sat up and tried to call out but my vocal cords appeared to have suddenly become atrophied. He saw that I was awake and he began to advance toward the bed. Not a lunge—just a slow deliberate walk—a cat closing in on a terrified mouse. Those strangely glittering eyes held mine and I couldn't utter a sound.

"To this day I've never figured out why I did then what I did do. As I look back, I almost feel it was at the prompting of some 'outside' agency, as you yourself might term it. All I can conclude is that the brain works in marvelous ways.

"As if it had a separate life of its own, my right arm shot out and my hand settled on the carapace of that metal turtle which still rested on my night table. I pressed the carapace with all my strength.

"I believe my sudden movement puzzled the jugular man. He hesitated momentarily. He had assumed, I imagine, that I was completely petrified with terror—literally incapable of movement.

"I suppose he quickly concluded that, in spite of my obvious and extreme fright, I was reaching for a gun. He leaped forward."

Marliss took out a handkerchief and patted his forehead. "He almost made it to the foot of my bed. But my hand remained on the carapace of that turtle and suddenly a bell was ringing—ringing loudly, filling the room with its clamor. It was louder than the average alarm clock.

"As the jugular man bounded toward the bed, something appeared there in front of him. At the time I could see only its back. In the moonlight it looked like a tall thin bundle of rotting black rags through which a few brown bones protruded. It blocked the face of the jugular man from my view. As I lifted my hand from the top of the turtle and it stopped ringing, I heard something strike the rug—the jugular man's knife.

"A second or so later he screamed. It was like a scream from the Pit. It made my hair stiffen. I heard him pounding across the floor, then the crash of window glass, then —silence."

Marliss wiped his forehead again. "I know the—thing—saved my life, but I wish it hadn't faced around. With the last tinkle of falling window glass, that tattered and hideous thing turned and looked right at me, that is, it would have looked if it had had any eyes. All I saw was a skull with empty eye sockets. I felt no sense of hostility —quite the opposite. I had the crazy feeling that it wanted to make sure I was all right. As I stared at it, still speechless, it vanished. I was left looking at the moonlight shining on the jagged edges of my shattered window pane."

He shook his head. "I knew there was no sense in telling the police the whole story. They found the midnight slasher on the ground near my front garden gate. His jugular had been pierced by a jagged fragment of protruding window glass and he had bled to death. In his panic to escape he had misjudged the height of the half-open window and as he smashed through the pane a thin but lethal sliver of glass had severed his jugular like a scalpel.

"I gave the police the basic facts, omitting the ringing of the bell and the appearance of that—whatever it was —in response to it. I told them that in desperation I had reached for the turtle, intending to hurl it at the jugular man. Assuming I was reaching for a loaded gun, I suggested to them, he had bolted. They accepted my story reluctantly. The jugular man had never been frightened off before. The papers, of course, had a field day as they described the method of the murderer's death. It did appear to be 'poetic justice,' as you chaps say—the throat slasher bleeding to death with a pierced jugular."

"And what about your own personal explanation?" I prodded him.

He rubbed his chin. "I never unearthed any further information about the turtle but I began to add things up. I finally concluded that the bazaar man had given me the basic truth—completely omitting the time element. The 'impoverished Southern family,' I decided, had become impoverished—like so many others—by the Civil War. The faithful 'old retainer,' Shift, had originally been a slave, a household servant devoted to a family whom he had probably catered to for generations.

"Somehow, the emotion kindled by my sudden and intense terror had traveled back through time as I pressed the carapace of that turtle. Whether the bell

52

really rang—it certainly seemed to—or rang only in another dimension of time I can't rightly say.

"But in any event the spirit of faithful old Shift heard it ringing back down through the dim corridors of time. He sensed my terror. Since I possessed the turtle and was pressing the carapace in a moment of mortal fright, he must have concluded that I was a member of that 'impoverished Southern family' which he had served so long.

"He came back, as well as he could, under the circumstances. Instead of appearing as in life, however, he simply materialized as he lay, after a hundred years or so in the grave."

"If he had come back as he appeared in life," I pointed out, "the jugular man might merely have brushed him aside."

Marliss nodded. "I've thought of that. I just don't know!" He sighed. "To tell you the truth, I don't like to ponder on the business at all. Gives me a headache—and it still conflicts with my basic beliefs."

"I don't want to nit-pick," I said, "but didn't you say the dealer told you he had *only just acquired* the turtle from an impoverished Southern family?"

Marliss shook his head impatiently. "No. He said that he himself had only just acquired it and that it came from such a family. What he meant, obviously, was that it had come *originally* from such a family. Heaven only knows how many other persons had owned the turtle at one time or another."

"One more question. What did you do with it?"

Marliss stood up. "Gave it to an art museum. It's now on display, locked under shatter-proof glass. I don't imagine anyone will ever press that carapace again under circumstances even remotely similar to mine."

He looked at his empty glass. "I'm going down to the cellar for another bottle of port. And you'd better have a funny story ready when I get back. I want to get some sleep tonight!"

Fritz Leiber is an amazing talent. In a long and much honored career he's written with brilliance in a variety of genres and sub-genres: satirical science fiction, sword and sorcery, "hard" science fiction in the Campbell tradition, supernatural horror stories in the Weird Tales manner, style-breaking virtuoso works such as "Gonna Roll The Bones," modern terror tales in urban settings. Which says nothing of writing poetry, acting and having done some of the most insightful literary criticism to date on two recent masters of fantasy fiction, Robert E. Howard and H.P. Lovecraft. There's no telling what Fritz Leiber will do next, or what he'll pull out of his idea-lined hat, but it's happy to anticipate. In the meanwhile, this pungent story from his Weird Tales period called . . . .

ALICE AND THE ALLERGY

by Fritz Leiber

THERE was a knocking. The doctor put down his pen. Then he heard his wife hurrying down the stairs. He resumed his history of old Mrs. Easton's latest blood-clot.

The knocking was repeated. He reminded himself to get after Engstrand to fix the bell.

After a pause long enough for him to write a sentence and a half, there came a third and louder burst of knocking. He frowned and got up.

It was dark in the hall. Alice was standing on the third step from the bottom, making no move to answer the door. As he went past her he shot her an inquiring glance. He noted that her eyelids looked slightly puffy, as if she were having another attack—an impression which the hoarseness of her voice a moment later confirmed.

"*He* knocked that way," was what she whispered. She sounded frightened. He looked back at her with an expression of greater puzzlement—which almost immediately, however, changed to comprehension. He gave her a sympathetic, semi-professional nod, as if to say, "I understand now. Glad you mentioned it. We'll talk about it later." Then he opened the door.

It was Renshaw from the Allergy Lab. "Got the new kit for you, Howard," he remarked in an amiable Southern drawl. "Finished making it up this afternoon and thought I'd bring it around myself."

"A million thanks. Come on in."

Alice had retreated a few steps farther up the stairs. Renshaw did not appear to notice her in the gloom. He was talkative as he followed Howard into his office.

"An interestin' case turned up. Very unusual. A doctor we supply lost a patient by broncho-spasm. Nurse mistakenly injected the shot into a vein. In ten seconds he

56

was strangling. Edema of the glottis developed. Injected aminophylline and epinephrine—no dice. Tried to get a bronchoscope down his windpipe to give him air, but couldn't manage. Finally did a tracheotomy, but by that time it was too late."

"You always have to be damned careful," Howard remarked.

"Right," Renshaw agreed cheerfully. He set the kit on the desk and stepped back. "Well, if we don't identify the substance responsible for your wife's allergy this time, it won't be for lack of imagination. I added some notions of my own to your suggestions."

"Good."

"You know, she's well on her way to becoming the toughest case I ever made kits for. We've tested all the ordinary substances, and most of the extraordinary."

Howard nodded, his gaze following the dark woodwork toward the hall door. "Look," he said, "do many doctors tell you about allergy patients showing fits of acute depression during attacks, a tendency to rake up unpleasant memories—especially old fears?"

"Depression seems to be a pretty common symptom," said Renshaw cautiously. "Let's see, how long is it she's been bothered?"

"About two years—ever since six months after our marriage." Howard smiled. "That arouses certain obvious suspicions, but you know how exhaustively we've tested myself, my clothes, my professional equipment."

"I should say so," Renshaw assured him. For a moment the men were silent. Then, "She suffers from depression and fear?"

Howard nodded.

"Fear of anything in particular?"

But Howard did not answer that question.

About ten minutes later, as the outside door closed on the man from the Allergy Lab, Alice came slowly down the stairs.

The puffiness around her eyes was more marked, emphasizing her paleness. Her eyes were still fixed on the door.

"You know Renshaw, of course," her husband said.

"Of course, dear," she answered huskily, with a little

laugh. "It was just the knocking. It made me remember *him*."

"That so?" Howard inquired cheerily. "I don't think you've ever told me that detail. I'd always assumed—"

"No," she said, "the bell to Auntie's house was out of order that afternoon. So it was his knocking that drew me through the dark hallway and made me open the door, so that I saw his white avid face and long strong hands —with the big dusty couch just behind me, where . . . and my hand on the curtain sash, with which he—"

"Don't think about it." Howard reached up and caught hold of her cold hand. "That chap's been dead for two years now. He'll strangle no more women."

"Are you sure?" she asked.

"Of course. Look, dear, Renshaw's brought a new kit. We'll make the scratch tests right away."

She followed him obediently into the examination room across the hall from the office. He rejected the forearm she offered him—it still showed faint evidences of the last test. As he swabbed off the other, he studied her face.

"Another little siege, eh? Well, we'll ease that with a mild ephedrine spray."

"Oh it's nothing," she said. "I wouldn't mind it at all if it weren't for those stupid moods that go with it."

"I know," he said, blocking out the test areas.

"I always have that idiotic feeling," she continued hesitantly, "that *he's* trying to get at me."

Ignoring her remark, he picked up the needle. They were both silent as he worked with practiced speed and care. Finally he sat back, remarking with considerably more confidence than he felt, "There! I bet you this time we've nailed the elusive little demon who likes to choke you!"—and looked up at the face of the slim, desirable, but sometimes maddeningly irrational person he had made his wife.

"I wonder if you've considered it from my point of view," he said, smiling. "I know it was a horrible experience, just about the worst a woman can undergo. But if it hadn't happened, I'd never have been called in to take care of you—and we'd never have got married."

"That's true," she said, putting her hand on his.

"It was completely understandable that you should have spells of fear afterwards," he continued. "Anyone would. Though I do think your background made a difference.

58

After all, your aunt kept you so shut away from people —men especially. Told you they were all sadistic, evil-minded brutes. You know, sometimes when I think of that woman deliberately trying to infect you with all her rotten fears, I find myself on the verge of forgetting that she was no more responsible for her actions than any other mis-educated neurotic."

She smiled at him gratefully.

"At any rate," he went on, "it was perfectly natural that you should be frightened, especially when you learned that he was a murderer with a record, who had killed other women and had even, in two cases where he'd been interrupted, made daring efforts to come back and com-plete the job. Knowing that about him, it was plain real-ism on your part to be scared—at least intelligently ap-prehensive—as long as he was on the loose. Even after we were married.

"But then, when you got incontrovertible proof—" He fished in his pocket. "Of course, he didn't formally pay the law's penalty, but he's just as dead as if he had." He smoothed out a worn old newspaper clipping. "You can't have forgotten this," he said gently, and began to read:

MYSTERY STRANGLER
UNMASKED BY DEATH

Lansing, Dec. 22. (Universal Press)—A mysteri-ous boarder who died two days ago at a Kinsey Street rooming house has been conclusively identi-fied as the uncaught rapist and strangler who in recent years terrified three Midwestern cities. Police Lieutenant Jim Galeto, interviewed by reporters in the death room at 1555 Kinsey Street . . .

She covered the clipping with her hand. "Please."

"Sorry," he said, "but an idea had occurred to me— one that would explain your continuing fear. I don't think you've ever hinted at it, but are you really completely satisfied that this was the man? Or is there a part of your mind that still doubts, that believes the police mistaken, that pictures the killer still at large? I know you identi-fied the photographs, but sometimes, Alice, I think it was a mistake that you didn't go to Lansing like they wanted you to and see with your own eyes—"

"I wouldn't want to go near that city, ever." Her lips had thinned.

"But when your peace of mind was at stake. . . ."

"No, Howard," she said. "And besides, you're absolutely wrong. From the first moment I never had the slightest doubt that *he* was the man who died—"

"But in that case—"

"And furthermore, it was only then, when my allergy started, that I really began to be afraid of him."

"But surely, Alice—" Calm substituted for anger in his manner. "Oh, I know you can't believe any of that occult rot your aunt was always falling for."

"No, I don't," she said. "It's something very different."

"What?"

But that question was not answered. Alice was looking down at the inside of her arm. He followed her gaze to where a white welt was rapidly filling one of the squares.

"What's it mean?" she asked nervously.

"Mean?" he almost yelled. "Why, you dope, it means we've licked the thing at last! It means we've found the substance that causes your allergy. I'll call Renshaw right away and have him make up the shots."

He picked up one of the vials, frowned, checked it against the area. "That's odd," he said. "HOUSEHOLD DUST. We've tried that a half dozen times. But then, of course, it's always different. . . ."

"Howard," she said, "I don't like it. I'm frightened."

He looked at her lovingly. "The little dope," he said to her softly. "She's about to be cured—and she's frightened." And he hugged her. She was cold in his arms.

But by the time they sat down to dinner, things were more like normal. The puffiness had gone out of her eyelids and he was briskly smiling.

"Got hold of Renshaw. He was very 'interested.' HOUSEHOLD DUST was one of his ideas. He's going down to the Lab tonight and will have the shots over early tomorrow. The sooner we start, the better. I also took the opportunity to phone Engstrand. He'll try to get over to fix the bell, this evening. Heard from Mrs. Easton's nurse too. Things aren't so well there. I'm pretty sure there'll be bad news by tomorrow morning at latest. I may have to rush over any minute. I hope it doesn't happen tonight, though."

It didn't and they spent a quiet evening—not even Engstrand showed up—which could have been very pleasant had Alice been a bit less preoccupied.

But about three o'clock he was shaken out of sleep by her trembling. She was holding him tight.

"*He's* coming." Her whisper was whistling, laryngitic.

"What?" He sat up, half pulling her with him. "I'd better give you another eph—"

"Sh! What's that? Listen."

He rubbed his face. "Look, Alice," after a moment, he said, "I'll go downstairs and make sure there's nothing there."

"No, don't!" she clung to him. For a minute or two they huddled there without speaking. Gradually his ears became attuned to the night sounds—the drone and mumble of the city, the house's faint, closer creakings. Something had happened to the street lamp and incongruous unmixed moonlight streamed through the window beyond the foot of the bed.

He was about to say something, when she let go of him and said, in a more normal voice, "There. It's gone."

She slipped out of bed, went to the window, opened it wider, and stood there, breathing deeply.

"You'll get cold, come back to bed," he told her.

"In a while."

The moonlight was in key with her flimsy nightgown. He got up, rummaged around for her quilted bathrobe and, in draping it around her, tried an embrace. She didn't respond.

He got back in bed and watched her. She had found a chair-arm and was looking out the window. The bathrobe had fallen back from her shoulders. He felt wide awake, his mind crawlingly active.

"You know, Alice," he said, "there may be a psychoanalytic angle to your fear."

"Yes?" She did not turn her head.

"Maybe, in a sense, your libido is still tied to the past. Unconsciously, you may still have that distorted conception of sex your aunt drilled into you, something sadistic and murderous. And it's possible your unconscious mind had tied your allergy in with it—you said it was a dusty couch. See what I'm getting at?"

She still looked out the window.

"It's an ugly idea and of course your conscious mind

wouldn't entertain it for a moment, but your aunt's influence set the stage and, when all's said and done, *he* was your first experience of men. Maybe in some small way, your libido is still linked to . . . him."

She didn't say anything.

Rather late next morning he awoke feeling sluggish and irritable. He got out of the room quietly, leaving her still asleep, breathing easily. As he was getting a second cup of coffee, a jarringly loud knocking summoned him to the door. It was a messenger with the shots from the Allergy Lab. On his way to the examination room he phoned Engstrand again, heard him promise he'd be over in a half hour sure, cut short a long-winded explanation as to what had tied up the electrician last night.

He started to phone Mrs. Easton's place, decided against it.

He heard Alice in the kitchen.

In the examination room he set some water to boil in the sterilizing pan, got out instruments. He opened the package from the Allergy Lab, frowned at the inscription HOUSEHOLD DUST, set down the container, walked over to the window, came back and frowned again, went to his office and dialed the Lab.

"Renshaw?"

"Uh huh. Get the shots?"

"Yes, many thanks. But I was just wondering . . . you know, it's rather odd we should hit it with household dust after so many misses."

"Not so odd, when you consider. . . ."

"Yes, but I was wondering exactly where the stuff came from."

"Just a minute."

He shifted around in his swivel chair. In the kitchen Alice was humming a tune.

"Say, Howard, look, I'm awfully sorry, but Johnson seems to have gone off with the records. I'm afraid I won't be able to get hold of them 'til afternoon."

"Oh, that's all right. Just curiosity. You don't have to bother."

"No, I'll let you know. Well, I suppose you'll be making the first injection this morning?"

"Right away. You know we're both grateful to you for having hit on the substance responsible."

"No credit due me. Just a . . ." Renshaw chuckled ". . . shot in the dark."

Some twenty minutes later, when Alice came into the examination room, Howard was struck, to a degree that quite startled him, with how pretty and desirable she looked. She had put on a white dress and her smiling face showed no signs of last night's attack. For a moment he had the impulse to take her in his arms, but then he remembered last night and decided against it.

As he prepared to make the injection, she eyed the hypodermics, bronchoscope, and scalpels laid out on the sterile towel.

"What are those for?" she asked lightly.

"Just routine stuff, never use them."

"You know," she said laughingly, "I was an awful ninny last night. Maybe you're right about my libido. At any rate, I've put *him* out of my life forever. He can't ever get at me again. From now on, you're the only one."

He grinned, very happily. Then his eyes grew serious and observant as he made the injection, first withdrawing the needle repeatedly to make sure there were no signs of venous blood. He watched her closely.

The phone jangled.

"Damn," he said. "That'll be Mrs. Easton's nurse. Come along with me."

He hurried through the swinging door. She started after him.

But it wasn't Mrs. Easton's nurse. It was Renshaw.

"Found the records. Johnson didn't have them after all. Just misplaced. And there *is* something out of the way. That dust didn't come from there at all. It came from . . ."

There came a knocking. He strained to hear what Renshaw was saying.

"What?" He whipped out a pencil. "Say that again. Don't mind the noise. It's just our electrician coming to fix the bell. What was that city?"

The knocking was repeated.

"Yes, I've got that. And the exact address of the place the dust came from?"

There came a third and louder burst of knocking, which grew to a violent tattoo.

Finishing his scribbling, he hung up with a bare

"Thanks," to Renshaw, and hurried to the door just as the knocking died.

There was no one there.

Then he realized. He hardly dared push open the door to the examination room, yet no one could have gone more quickly.

Alice's agonizingly arched, suffocated body was lying on the rug. Her heels, which just reached the hardwood flooring, made a final, weak knock-knock. Her throat was swollen like a toad's.

Before he made another movement he could not stop himself from glaring around, window and door, as if for an escaping intruder.

As he snatched for his instruments, knowing for an absolute certainty that it would be too late, a slip of paper floated down from his hand.

On it was scribbled, "Lansing. 1555 Kinsey Street."

L.P. Hartley, who died in his native England in 1973, is chiefly known as a distinguished mainstream novelist and perhaps best remembered for his novel The Go-Between, *made into an award-winning film with Julie Christie and Alan Bates. What Hartley's name may well endure for, however, are his tales of terror and fright. He was an unqualified master of the form, not just for frequently reprinted gems such as "The Travelling Grave" and "A Visitor From Down Under", but for approximately two dozen stories written over a period of almost fifty years, many of which are authentic masterpieces. "The Island", a subtle and scary depiction of strange events in the night hours, first saw publication in one of Hartley's early books in the 1920s and was reprinted later in his collection* The Travelling Grave, *a must book for any connoisseur of the horror tale.*

THE ISLAND

by L. P. Hartley

How WELL I remembered the summer aspect of Mrs. Santander's island, and the gratefully deciduous trees among the pines of that countryside coming down to the water's edge and over it! How their foliage, sloping to a shallow dome, sucked in the sunlight, giving it back all grey and green! The sea, tossing and glancing, refracted the light from a million spumy points; the tawny sand glared, a monochrome unmitigated by shades; and the cliffs, always bare, seemed to have achieved an unparalleled nudity, every speck on their brown flanks clamouring for recognition.

Now every detail was blurred or lost. In the insufficient, ill-distributed November twilight the island itself was invisible. Forms and outlines survive but indistinctly in the memory; it was hard to believe that the spit of shingle on which I stood was the last bulwark of that huge discursive land-locked harbour, within whose meagre mouth Mrs. Santander's sea-borne territory seemed to ride at anchor. In the summer I pictured it as some crustacean, swallowed by an ill-turned starfish, but unassimilated. How easy it had been to reach it in Mrs. Santander's gay plunging motorboat! And how inaccessible it seemed now, with the motorboat fallen, as she had written to tell me, into war-time disuse, with a sea running high and so dark that save for the transparent but scarcely luminous wave-tips, it looked like an agitated solid. The howling of the wind, and the oilskins in which he was encased, made it hard to attract the ferryman's attention. I shouted to him: "Can you take me over to the island?"

"No, I can't," said the ferryman, and pointed to the tumultuous waves in the harbour.

"What are you here for?" I bawled. "I tell you I must get across; I have to go back to France tomorrow."

In such circumstances it was impossible to argue without heat. The ferryman turned, relenting a little. He asked querulously in the tone of one who must raise a difficulty at any cost: "What if we both get drowned?"

What a fantastic objection! "Nonsense," I said. "There's no sea to speak of; anyhow, I'll make it worth your while."

The ferryman grunted at my unintentional pleasantry. Then, as the landing stage was submerged by the exceptionally high tide, he carried me on his back to the boat, my feet trailing in the water. The man lurched at every step, for I was considerably heavier than he; but at last, waist-deep in water, he reached the boat and turned sideways for me to embark. How uncomfortable the whole business was. Why couldn't Mrs. Santander spend November in London like other people? Why was I so infatuated as to follow her here on the last night of my leave when I might have been lolling in the stalls of a theatre? The craft was behaving oddly, rolling so much that at every other stroke one of the boatman's attenuated seafaring oars would be left high and dry. Once, when we happened to be level with each other, I asked him the reason of Mrs. Santander's seclusion. At the top of his voice he replied: "Why, they do say she be lovesick. Look out!" he added, for we had reached the end of our short passage and were "standing by" in the surf, a few yards from the shore, waiting for an "easy" in the succession of breakers. But the ferryman misjudged it. Just as the keel touched the steep shingle bank, a wave caught the boat, twisted it round and half over, and I lost my seat and rolled about in the bottom of the boat, getting very wet.

How dark it was among the trees. Acute physical discomfort had almost made me forget Mrs. Santander. But as I stumbled up the grassy slope I longed to see her.

She was not in the hall to welcome me. The butler, discreetly noticing my condition, said: "We will see about your things, sir." I was thankful to take them off, and I flung them about the floor of my bedroom—that huge apartment that would have been square but for the bow-window built on to the end. The wind tore at this window, threatening to drive it in; but not a curtain moved. Soundlessness, I remembered, was characteristic of the house. Indeed, I believe you might have screamed yourself hoarse in that room and not have been heard in the adjoining bathroom. Thither I hastened and wallowed long and luxuriously in the marble bath; deliberately I splashed the water over the side, simply to see it collected and marshalled away down the little grooves that unerringly received it. When I emerged, swathed in hot towels, I found my clothes already dried and pressed. Wonderful household. A feeling of unspeakable well-being descended upon me as, five minutes before dinner-time, I entered the drawing-room. It was empty. What pains Mrs. Santander must be bestowing on her toilette! Was it becoming her chief asset? I wondered. Perish the thought! She had a hundred charms of movement, voice and expression, and yet she defied analysis. She was simply irresistible! How Santander, her impossible husband, could have retired to South America to nurse an injured pride, or as he doubtless called it, an injured honour, passed my comprehension. She had an art to make the most commonplace subject engaging. I remembered having once admired the lighting of the house. I had an odd fancy that it had a quality not found elsewhere, a kind of whiteness, a power of suggesting silence. It helped to give her house its peculiar hush. "Yes," she had said, "and it's all so simple; the sea makes it, just by going in and out!" A silly phrase, but her intonation made it linger in the memory like a charm.

I sat at the piano and played. There were some songs on the music-rest—Wolf, full of strange chords and accidentals so that I couldn't be sure I was right. But they interested me; and I felt so happy that I failed to notice how the time was drawing on—eight o'clock, and dinner should have been at a quarter to. Growing a little restless, I rose and walked up and down the room. One corner of it was in shadow, so I turned on all the lights. I had found it irritating to watch the regular expansion and shrinkage of my shadow. Now I could see everything; but I still felt constrained, sealed up in that admirable room. It was always a shortcoming of mine not to be able to wait patiently. So I wandered into the dining-room and almost thought—such is the power of overstrung anticipation—that I saw Mrs. Santander sitting at the head of the oval table. But it was only an effect of the candlelight.

The two places were laid, hers and mine; the glasses with twisty stems were there, such a number of glasses for the two of us! Suddenly I remembered I was smoking and, taking an almond, I left the room to its four candles. I peeped inside the library; it was in darkness, and I realized, as I fumbled for the switch without being able to find it, that I was growing nervous. How ridiculous! Of course, Mrs. Santander wouldn't be in the library and in the dark. Abandoning the search for the switch, I returned to the drawing-room.

I vaguely expected to find it altered, and yet I had ceased to expect to see Mrs. Santander appear at any moment. That always happens when one waits for a person who doesn't come. But there *was* an alteration—in me. I couldn't find any satisfaction in struggling with Wolf; the music had lost its hold. So I drew a chair up to the china-cabinet; it had always charmed me with its figures of Chinamen, those white figures, conventional and stiff, but so smooth and luminous and significant. I found myself wondering, as often before, whether the ferocious pleasure in their expressions was really the Oriental artist's conception of unqualified good humour, or whether they were not, after all, rather cruel people. And this disquieting topic aroused others that I had tried succesfully to repress: the exact connotation of my staying in the house as Mrs. Santander's guest, an unsporting little mouse playing when the cat was so undeniably, so effectually away. To ease myself of these obstinate questionings, I leant forward to open the door of the cabinet, intending to distract myself by taking one of the figures into my hands. Suddenly I heard a sound and looked up. A man was standing in the middle of the room.

"I'm afraid the cabinet's locked," he said.

In spite of my bewilderment, something in his appearance struck me as odd: he was wearing a hat. It was a grey felt hat, and he had an overcoat that was grey too.

"I hope you don't take me for a burglar," I said, trying to laugh.

"Oh no," he replied, "not that." I thought his eyes were smiling, but his mouth was shadowed by a dark moustache. He was a handsome man. Something in his face struck me as familiar; but it was not an unusual type and I might easily have been mistaken.

In the hurry of getting up I knocked over a set of fire-irons—the cabinet flanked the fireplace—and there was a tremendous clatter. It alarmed and then revived me. But I had a curious feeling of defencelessness as I stooped down to pick the fire-irons up, and it was difficult to fix them into their absurd sockets. The man in grey watched my operations without moving. I began to resent his presence. Presently he moved and stood with his back to the fire, stretching out his fingers to the warmth.

"We haven't been introduced," I said.

"No," he replied, "we haven't."

Then, while I was growing troubled and exasperated by his behaviour, he offered an explanation. "I'm the engineer Mrs. Santander calls in now and then to superintend her electric plant. That's how I know my way about. She's so inventive, and she doesn't like to take risks." He volunteered this. "And I came in here in case any of the fittings needed adjustment. I see they don't."

"No," I said, secretly reassured by the stranger's account of himself; "but I wish—of course, I speak without Mrs. Santander's authority—I wish you'd have a look at the switches in the library. They're damned inconvenient." I was so pleased with myself for having compassed the expletive that I scarcely noticed how the engineer's fingers, still avid of warmth, suddenly became rigid.

"Oh, you've been in the library, have you?" he said.

I replied that I had got no further than the door. "But if you can wait," I added politely to this superior mechanic who liked to style himself an engineer, "Mrs. Santander will be here in a moment."

"You're expecting her?" asked the mechanic.

"I'm staying in the house," I replied stiffly. The man was silent for several moments. I noticed the refinement in his face, the good cut of his clothes. I pondered upon the physical disability that made it impossible for him to join the army.

"She makes you comfortable here?" he asked; and a physical disturbance, sneezing or coughing, I supposed, seized him, for he took out his handkerchief and turned from me with all the instinct of good breeding. But I felt that the question was one his station scarcely entitled him to make, and ignored it. He recovered himself.

70

"I'm afraid I can't wait," he said. "I must be going home. The wind is dropping. By the way," he added, "we have a connection in London. I think I may say it's a good firm. If ever you want an electric plant installed! —I left a card somewhere." He searched for it vainly. "Never mind," he said, with his hand on the door, "Mrs. Santander will give you all particulars." Indulgently I waved my hand, and he was gone.

A moment later it seemed to me that he wouldn't be able to cross to the mainland without notifying the ferryman. I rang the bell. The butler appeared. "Mrs. Santander is very late, sir," he said.

"Yes," I replied, momentarily dismissing the question. "But there's a man, a mechanic or something—you probably know." The butler looked blank. "Anyhow," I said, "a man has been here attending to the lighting; he wants to go home; would you telephone the boatman to come and fetch him away?"

When the butler had gone to execute my order, my former discomfort and unease returned. The adventure with the engineer had diverted my thoughts from Mrs. Santander. Why didn't she come? Perhaps she had fallen asleep, dressing. It happened to women when they were having their hair brushed. Gertrude was imperious and difficult; her maid might be afraid to wake her. Then I remembered her saying in her letter, "I shall be an awful fright because I've had to give my maid the sack." It was funny how the colloquialisms jarred when you saw them in black and white; it was different when she was speaking. Ah, just to hear her voice! Of course, the loss of her maid would hinder her, and account for some delay. Lucky maid, I mused confusedly, to have her hair in your hands! Her image was all before me as I walked aimlessly about the room. Half tranced with the delight of that evocation, I stopped in front of a great bowl, ornamented with dragons, that stood on the piano. Half an hour ago I had studied its interior that depicted terra-cotta fish with magenta fins swimming among conventional weeds. My glance idly sought the pattern again. It was partially covered by a little slip of paper. Ah! the engineer's card! His London connection! Amusedly I turned it over to read the engineer's name.

"Mr. Maurice Santander."

I started violently, the more that at the same moment there came a knock at the door. It was only the butler; but I was so bewildered I scarcely recognized him. Too well-trained perhaps to appear to notice my distress, he delivered himself almost in a speech. "We can't find any trace of the person you spoke of, sir. The ferryman's come across and he says there's no one at the landing-stage."

"The gentleman," I said, "has left this," and I thrust the card into the butler's hand.

"Why, that must be Mr. Santander!" the servant of Mr. Santander's wife at last brought out.

"Yes," I replied, "and I think perhaps as it's getting late, we ought to try and find Mrs. Santander. The dinner will be quite spoiled."

Telling the butler to wait and not to alarm the servants, I went alone to Gertrude's room. From the end of a long passage I saw the door standing partly open; I saw, too, that the room was in darkness. There was nothing strange in that, I told myself; but it would be methodical, it would save time, to examine the intervening rooms first. Examine! What a misleading word. I banished it, and "search" came into my mind. I rejected that too. As I explored the shuttered silences I tried to find a formula that would amuse Gertrude, some facetious understatement of my agitated quest. "A little tour of inspection"— she would like that. I could almost hear her say: "So you expected to find me under a sofa!" I wouldn't tell her that I had looked under the sofas, unless to make a joke of it: something about dust left by the housemaid. I rose to my knees, spreading my hands out in the white glow. Not a speck. But wasn't conversation—conversation with Gertrude—made up of little half-truths, small forays into fiction? With my hand on the door—it was of the last room and led on to the landing—I rehearsed the pleasantry aloud: "During the course of a little tour of inspection, Gertrude, I went from one dust-heap to another, from dust unto dust I might almost say. . . ." This time I must overcome my unaccountable reluctance to enter her room. Screwing up my courage, I stepped into the passage, but for all my resolution I got no further.

The door still stood as I had first seen it—half open; but there was a light in the room—a rather subdued light, possibly from the standard-lamp by the bed. I knocked and called "Gertrude!" and when there was no reply I pushed open the door. It moved from right to left so as not to expose the bulk of the room, which lay on the left side. It seemed a long time before I was fairly in.

I saw the embers of the fire, the pale troubled lights of the mirror, and, vivid in the pool of light by the bed, a note. It said: "Forgive me dearest, I have had to go. I can't explain why, but we shall meet some time. All my love., G." There was no envelope, no direction, but the handwriting was hers and the informality characteristic of her. It was odd that the characters, shaky as they were, did not seem to have been written in haste. I was trying to account for this, trying to stem, by an act of concentration, the tide of disappointment that was sweeping over me, when a sudden metallic whirr sounded in my ear. It was the telephone—the small subsidiary telephone that communicated with the servants' quarters. "It will save their steps," she had said, when I urged her to have it put in; and I remembered my pleasure in this evidence of consideration, for my own motives had been founded in convenience and even in prudence. Now I loathed the black shiny thing that buzzed so raucously and never moved. And what could the servants have to say to me except that Mr. Santander had—well, gone. What else was there for him to do? The instrument rang again and I took up the receiver.

"Yes?"

"Please, sir, dinner is served."

"Dinner!" I echoed. It was nearly ten, but I had forgotten about that much-postponed meal.

"Yes, sir. Didn't you give orders to have it ready immediately? For two, I think you said, sir." The voice sounded matter-of-fact enough, but in my bewilderment I nearly lost all sense of what I was doing. At last I managed to murmur in a voice that might have been anybody's: "Yes, of course, for two."

On second thoughts, I left the telephone disconnected. I felt just then that I couldn't bear another summons. And, though my course was clear, I did not know what to do next; my will had nothing but confusion to work with. In the dark perhaps, I might collect myself. But it didn't occur to me to turn out the light; instead, I parted the heavy curtains that shut off the huge bow-window and drew them behind me. The rain was driving furiously

73

against the double casements, but not a sound vouched for its energy. A moon shone at intervals, and by the light of one gleam, brighter than the rest, I saw a scrap of paper, crushed up, lying in a corner. I smoothed it out, glad to have employment for my fingers, but darkness descended on the alcove again and I had to return to the room. In spite of its crumpled condition I made out the note—easily, indeed, for it was a copy of the one I had just read. Or perhaps the original; but why should the same words have been written twice and even three times, not more plainly, for Gertrude never tried to write plainly, but with a deliberate illegibility?

There was only one other person besides Gertrude, I thought, while I stuffed the cartridges into my revolver, who could have written that note, and he was waiting for me downstairs. How would he look, how would he explain himself? This question occupied me to the exclusion of a more natural curiosity—*my* appearance, *my* explanation. They would have to be of the abruptest. Perhaps, indeed, they wouldn't be needed. There were a dozen corners, a dozen points of vantage all well known to Mr. Santander between me and the dining-room door. It came to me inconsequently that the crack of a shot in that house would make no more noise than the splintering of a toilet-glass on my washing-stand. And Mr. Santander, well versed no doubt in South American revolutions, affrays, and shootings-up, would be an adept in the guerrilla warfare to which military service hadn't accustomed me. Wouldn't it be wiser, I thought irresolutely contemplating the absurd bulge in my dinner jacket to leave him to his undisputed mastery of the situation, and not put it to the proof? It was not like cutting an ordinary engagement. A knock on the door interrupted my confused consideration of social solecisms.

"Mr. Santander told me to tell you he is quite ready," the butler said. Through his manifest uneasiness I detected a hint of disapproval. He looked at me askance; he had gone over. But couldn't he be put to some use? I had an idea.

"Perhaps you would announce me," I said. He couldn't very well refuse, and piloted by him I should have a better chance in the passages and an entry valuably disconcerting. "I'm not personally known to Mr. Santander," I explained. "It would save some little awkwardness."

74

Close upon the heels of my human shield I threaded the passages. Their bright emptiness reassured me; it was inconceivable, I felt, after several safely negotiated turns, that anything sinister could lurk behind those politely rounded corners—Gertrude had had their angularities smoothed into curves; it would be so terrible, she said, if going to bed one stumbled (one easily might) and fell against an *edge!* But innocuous as they were, I preferred to avoid them. The short cut through the library would thus serve a double purpose, for it would let us in from an unexpected quarter, from that end of the library, in fact, where the large window, so perilous-looking—really so secure on its struts and stays—perched over the roaring sea.

"This is the quickest way," I said to the butler, pointing to the library door. He turned the handle. "It's locked, sir."

"Oh, well."

We had reached the dining-room at last. The butler paused with his hand on the knob as though by the mere sense of touch he could tell whether he were to be again denied admittance. Or perhaps he was listening or just thinking. The next thing I knew was that he had called out my name and I was standing in the room. Then I heard Mr. Santander's voice. "You can go, Collins." The door shut.

My host didn't turn round at once. All I could make out, in the big dim room lighted only by its four candles and the discreet footlights of dusky pictures, was his back and his face—the eyes and forehead—reflected in the mirror over the mantelpiece. The same mirror showed my face too, low down on the right-hand side, curiously unrelated. His arms were stretched along the mantelpiece and he was stirring the fire with his foot. Suddenly he turned and faced me.

"Oh, you're there," he said. "I'm so sorry."

We moved to the table and sat down. There was nothing to eat.

I fell to studying his appearance. Every line of his dinner-jacket, every fold in his soft shirt, I knew by heart; I seemed always to have known them.

"What are you waiting for?" he suddenly demanded rather loudly. "Collins!" he called. "Collins!" His voice reverberated through the room, but no one came. "How stupid of me," he muttered; "of course, I must ring."

Oddly enough he seemed to look to me for confirmation. I nodded. Collins appeared, and the meal began.

Its regular sequence soothed him, for presently he said: "You must forgive my being so distrait. I've had rather a tiring journey—come from a distance, as they say. South America, in fact." He drank some wine reflectively. "I had one or two things to settle before . . . before joining the army. Now I don't think it will be necessary."

"Necessary to settle them?" I said.

"No," he replied. "I have settled them."

"You mean that you will claim exemption as an American citizen?"

Again Mr. Santander shook his head. "It would be a reason, wouldn't it? But I hadn't thought of that."

Instinct urged me to let so delicate a topic drop; but my nerves were fearful of a return to silence. There seemed so little, of all that we had in common, to draw upon for conversation.

"You suffer from bad health, perhaps?" I suggested. But he demurred again.

"Even Gertrude didn't complain of my health," he said, adding quickly, as though to smother the sound of her name: "But you're not drinking."

"I don't think I will," I stammered. I had meant to say I was a teetotaller.

My host seemed surprised. "And yet Gertrude had a long bill at her wine merchant's," he commented, half to himself.

I echoed it involuntarily: "Had?"

"Oh," he said, "it's been paid. That's partly," he explained, "why I came home—to pay."

I felt I couldn't let this pass.

"Mr. Santander," I said, "there's a great deal in your behaviour that I don't begin (is that good American?) to understand."

"No?" he murmured, looking straight in front of him.

"But," I proceeded, as truculently as I could, "I want you to realise—"

He cut me short. "Don't suppose," he said, "that I attribute all my wife's expenditure to you."

I found myself trying to defend her. "Of course," I said, "she has the house to keep up; it's not run for a mere song, a house like this." And with my arm I tried to indicate to Mr. Santander the costly immensity of his domain.

"You wouldn't like her to live in a pigsty, would you? And there's the sea to keep out—why, a night like this must do pounds' worth of damage!"

"You are right," he said with a strange look; "you even underestimate the damage it has done."

Of course, I couldn't fail to catch his meaning. He meant the havoc wrought in his affections. They had been strong, report said—strong enough for her neglect of them to make him leave the country. They weren't expressed in half-measures, I thought, looking at him with a new sensation. He must have behaved with the high-hand, when he arrived. How he must have steeled himself to drive her out of the house, that stormy night, ignoring her piteous protestations, her turns and twists which I had never been able to ignore! She was never so alluring, never so fertile in emotional appeals, as when she knew she was in for a scolding. I could hear her say, "But, Maurice, however much you hate me, you couldn't really want me to get *wet!*" and his reply: "Get out of this house, and don't come back till I send for you. As for your lover, leave me to look after him." He was looking after me, and soon, no doubt, he would send for her. And for her sake, since he had really returned to take part in her life, I couldn't desire this estrangement. Couldn't I even bridge it over, bring it to a close? *Beati pacifici*. Well, I would be a peace-maker too.

Confident that my noble impulses must have communicated themselves to my host, I looked up from my plate and searched his face for signs of abating rigour. I was disappointed. But should I forego or even postpone my atonement because he was stiff-necked? Only it was difficult to begin. At last I ventured.

"Gertrude is really very fond of you, you know."

Dessert had been reached, and I, in token of amity and good-will, had helped myself to a glass of port wine.

For answer he fairly glared at me. "Fond of me!" he shouted.

I was determined not to be browbeaten out of my kind offices.

"That's what I said; she has a great heart."

"If you mean," he replied, returning to his former tone, "that it has ample accommodation!—but your recommendations come too late; I have delegated her affections."

"To me?" I asked, involuntarily.

He shook his head. "And in any case, why to you?"

"Because I—"

"Oh, no," he exclaimed passionately. "Did she deceive you—has she deceived you into believing *that*—that *you* are the alternative to *me*? You aren't unique—you have your reduplications, scores of them!"

My head swam, but he went on, enjoying his triumph. "Why, no one ever told me about you! She herself only mentioned you once. You are the least—the least of all her lovers!" His voice dropped. "Otherwise you wouldn't be here."

"Where should I be?" I fatuously asked. But he went on without regarding me.

"But I remember this house when its silence, its comfort, its isolation, its uniqueness were for us, Gertrude and me and . . . and for the people we invited. But we didn't ask many—we preferred to be alone. And I thought at first she was alone," he wound up, "when I found her this evening."

"Then why," I asked, "did you send her away and not me?"

"Ah," he replied with an accent of finality, "I wanted you."

While he spoke he was cracking a nut with his fingers and it must have had sharp edges, for he stopped, wincing, and held the finger to his mouth.

"I've hurt my nail," he said. "See?"

He pushed his hand towards me over the polished table. I watched it, fascinated, thinking it would stop; but still it came on, his body following, until if I hadn't drawn back, it would have touched me, while his chin dropped to within an inch of the table, and one side of his face was pillowed against his upper arm.

"It's a handicap, isn't it?" he said, watching me from under his brows.

"Indeed it is," I replied; for the fine acorn-shaped nail was terribly torn, a jagged rent revealing the quick, moist and gelatinous. "How did you manage to do that?" I went on, trying not to look at the mutilation which he still held before my eyes.

"Do you really want to know how I did it?" he asked. He hadn't moved, and his question, in its awkward irregular delivery, seemed to reflect the sprawled unnatural position of his body.

"Do tell me," I said, and added, nervously jocular, "But

78

first let me guess. Perhaps you met with an accident in the course of your professional activities, when you were mending the lights, I mean, in the library."

At that he jumped to his feet. "You're very warm," he said, "you almost burn. But come into the library with me, and I'll tell you."

I prepared to follow him.

But unaccountably he lingered, walked up and down a little, went to the fireplace and again (it was evidently a favourite relaxation) gently kicked the coals. Then he went to the library door, meaning apparently to open it, but he changed his mind and instead turned on the big lights of the dining-room. "Let's see what it's really like," he said. "I hate this half-light." The sudden illumination laid bare that great rich still room, so secure, so assured, so content. My host stood looking at it. He was fidgeting with his dinner-jacket and had so little self-control that, at every brush of the material with his damaged finger, he whimpered like a child. His face, now that I saw it fairly again, was twisted and disfigured with misery. There wasn't one imaginable quality that he shared with his sumptuous possessions.

In the library darkness was absolute. My host preceded me, and in a moment I had lost all sense of even our relative positions. I backed against the wall, and by luck my groping fingers felt the switch. But its futile click only emphasized the darkness. I began to feel frightened, with an acute immediate alarm very different from my earlier apprehensions and forebodings. To add to my uneasiness my ears began to detect a sound, a small irregular sound; it might have been water dripping, yet it seemed too definitely consonantal for that; it was more like an inhuman whisper. "Speak up," I cried, "if you're talking to me!" But it had no more effect, my petulant outcry, than if it had fallen on the ears of the dead. The disquieting noise persisted, but another note had crept into it—a soft labial sound, like the licking of lips. It wasn't intelligible, it wasn't even articulate, yet I felt that if I listened longer it would become both. I couldn't bear the secret colloquy; and though it seemed to be taking place all round me, I made a rush into what I took to be the middle of the room. I didn't get very far, however. A chair sent me sprawling, and when I picked myself up it was to the accompaniment of a more familiar sound. The curtains were being drawn apart and the moonlight, struggling in, showed me shapes of furniture and my own position, a few feet from the door. It showed me something else, too.

How could my host be drawing the curtains when I could see him lounging, relaxed and careless, in an armchair that, from its position by the wall, missed the moon's directer ray? I strained my eyes. Very relaxed, very careless he must be, after what had passed between us, to stare at me so composedly over his shoulder, no, more than that, over his very back! He faced me, though his shoulder, oddly enough, was turned away. Perhaps he had practised it—a contortionist's trick to bewilder his friends. Suddenly I heard his voice, not from the armchair at all but from the window.

"Do you know now?"

"What?" I said.

"How I hurt my finger?"

"No," I cried untruthfully, for that very moment all my fears told me.

"I did it strangling my wife!"

I rushed towards the window, only to be driven back by what seemed a solid body of mingled sleet and wind. I heard the creak of the great casement before it whirled outwards, crashing against the mullion and shattering the glass. But though I fought my way to the opening I wasn't quick enough. Sixty feet below the eroding sea sucked, spouted and roared. Out of it jags of rock seemed to rise, float for a moment and then be dragged under the foam. Time after time great arcs of spray sprang hissing from the sea, lifted themselves to the window as though impelled by an insatiable curiosity, condensed and fell away. The drops were bitter on my lips. Soaked to the skin and stiff with cold, I turned to the room. The heavy brocade curtains flapped madly or rose and streamed level with the ceiling, and through the general uproar I could distinguish separate sounds, the clattering fall of small objects and the banging and scraping of pictures against the walls. The whole weatherproof, soundproof house seemed to be ruining in, to be given up to darkness and furies . . . and to me. But not wholly, not unreservedly, to me. Mrs. Santander was still at her place in the easy chair.

Gahan Wilson is a man needing a minimum of introduction. Mention his name and chances are you'll get in response a gleam in the eye, a chuckle, and a happy nodding of the head. His cartoons in Playboy *and elsewhere, alternately droll and zany, macabre yet touchingly human, are the delight of millions, and his Sunday comic strip is gaining for him even more fans. He also writes a column of reviews on spooky books for* Fantasy & Science Fiction *and, not surprisingly, writes splendid short stories. This story, premiered in* Witchcraft & Sorcery, *and apparently rooted in Wilson's Illinois childhood, is a warmly nostalgic bit of eeriness, for everyone who once carried around a brown paper bag on the last night of October.*

YESTERDAY'S WITCH

by Gahan Wilson

HER HOUSE is gone now. Someone tore it down and bull-dozed away her trees and set up an ugly apartment build-ing made of cheap bricks and cracking concrete on the flattened place they'd built. I drove by there a few nights ago; I'd come back to town for the first time in years to give a lecture at the university, and I saw blue TV flickers glowing in the building's living rooms.

Her house sat on a small rise, I remember, with a wide stretch of scraggly lawn between it and the ironwork fence which walled off her property from the sidewalk and the rest of the outside world. The windows of her house peered down at you through a thick tangle of oak tree branches, and I can remember walking by and knowing she was peering out at me and hunching up my shoulders. Because I couldn't help it, but never, ever, giving her the satisfaction of seeing me hurry because of fear.

To the adults she was Miss Marble, but we children knew better. We knew she had another name, though none of us knew just what it was, and we knew she was a witch. I don't know who it was told me first about Miss Marble's being a witch; it might have been Billy Drew. I think it was, but I had already guessed in spite of being less than six. I grew up, all of us grew up, sure and certain of Miss Marble's being a witch.

You never managed to get a clear view of Miss Marble, or I don't ever remember doing so, except that once. You just got peeks and hints. A quick glimpse of her wide, short body as she scuttled up the front porch steps; a brief hint of her brown-wrapped form behind a thick clump of bushes by the garage where, it was said, an electric run-about sat rusting away; a sudden flash of her fantastically wrinkled face in the narrowing slot of a closing door, and that was all.

Fred Pulley claimed he had gotten a good long look at her one afternoon. She had been weeding, or something, absorbed at digging in the ground, and off-guard and careless even though she stood a mere few feet from the fence. Fred had fought down his impulse to keep on going by, and he had stood and studied her for as much as two or three minutes before she looked up and saw him and snarled and turned away.

We never tired of asking Fred about what he had seen.

"Her teeth, Fred," one of us would whisper—you almost always talked about Miss Marble in whispers—"Did you see her *teeth?*"

"They're long and yellow," Fred would say. "And they come to points at the ends. And I think I saw blood on them."

None of us really believed Fred had seen Miss Marble, understand, and we certainly didn't believe that part about the blood, but we were so very curious about her, and when you're really curious about something, especially if you're a bunch of kids, you want to get all the information on the subject even if you're sure it's lies.

So we didn't believe what Fred Pulley said about Miss Marble's having blood on her teeth, nor about the bones he'd seen her pulling out of the ground, but we remembered it all the same, just in case, and it entered into any calculations we made about Miss Marble.

Hallowe'en was the time she figured most prominently in our thoughts. First because she was a witch, of course, and second because of a time-honored ritual among the neighborhood children concerning her and ourselves and that evening of the year. It was a kind of test by fire that every male child had to go through when he reached the age of thirteen, or to be shamed forever after. I have no idea when it originated; I only know that when I attained my thirteenth year and was thereby qualified and doomed for the ordeal, the rite was established beyond question.

I can remember putting on my costume for that memorable Hallowe'en, an old Prince Albert coat and a papier-mâché mask which bore a satisfying likeness to a decayed cadaver, with the feeling I was girding myself for a great battle. I studied my reflection in a mirror affixed by swivels to my bedroom bureau and wondered gravely if I would be able to meet the challenge this night would bring. Unsure, but determined, I picked up my brown paper shopping bag, which was very large so as to accommodate as much candy as possible, said goodbye to my mother and father and dog, and went out. I had not gone a block before I met George Watson and Billy Drew.

"Have you got anything yet?" asked Billy.

"No." I indicated the emptiness of my bag. "I just started."

"The same with us," said George. And then he looked at me carefully. "Are you ready?"

"Yes" I said, realizing I had not been ready until that very moment, and feeling an encouraging glow at knowing I was. "I can do it alright."

Mary Taylor and her little sister Betty came up, and so did Eddy Baker and Phil Myers and the Arthur brothers. I couldn't see where they all had come from, but it seemed as if every kid in the neighborhood was suddenly there, crowding around under the street lamp, costume flapping in the wind, holding bags and boxes and staring at me with glistening, curious eyes.

"Do you want to do it now," asked George, "Or do you want to wait?"

George had done it the year before and he had waited.

"I'll do it now," I said.

I began walking along the sidewalk, the others following after me. We crossed Garfield Street and Peabody Street and that brought us to Baline Avenue where we turned left. I could see Miss Marble's iron fence half a block ahead, but I was careful not to slow my pace. When we arrived at the fence I walked to the gate with as firm a tread as I could muster and put my hand upon its latch. The metal was cold and made me think of coffin handles and graveyard diggers' picks. I pushed it down and the gate swung open with a low, rusty groaning.

Now it was up to me alone. I was face to face with the ordeal. The basic terms of it were simple enough: walk down the crumbling path which led through the tall, dry grass to Miss Marble's porch, cross the porch, ring Miss Marble's bell and escape. I had seen George Watson do it last year and I had seen other brave souls do it before him. I knew it was not an impossible task.

It was a chilly night with a strong, persistent wind and

clouds scudding overhead. The moon was three-fourths full and it looked remarkably round and solid in the sky. I became suddenly aware, for the first time in my life, that it was a real *thing* up there. I wondered how many Hallowe'ens it had looked down on and what it had seen.

I pulled the lapels of my Prince Albert coat close about me and started walking down Miss Marble's path. I walked because all the others had run or skulked, and I was resolved to bring new dignity to the test if I possibly could.

From afar the house looked bleak and abandoned, a thing of cold blues and greys and greens, but as I drew nearer a peculiar phenomenon began to assert itself. The windows, which from the sidewalk had seemed only to reflect the moon's glisten, now began to take on a warmer glow; the walls and porch, which had seemed all shriveled, peeling paint and leprous patches of rotting wood now began to appear well-kept. I swallowed and strained my eyes. I had been prepared for a growing feeling of menace, for ever darker shadows, and this increasing evidence of warmth and tidiness absolutely baffled me.

By the time I reached the porch steps the place had taken on a positively cozy feel. I now saw that the building was in excellent repair and that it was well-painted with a smooth coat of reassuring cream. The light from the windows was now unmistakably cheerful, a ruddy, friendly pumpkin kind of orange suggesting crackling fireplaces all set and ready for toasting marshmallows. There was a very unwitchlike clump of Indian corn fixed to the front door, and I was almost certain I detected an odor of sugar and cinnamon wafting into the cold night air.

I stepped onto the porch, gaping. I had anticipated many awful possibilities during this past year. Never far from my mind had been the horrible pet Miss Marble was said to own, a something-or-other which was all claws and scales and flew on wings with transparent webbing. Perhaps, I had thought, this thing would swoop down from the bare oak limbs and carry me off while my friends on the sidewalk screamed and screamed. Again, I had not dismissed the notion Miss Marble might turn me into a frog with a little motion of her fingers and then step on me with her foot and squish me.

But here I was feeling foolish, very young, crossing

this friendly porch and smelling, I was sure of it now, sugar and cinnamon and cider and, what's more, butter-scotch on top of that. I raised my hand to ring the bell and was astonished at myself for not being the least bit afraid when the door softly opened and there stood Miss Marble herself.

I looked at her and she smiled at me. She was short and plump, and she wore an apron with a thick ruffle all along its edges, and her face was smooth and red and shiny as an autumn apple. She wore bifocals on the tip of her tiny nose and she had her white hair fixed in a perfectly round bun in the exact center of the top of her head. Delicious odors wafted round her through the open door and I peered greedily past her.

"Well," she said in a mild, old voice, "I am so glad that someone has at last come to have a treat. I've waited so many years, and each year I've been ready, but no-body's come."

She stood to one side and I could see a table in the hall piled with candy and nuts and bowls of fruit and platesful of pies and muffins and cake, all of it shining and glittering in the warm, golden glow which seemed everywhere. I heard Miss Marble chuckle warmly.

"Why don't you call your friends in? I'm sure there will be plenty for all."

I turned and looked down the path and saw them, huddled in the moonlight by the gate, hunched wide-eyed over their boxes and bags. I felt a sort of generous pity for them. I walked to the steps and waved.

"Come on! It's all right!"

They would not budge.

"May I show them something?"

She nodded yes and I went into the house and got an enormous orange-frosted cake with numbers of golden sugar pumpkins on its sides.

"Look," I cried, lifting the cake into the moonlight, "Look at this! And she's got lots more! She always had, but we never asked for it!"

George was the first through the gate, as I knew he would be. Billy came next, and then Eddy, then the rest. They came slowly, at first, timid as mice, but then the smells of chocolate and tangerines and brown sugar got to their noses and they came faster. By the time they had arrived at the porch they had lost their fear, the same as I, but their astonished faces showed me how I must have looked to Miss Marble when she'd opened the door.

"Come in, children. I'm so glad you've all come at last!"

None of us had ever seen such candy or dared to dream of such cookies and cakes. We circled the table in the hall, awed by it's contents, clutching at our bags.

"Take all you want, children. It's all for you."

Little Betty was the first to reach out. She got a gumdrop as big as a plum and was about to pop it into her mouth when Miss Marble said:

"Oh, no, dear, don't eat it now. That's not the way you do with tricks or treats. You wait till you get out on the sidewalk and then you go ahead and gobble it up. Just put it in your bag for now, sweetie."

Betty was not all that pleased with the idea of putting off eating her gumdrop, but she did as Miss Marble asked and plopped it into her bag and quickly followed it with other items such as licorice cats and apples dipped in caramel and pecans lumped together with some lovely-looking brown stuff and soon all the other children, myself very much included, were doing the same, filling our bags and boxes industriously, giving the task of clearing the table as rapidly as possible our entire attention.

Soon, amazingly soon, we had done it. True, there was the occasional peanut, now and then a largish crumb survived, but by and large, the job was done. What was left was fit only for rats and roaches, I thought, and then was puzzled by the thought. Where had such an unpleasant idea come from?

How our bags bulged! How they strained to hold what we had stuffed into them! How wonderfully heavy they were to hold!

Miss Marble was at the door, now, holding it open and smiling at us.

"You must come back next year, sweeties, and I will give you more of the same."

We trooped out, some of us giving the table one last glance just to make sure, and then we headed down the path, Miss Marble waving us goodbye. The long, dead grass at the sides of the path brushed stiffly against our bags making strange hissing sounds. I felt as cold as if I had been standing in the chill night air all along, and not comforted by the cozy warmth inside Miss Marble's house. The moon was higher, now, and seemed, I didn't know how or why, to be mocking us.

I heard Mary Taylor scolding her little sister: "She said not to eat any till we got to the sidewalk!"

"I don't care. I want some!"

The wind had gotten stronger and I could hear the stiff tree branches growl high over our heads. The fence seemed far away and I wondered why it was taking us so long to get to it. I looked back at the house and my mouth went dry when I saw that it was grey and old and dark, once more, and that the only light from its windows were reflections of the pale moon.

Suddenly little Betty Taylor began to cry, first in small, choking sobs, and then in loud wails. George Watson said: "What's wrong?" and then there was a pause, and then George cursed and threw Betty's bag over the lawn toward the house and his own box after it. They landed with a queer rustling slither that made the small hairs on the back of my neck stand up. I let go of my own bag and it flopped, bulging, into the grass by my feet. It looked like a huge, pale toad with a gaping, grinning mouth.

One by one the others rid themselves of what they carried. Some of the younger ones, whimpering, would not let go, but the older children gently separated them from the things they clutched.

I opened the gate and held it while the rest filed out onto the sidewalk. I followed them and closed the gate firmly. We stood and looked into the darkness beyond the fence. Here and there one of our abandoned boxes or bags seemed to glimmer faintly, some of them moved, I'll swear it, though others claimed it was just an illusion produced by the waving grass. All of us heard the high, thin laughter of the witch.

WET SEASON

by Dennis Etchison

MADDEN watched the black crowd on the other side of the moving gelatin wall, as rainwater poured down in translucent sheets over the windshield. He did not listen to the patternless tattoo. Instead he followed with his eyes the group of black shadows floating past the car.

"I . . . I shouldn't have made you come, Lorie," he said at last to the black figure next to him.

She turned from the window, her lidded eyes not disapproving. "That's enough, Jim. I wouldn't have felt right, otherwise."

Madden pressed his chin to his chest, squeezing his eyelids shut. He cleared his throat and rubbed his eyes, and his fingers came away moist.

Again his wife spoke, very quietly. "You . . . were very close to her, I suppose. James, I only wish there were something. . . . Forgive me if I'm crude. But I only wish I could have gotten to know her better. That she might have become, in time, my little girl as well."

He pressed her cool hand.

"It was—just—all the *mud* around her—" He bit his lips and started the engine and roared up the cemetery road, spinning out and spattering mud as he went.

The Ford geared to a slippery halt under the wet sycamores.

Bart stood at the end of the cracked driveway, behind the main house, propping open the sagging screen door to his apartment.

Through mist Madden saw the controlled, mildly pleasant line shaping his mouth, leaving the face somber in a new and ill-fitting mask.

"Forget about the rug," said Bart. "It's filthy anyway."

"We're so sorry to do this to you, Bart." Madden's wife brushed water from her clothing. "But we thought the twins were really too young to, well, exactly have their faces rubbed in."

Bart smoothed a hand over his protruding, black-T-shirted belly. "The kids are in the bedroom. Rain must have got 'em drowsy. Left them staring out the window, counting drops or something," he added gently to Madden, testing a smile.

"Let me see to them." Madden's wife started across the room.

The men waited until she was gone.

Bart faced him. "Come over here and have a drink."

"No."

"Really, boy, really now. You know how I mean it. Come on."

At once Madden felt his joints chilled and tired. "No, Bart. I . . . I don't need it." He lowered himself to the sofa that was bulging and splitting like a fat man's incisions.

Bart watched the misty screen door and compared it to the pale Scotch and water in his hand. Twice he shaped his lips to stillborn beginnings. He shook his head and said nothing.

"You look at the hole, and the mud," Madden began finally in a low voice, "and you think of . . . that human being there in a box, being lowered into the ground, and you wonder how it can be that—that a part of your body, a piece that has come *from* you like an arm or leg, can be cut off, killed and buried away, and you never being able to feel with it again.

"But you know, I worked with a man once who had lost an arm in the Korean War; and he said he could close his eyes anytime and suddenly it was *there* again, the nerves were restored and he could feel down into his fingertips. But when he opened his eyes to see why he hadn't touched what he was reaching for, his eyes told him there was nothing there anymore."

Rain began to tap erratically on a metal vent somewhere in the roof.

"And you know, I can still see the world through my little girl's eyes, feel it as she felt it, even . . . even though she's been cut off me, like one of my sense organs. I still

91

feel her, feel *through* her, and my nerves, my ganglia just won't listen to the goddamn facts."

Outside, water continued to fall and fall illogically, relentlessly, in what seemed to be the result of a vast macrocosmic defrosting.

Giggling, the twins came out of the bedroom.

Madden saw them and smiled wanly from the sofa. The two little boys acknowledged him peripherally and grinned, grasping their mother's hands more securely.

"How did it go, boys?" inquired Madden, generating concern, and immediately hated his own detachment. *You are my sons, now,* he thought, *my only sons, and I should hold you tight against me—*

"We had fun, Da-da. We had samiches."

"An' we tooka nap an' went out an' played an'—"

Why, noted Madden wearily, *they're actually speaking directly to me. . . . She almost never lets them do that—what is this, some kind of show for Bart?*

"Out? But it didn't let up today, did it, Bart?" he said.

"Well, uh," the dark man gestured firmly to Madden, "they—" and he dropped his voice, ready to spell out words before the children, "they begged to go out. You brought them in their raincoats and, you know, it was one of those things. For a few minutes is all. Made 'em real happy. God knows I have no practice in child-rearing. Jesus, Jim, I hope they didn't catch anything."

"Tad and Ray never catch colds," stated Madden's wife, smiling her wide, smooth, peculiar kind of smile. "You did fine, Bart."

Madden watched his wife. Svelte in the gray light, she snaked an arm around each of her children's shoulders.

"We'd better go," she said. "It's Sunday and I have a Women's Guild meeting tonight."

"Thanks, Bart. I mean it more than I can say."

They walked together, heads down, to the door. A Sunday comics section for her hair and Lorelei and the giggly children clamored down the shiny, fragmented driveway.

Bart gripped his arm, looking deep in his eyes and nodding.

"You know I know. I can't say it. But I remember the Sunday we buried Mama." Hearing it said now, Madden felt no longer a memory of pain but a bond with manhood. "Just so's you know I know." And a slap caught Madden between the shoulder blades and sent him into the rain.

To a car where a somehow strange woman and children waited.

He switched off the ignition and sat very still, staring into the liquid pattern on the windshield.

"Ready, children?" asked Mrs. Madden, not looking to the back seat, taking her purse into her lap.

From the back seat came giggling.

Madden lay his head back to let his eyes trace the headliner of the car. Half a minute earlier, shutting off the wipers, he had caught himself hypnotized as the twin arcs of the wiper blades melted away. Now, motor silenced, he listened to the sound of endless beads beating their pattern into the top of the automobile.

In the back seat, there was whispering like the swishing of cars down an empty street.

"Let's go, children," prompted their mother. "There'll be plenty of time for secrets when we get in the house."

Abruptly Madden snapped to. He focused his eyes from the windshield to the woman next to him, attuned his ears from the drumming overhead to the whisper of cloth on plastic as the children slid across the back seat. He touched the handle of his wife's door; it was cold. Almost as cold as his hand.

Behind him, someone giggled.

Outside the picture window, premature dusk settled along the block like silent black wings.

"Won't . . . won't you eat something?" asked Mrs. Madden tenuously. She leaned into the living room, spoon in hand and spoke in silhouette from the yellow kitchen doorway.

He cleared his throat. "What?" Madden's five fingertips moved involuntarily to the pane. The glass was cold.

"Well," she intoned maternally, "you should have something. It's almost dark. Let me turn on the—"

"It's all right, Lorelei." *For God's sake*, he thought, *don't patronize me. Not now.*

Chilled and fatigued to the marrow, he sat in the newly rearranged and alien living room and tried to release his senses from the pain of here-and-now. He shut his eyes and tried to let his thoughts blow with the storm on down the blurred panorama of empty street.

She puttered for a time in the kitchen and Madden, curiously detached in the dark and the overstuffed chair, noticed again her effortless, liquid movements. The way she had of gliding over a floor as though it were polished glass, her legs flowing out and back with each step in a charming suggestion of no gristle or bone. No deliberate, angular bend to Lorie's arm, no; in her, stirring and pouring out and rinsing away became a Siamese rubber-arm ballet.

"Your soup is in the oven, keeping warm. And the twins are tucked in, so don't—I mean, they shouldn't give you any trouble."

Mrs. Madden paused in silhouette, then glided behind the enormous sagging hand that enclosed her husband.

"Lorie," he swallowed. Away in the bright kitchen, an electric clock hummed.

She sat on the armrest.

"Lorelei, do you ever . . . think about the decision you made ten months ago?" He tried to stop his teeth from chattering. "I mean—"

Her arms reached a pale circle around his shoulders. "You are the finest father my boys could possibly have. And I . . ." And she smoothed his hair with her oddly flat hands and did not finish.

"Do you need to talk, Jim? The Guild meeting—"

Yes, he thought, pressing his eyes tightly shut until shards of gray light fired inside his eyelids, *yes, I need something, I hear your words but they are only words, I need more than talk, I need you warm against me, I need to live—*

He drew her into his lap. And at once it struck him. She was *not* warm. Her skin was cold, cold almost as— He pushed her away.

"Jim, I'm sorry. Is there something I can do for you?"

"No." He stared ahead into the night-filled room. "They're waiting for you already. There isn't anything you can do for me."

Picking up coat, purse and overshoes, Mrs. Madden pulled back the front door to a sheet of rain. A reminder about the soup, and she entered the falling sea.

The telephone refused to warm in his hands.

A sputter and crackle of rain and whispers on the wires between and across town, a mile away, a phone purred to life.

And purred. And purred.

"Yeah?"

"Hello, Bart. What am I interrupting?"

"Jimmy? That you, boy?"

"I hope I'm not interrupting anything."

"No, no. Listen. Lorie gone to her meeting?"

"That's right."

"Then you're alone." Pause. "Everything all right over there?"

"Yes. Aw, look, I shouldn't have called."

"You wanna talk, Jim?"

"I guess. No. . . . Look. Bart, is someone coming over tonight? You going out?"

"In this weather? Look, is everything all right?"

Pause. "Uh, Bart, I wonder . . . I just wondered if . . . aw, never mind, I shouldn't have bothered you."

"Look. You wanna come over here? We could talk, if you want."

"Can't leave the kids."

"They're asleep, then, and you're alone over there. Look, you want me to come over? Talk or something till Lorie gets back?"

Pause. "I have no business bothering you."

"Crap. Look, I'll come over, okay? We can talk, you know, like we used to."

"I'm pretty bad company tonight, I'm afraid. And the weather. Sure you want to?"

"My idea, isn't it? And look, how can you turn down a lonely ol' bachelor like me? See you in ten minutes."

"Thanks very much, Bart," but he had hung up.

Madden waited on the back porch, listening.

Far down in the darkness, the throaty thrumming of the frogs met with the rushing of running water.

All about his thin figure, dirty streams dripped from the roof to mingle with puddles at his cold feet, to slip on down over the slanting yard, to join larger tributaries that splashed their way through the thorny shrubbery of the ravine to feed at last with violent churning into the shrouded riverbed far below.

From in front, Madden heard wet brakes grip to a splashing stop. Shivering, he turned inside.

The two men sat across from one another in the living room, two men who knew each other best of all in the world. There was only a pale-moth glow from the kitchen. They spoke, and they did not speak, and from time to time Bart laughed and sipped from the brandy snifter in his lap.

". . . but then they threw the next game to the motherin' Angels," Bart was saying.

"Yes," said Madden.

Bart rose and ambled to the black picture window.

Abruptly Madden was aware that his brother had stopped talking.

Madden stared with him. He saw his brother frown. *Do you feel it too?* he thought. Vaguely illumined beneath the street lamp was Bart's car, leaned against the curb, weathering the storm. Idly, Madden had a vision of the rain pouring off the metal top, streaming down the rolled-up windows and down into the innards of the door, where the handle and lock mechanism were.

"Jimbo. God damn it."

Madden watched him. "What's wrong?"

Bart drained his glass. "I don't wanna say it. I don't even know I'm right. Or if I oughta say it."

"It's all right—I can talk about Darla. Probably it would do me good." He massaged his face, trying to relax. "I know I have to face—"

"No. That's not what I'm talking about." Bart pivoted from the window and the rain. "Listen to me, kid. *Do you feel it?*"

"Feel what?"

"Something, about this house, this town. I don't know how to say it. But can't you feel it?" Bart glared into the empty brandy glass.

"Something like what?" Madden lounged back into the cushion, ready to listen. *Now,* thought Madden, *this is the way. It won't prove a thing unless he says it first.*

"Damn," breathed Bart. He turned back to the night and lit a cigaret. "Maybe I'm going off the deep end. Look. Can I ask you a question?"

"Shoot."

"Something about this house. I don't know. The way it

smells now, the way the chairs creak when I sit down, the color of the *light*, for God's sake, like the room is underwater or something. And all since she moved in." The cigaret reflection burned in the window. "Naw. Man, you're the one needs to talk at a time like this. I'm supposed to cheer *you*."

"So you're cheerin'. Shoot."

"Look, it's just that—haven't you noticed anything, well, different about the place since Lorie and her kids moved in? That it isn't really yours anymore? I mean, it's like every person has a rhythm, a pattern to his everyday life. You go into a man's bedroom, it *smells* like him, the bed bends a certain way when you sit on it, because it's been shaped to fit every angle and bulge just right over the years. And you go into the kitchen, the way the dishes are piled up in the sink tells you more about the guy than a look at his diary, if you know what I mean. It's like the house soaks up what you are, the way you feel about life, and everything in the house gets to feeling the same way, too. And not only the place, but the woman he marries: she seems to fit right in, fit him, and the house . . . and that's part of it, too, Jimbo. She's—and I know I'm steppin' way over the bounds on this, but dammit, man, she's *not you*, you know? Let me ask: don't you notice anything unusual about Lorie?"

Madden shut his eyes impatiently. "She's an unusually attractive woman, if that's what you mean."

"No. But then I promised myself not to bring up any of this with you, at least not for a long time . . . .

"But it isn't just this house. Hell, we both grew up in Greenworth, I knew every turn in the river like the lines on my hand years before the government moved in. And it's changed now, somehow. First, it was just the way the trees started growing crooked along the banks, but lately the whole town seems, I don't know, *funny*. The way the air smells, the paint on the houses . . . I don't know. I just don't know. But I'll tell you this: if I were blindfolded and left here, I'd never in a year guess this was the same town we grew up in."

Outside, the moon slipped for a moment through a pocket in the clouds, washing Bart's face fishlike-pale by the window.

"Bart. What is it?"

"I wish I could be sure, kid. Maybe you should forget

it. I pray to God I could. Jim, do you know how many storms like this we've had in Greenworth in the last twenty-five years?"

Madden stirred.

"I'll tell you: three, before two years ago. And not one raised the river more than a few inches. But in two years, five big ones. Here." Bart spilled his coat pocket onto the coffee table. "What the hell—I spent yesterday in the library looking things up, I don't know what for. Something made me do it. But God, I've gotta show you."

Madden reached to the lamp.

Little white slips of paper fluttered in Bart's hands. For the first time in his life Madden saw his brother trembling.

"God!" he laughed nervously. "Help me, will you, Jim? Here are the pieces to a crazy jigsaw, it doesn't make any sense, but something in the back of my head keeps me from getting any sleep lately. Here, look, read it all and then tell me I'm nuts and send me home, but *do something!*"

" 'Deaths by drowning, County Beach: this year and last, total 31. Previous two years' total, 9.' What's this for?"

"Don't stop now." Bart fumbled at the liquor cabinet.

" 'Total rainfall in inches, adjacent counties last year, up 300%.' "

"See! It's spreading."

Another slip of paper. " 'New residents in Greenworth, past 24 months: Broadbent, Mr. and Mrs. C.L.; Marber, G.; Nottingham, Mr. and Mrs. Frank R. . . .' " Madden leaned intently forward.

"There's two dozen more."

He scrutinized his brother's now twisted face. "So?"

"So? So you're right, they're nothing separately, but put them all together—Let me ask you: Lorie never told you where she moved from when she came here, did she?"

"Now that you bring it up, no. But what—?"

"Listen to this. Last night I got out the phone book and dialed these new listings. Twenty-one are married couples. And every woman—" Bart emptied his glass. ". . . Every woman is in the Women's Guild."

Ice water poured into Madden's stomach. "So?"

Bart jerked forth a folded clipping. "This was in the

Gazette when one finally moved in twenty months ago."

Madden fingered the newspaper photo of 'Mr. and Mrs. Peter Hallendorf, newly established real estate broker and his lovely bride.'

"Use this." A pocket magnifier hit the coffee table.

She *was* lovely. There in the enlarged dots was a face that was— "I don't see—"

Bart's shaking finger jabbed at the indistinct eyes, the mouth.

At first he didn't see it. Just that her eyes were softly, lethargically lidded.

Bart snatched a framed photograph from the bookcase and tossed it to his lap.

And there.

There were the two sets of lidded eyes, two wide, smooth, peculiar smiles, side by side. They might have been sisters.

Madden groped. At the bottom of his consciousness, the pressure was rising now and he felt his finger giving way in the dike.

"Jim," grunted Bart. "I called the Community Center this evening. They never heard of it. *There is no Women's Guild!*

"And now. Just one more question. I hate to remind you, boy, but you've got to have all the pieces in front of you." Bart leaned over him, breath coming fast and pungent. "Tell me again how it was your little girl died."

Madden bit his knuckle. "Man, I don't know what you're driving at. Please—"

"Just say it!"

"She . . . she, you know. She drowned—in the—bottom of the tub." He fought up out of the chair.

Both men faced each other, white-faced.

"Goddamn," breathed Bart, turning back to the darkness. "Goddamn me for saying it."

Walking in the wet, Madden knew at last that he could leave the house behind and give himself up to the storm. Slimy, tangled brush grabbed at his sopping clothes, but he did not think of it and slid down the ravine to the churning riverbed. In the glistening night he saw the swelling rush muddying over collapsing banks, and he remembered the first and worst storm, two seasons ago: how the ravine filled steadily to the brim, spilling up over the backyard; and then, weeks later, how the yard blossomed alive with all manner of new, unnamed wild plants and shoots and bloom-faced flowers. And how he suddenly awoke one night to discover the moldering ravine an amphitheater of swollen hordes of singing insect life, a thundering of bullfrogs, a sweltering din of mosquitoes, a screeching chorus of crickets. Latent with life, pollen and cyst and egg had been carried by the water and given birth at long last.

Madden stretched through the wet growth to the river's edge. Facts and meanings swirled and eddied within him.

He saw the fresh water flowing on past, headed for the sea.

A paper boat or a leaf could float the five miles to the turbines, and beyond to the sea. But only something living could do the opposite.

Suddenly, as if by a signal, frog and insect ceased their noise.

In the new silence, above the rain, Madden heard a car door slam.

He began tearing savagely at the shrubbery. His hair and chin dripped and his clothes were torn and caked with mud below the waist, but he did not think of these things as he climbed his way to the porch.

He smeared a wet trail across the kitchen.

Lorelei came through the unlighted living room.

"Why James, I thought you'd be in bed. And your clothes, why—"

"Wh-where have you been?" he shivered.

She reached to touch his clothes. He jumped back.

He saw that her clothing, too, was dripping. Much more than from a run from the car.

"Why, James—"

"Get away! Who are you?"

The sound of giggling.

He ran to the bathroom door. He kicked it in.

Grinning in the stark white porcelain bathtub were the twins, Tad and Ray. They splashed and curled eel-like appendages up over the edge.

"What is this?" muttered Madden, blinded by the light. "What are you boys bathing for at . . ." Then he saw their smooth, shining skins glistening in the water in a strange new way.

So this is the way Darla came upon them that day,

he thought. *So that was why, that was why. So now I have no choice . . .*

He fell upon them, pushing their small heads under the water until bubbles floated up.

They came up grinning.

"So you know," she said.

He turned.

The bright, white tiles around him.

Lorelei, dripping, came toward him, holding out her arms as if to embrace him. An alien scaliness glittered anew along her neck, her boneless arms.

Behind him, the little ones giggled.

Madden stepped back before she could touch him. His legs met the tub and he tumbled backwards, seeing in a flash the bright walls and ceiling.

There was a resounding splash and then violent churning. And giggling.

And the sound of the rain outside.

Except for two years in New York in the mid-1920s, H.P. Lovecraft lived all his life in Providence, Rhode Island. Most of his stories, with their regional flavor and antiquarianism and their compelling visions of cosmic fright and horror, are set in that city or within a hundred miles of it, the real-world counterparts to his fictional Arkham country. In the four decades since his death, Lovecraft's place as one of the most important authors of supernatural literature has been firmly established. His stories have become classics and his life, his letters and his world-view have attracted the attention of many scholars and biographers.

August Derleth, who wrote this story from notes left by Lovecraft, died in 1971 at the age of sixty-two. Derleth himself wrote and edited many effective books of supernatural stories but seems destined to be best remembered for his writings about his native Wisconsin and for the writers he championed and published: Henry S. Whitehead, Clark Ashton Smith, Robert E. Howard, Fritz Leiber, Robert Bloch, and, of course, Lovecraft himself. The story presented here takes place in and near the Arkham country ocean town of Innsmouth, setting of Lovecraft's powerful tale, "The Shadow Over Innsmouth."

INNSMOUTH CLAY

by H. P. Lovecraft and August Derleth

THE FACTS relating to the fate of my friend, the late sculptor, Jeffrey Corey—if indeed "late" is the correct reference—must begin with his return from Paris and his decision to rent a cottage on the coast south of Innsmouth in the autumn of 1927. Corey came from an armigerous family with some distant relationship to the Marsh clan of Innsmouth—not, however, such a one as would impose upon him any obligation to consort with his distant relatives. There were, in any case, odd rumors abroad about the reclusive Marshes who still lived in that Massachusetts seaport town, and these were hardly calculated to inspire Corey with any desire to announce his presence in the vicinity.

I visited him a month after his arrival in December of that year. Corey was a comparatively young man, not yet forty, six feet in height, with a fine, fresh skin, which was free of any hirsute adornment, though his hair was worn rather long, as was then the custom among artists in the Latin Quarter of Paris. He had very strong blue eyes, and his lantern-jawed face would have stood out in any assemblage of people, not alone for the piercing quality of his gaze, but as much for the rather strange, wattled appearance of the skin back from his jaws, under his ears and down his neck a little way below his ears. He was not ill-favored in looks, and a queer quality, almost hypnotic, that informed his fine-featured face had a kind of fascination for most people who met him. He was well settled in when I visited him, and had begun to work on a statue of Rima, the Bird-Girl, which promised to become one of his finest works.

He had laid in supplies to keep him for a month, having gone into Innsmouth for them, and he seemed to me more

104

than usually loquacious, principally about his distant relatives, about whom there was a considerable amount of talk, however guarded, in the shops of Innsmouth. Being reclusive, the Marshes were quite naturally the object of some curiosity; and since that curiosity was not satisfied, an impressive lore and legendry had grown up about them, reaching all the way back to an earlier generation which had been in the South Pacific trade. There was little definite enough to hold meaning for Corey, but what there was suggested all manner of arcane horror, of which he expected at some nebulous future time to learn more, though he had no compulsion to do so. It was just, he explained, that the subject was so prevalent in the village that it was almost impossible to escape it.

He spoke also of a prospective show, made references to friends in Paris and his years of study there, to the strength of Epstein's sculpture, and to the political turmoil boiling in the country. I cite these matters to indicate how perfectly normal Corey was on the occasion of this first visit to him after his return from Europe. I had, of course, seen him fleetingly in New York when he had come home, but hardly long enough to explore any subject as we were able to do that December of 1927.

Before I saw him again, in the following March, I received a curious letter from him, the gist of which was contained in the final paragraph, to which everything else in his letter seemed to mount as to a climax—

"You may have read of some strange goings-on at Innsmouth in February. I have no very clear information about it, but it must surely have been in the papers somewhere, however silent our Massachusetts papers seem to have been. All I can gather about the affair is that a large band of Federal officers of some kind descended upon the town and spirited away some of the citizens—among them some of my own relatives, though which I am at a loss to say since I've never troubled to ascertain how many of them there are—or were, as the case may be. What I can pick up in Innsmouth has reference to some kind of South Pacific trade in which certain shipping interests in the town were still evidently engaged, though this seems to be pretty farfetched, insofar as the docks are all but abandoned, and actually largely useless for the ships now plying the Atlantic, most of which go to the larger and more modern ports. Quite apart from the reasons for the Federal action

—and considerably of more importance to me, as you will see—is the indisputable fact that, coincident with the raid on Innsmouth, some naval vessels appeared off the coast in the vicinity of what is known as Devil's Reef, and there dropped a power of depth charges! These set off such turmoil in the depths that a subsequent storm washed ashore all manner of debris, of which a peculiar blue clay came in along the water's edge here. It seemed to me very much like that moulding clay of similar color found in various parts of interior America and often used for the manufacture of bricks, particularly years ago when more modern methods of brick-making were not available to builders. Well, what is important about all this is that I gathered up the clay I could find before the sea took it back again, and I have been working on an entirely new piece I've tentatively titled 'Sea Goddess'—and I am wildly enthusiastic about its possibilities. You will see it when you come down next week, and I am certain you will like it even more than my 'Rima.' "

Contrary to his expectations, however, I found myself oddly repelled at my first sight of Corey's new statue. The figure was lissome, save for rather heavier pelvic structure than I thought fitting, and Corey had chosen to alter the feet with webbing between the toes.

"Why?" I asked him.

"I really don't know," he said. "The fact is I hadn't planned to do it. It just happened."

"And those disfiguring marks on the neck?" He was apparently still at work in that area.

He gave an embarrassed laugh, and a strange expression came into his eyes. "I wish I could explain those marks to my own satisfaction, Ken," he said. "I woke up yesterday morning to find that I must have been working in my sleep, for there were slits in the neck below her ears—on both sides—slits like—well, like gills. I'm repairing the damage now."

"Perhaps a 'sea goddess' ought to have gills," I said.

"I'd guess it came about as a result of what I picked up in Innsmouth day before yesterday when I went in for some things I needed. More talk of the Marsh clan. It boiled down to the suggestion that members of the family were reclusive by choice because they had some kind of physical deformity that related to a legend tying them to certain South Sea Islanders. This is the kind of fairy tale that ignorant people take up and embellish—though I grant that this one is more unusual than the kind one commonly picks up, related to the Judaeo-Christian morality pattern. I dreamed about it that night—and evidently walked in my sleep and worked out some part of the dream on my 'Sea Goddess.' "

However strange I thought it, I made no further comment on the incident. What he said was logical, and I confess that I was appreciably more interested in the Innsmouth lore than in the disfigurement of the "Sea Goddess."

Moreover, I was somewhat taken aback at Corey's evident preoccupation. He was animated enough when we were in conversation, no matter what the subject, but I could not help noticing an air of abstraction whenever we were not—as if he had something on his mind of which he was reluctant to speak, something that vaguely troubled him, but of which he had no certain knowledge himself, or knowledge insufficient to permit him to speak. This showed itself in various ways—a distant look in his eyes, an occasional expression of bafflement, a far gazing out to sea, and now and then a bit of wandering in his talk, an edging off the subject, as were some more demanding thought intruding upon the subject under discussion.

I have thought since that I ought to have taken the initiative and explored the preoccupation so manifest to me; I deferred doing so because I thought it did not concern me and to have done so seemed to me an invasion of Corey's privacy. Though we were friends of long standing, it did not seem that it should be incumbent upon me to intrude upon matters that were patently his alone, and he did not offer to introduce the subject himself, which, I felt, precluded my doing so.

Nevertheless, if I may digress here and leap forward to that period after Corey's disappearance, when I had come into possession of his estate—as directed by him in a formally drawn-up document—it was at about this time that Corey began to jot down disturbing notes in a journal or diary he kept, one that had begun as a commonplace book relating solely to his creative life. Chronologically, these jottings fit at this point into any account of the facts about Jeffrey Corey's last months.

"March 7. A very strange dream last night. Something impelled me to baptize Sea Goddess. This morning found the piece *wet* about the head and shoulders, as if I had done it. I repaired the damage, as if no alternative were offered me, though I had planned to crate Rima. The *compulsion* troubles me."

"March 8. A dream of swimming accompanied by shadowy men and women. Faces, when seen, hauntingly familiar—like something out of an old album. This undoubtedly took rise in the grotesque hints and sly innuendos heard at Hammond's Drug Store today—about the Marshes, as usual. A tale of great-grandfather Jethro *living* in the sea. Gilled! The same thing said of some members of the Waite, Gilman, and Eliot families. Heard the identical stuff when I stopped to make an inquiry at the railroad station. The natives here have fed upon this for decades."

"March 10. Evidently sleep-walked in the night, for some slight alterations had been made in Sea Goddess. Also curious indentations as if someone's arms had been around the statue, which was yesterday far too hard to take any sort of impression not made by a chisel or some such tool. The marks bore the appearance of having been *pressed into soft clay*. The entire piece *damp* this morning."

"March 11. A really extraordinary experience in the night. Perhaps the most vivid dream I've ever had, certainly the most erotic. I can hardly even now think of it without being aroused. I dreamed that a woman, *naked*, slipped into my bed after I had gone to sleep, and remained there all night. I dreamed that the night was spent at love—or perhaps I ought to call it lust. Nothing like it since Paris! And as real as those many nights in the Quarter! Too real, perhaps, for I woke exhausted. And I had undoubtedly spent a restless night, for the bed was much torn up."

"March 12. Same dream. Exhausted."

"March 13. The dream of swimming again. In the seadepths. A sort of city far below. Ryeh or R'lyeh? Something named 'Great Thooloo'?"

Of these matters, these strange dreams, Corey said very little on the occasion of my March visit. His appearance at that time seemed to me somewhat drawn. He did speak of some difficulty sleeping; he was not, he said, getting his "rest"—no matter when he went to bed. He did ask me then if I had ever heard the names "Ryeh" or "Thooloo"; of course, I never had, though on the second day of my visit, we had occasion to hear them.

We went into Innsmouth that day—a short run of less than five miles—and it was evident to me soon that the supplies Corey said he needed did not form the principal reason for going to Innsmouth. Corey was plainly on a fishing expedition; he had come deliberately to find out what he could learn about his family, and to that end led the way from one place to another, from Ferrand's Drug Store to the public library, where the ancient librarian showed an extraordinary reserve on the subject of the old families of Innsmouth and the surrounding countryside, though she did at last mention two names of very old men who might remember some of the Marshes and Gilmans and Waites, and who might be found in their usual haunt, a saloon on Washington Street.

Innsmouth, for all that it had much deteriorated, was the kind of village that must inevitably fascinate anyone with archeological or architectural interests, for it was well over a century old, and the majority of its buildings—other than those in the business-section, dated back many decades before the turn of the century. Even though many were now deserted, and in some cases fallen into ruin, the architectural features of the houses reflected a culture long since gone from the American scene.

As we neared the waterfront, on Washington Street, the evidence of catastrophe was everywhere apparent. Buildings lay in ruins—"Blown up," said Corey, "by the Federal men, I'm told."—and little effort had been made to clean up anything, for some side streets were still blocked by brick rubble. In one place an entire street appeared to have been destroyed, and all the old buildings once used as warehouses along the docks—long since abandoned—had been destroyed. As we neared the seashore, a nauseating, cloying musk, icthyic in origin, pervaded everything; it was more than the fishy odor often encountered in stagnant areas along the coast or, too, in inland waters.

Most of the warehouses, Corey said, had once been

Marsh property; so much he had learned at Ferrand's Drug Store. Indeed, the remaining members of the Waite and Gilman and Eliot families had suffered very little loss; almost the entire force of the Federal raid had fallen upon the Marshes and their holdings in Innsmouth, though the Marsh Refining Company, engaged in manufacturing gold ingots, had not been touched, and still allowed employment to some of the villagers who were not engaged in fishing, though the Refining Company was no longer directly controlled by members of the Marsh clan.

The saloon, which we finally reached, was plainly of nineteenth-century origin; and it was equally clear that nothing in the way of improvement had been done to the building or its interior since it had gone up, for the place was unbelievably rundown and shabby. A slovenly middle-aged man sat behind the bar reading a copy of *The Arkham Advertiser,* and two old men, one of them asleep, sat at it, far apart.

Corey ordered a glass of brandy, and I did likewise.

The bartender did not disguise a cautious interest in us.

"Seth Akins?" asked Corey presently.

The bartender nodded toward the customer who slept at the bar.

"What'll he drink?" asked Corey.

"Anything."

"Let's have a brandy for him."

The bartender poured a shot of brandy into an ill-washed glass and put it down on the bar. Corey took it down to where the old man slept, sat down beside him, and nudged him awake.

"Have one on me," he invited.

The old fellow looked up, revealing a grizzled face and bleary eyes under tousled grey hair. He saw the brandy, grabbed it, grinning uncertainly, and drank it down.

Corey began to question him, at first only establishing his identity as an old resident of Innsmouth, and talking in a general fashion about the village and the surrounding country to Arkham and Newburyport. Akins talked freely enough; Corey bought him another drink, and then another.

But Akins's ease of speech faded as soon as Corey mentioned the old families, particularly the Marshes. The old man grew markedly more cautious, his eyes darting longingly toward the door, as if he would have liked to escape. Corey, however, pressed him hard, and Akins yielded.

"Guess thar ain't no harm sayin' things naow," he said finally. "Most o' them Marshes is gone since the guv'mint come in last month. And no one knows whar to, but they ain't come back." He rambled quite a bit, but, after circling the subject for some time, he came at last to the "East Injy trade" and "Cap'n Obed Marsh—who begun it all. He had some kind a truck with them East Injuns—brung back some o' thar women an' kep' 'em in that big haouse he'd built—an' after that, the young Marshes got that queer look an' took to swimmin' aout to Devil Reef an' they'd be gone fer a long time—haours—an' it wan't natural bein' underwater so long. Cap'n Obed married one o' them women—an' some o' the younger Marshes went aout to the East Injys an' brung back more. The Marsh trade never fell off like the others'. All three o' Cap'n Obed's ships—the brig *Columby,* an' the barque *Sumatry Queen,* an' another brig, *Hetty*—sailed the oceans for the East Injy an' the Pacific trade withaout ever a accident. An' them people—them East Injuns an' the Marshes—they begun a new kind a religion—they called it the Order o' Dragon—an' there was a lot o' talk, whisperin' whar nobuddy heerd it, abaout what went on at their meetin's, an' young folk—well, maybe they got lost, but nobuddy ever saw 'em again, an' thar was all that talk about sacreefices —*human* sacreefices—abaout the same time the young folks dropped aout o' sight—none o' them Marshes or Gilmans or Waites or Eliots, though, none o' thar young folk ever got lost. An' thar was all them whispers abaout some place called 'Ryeh' an' somethin' named 'Thooloo' —some kin t' Dagon, seems like . . ."

At this, Corey broke in with a question, seeking to clarify Akins's reference; but the old man knew nothing, and I did not understand until later the reason for Corey's sudden interest.

Akins went on. "People kep' away from them Marshes —an' the others, too. But it was the Marshes that had that queer look mostly. It got so bad some o' them never went aout o' the house, unless it was at night, an' then it was most o' the time to go swimmin' in the ocean. They cud swim like fish, people said—I never saw 'em myself, and nobuddy talked much cuz we noticed whenever anybuddy talked a lot he sort o' dropped aout o' sight—like the young people—and were never heerd from again.

"Cap'n Obed larnt a lot o' things in Ponape an' from the Kanakys—all abaout people they called the 'Deep Ones' that lived under the water—an' he brought back all kinds o' carved things, queer fish things and things from under the water that wan't fish-things—Gawd knows what them things wuz!"

"What did he do with those carvings?" put in Corey.

"Some as didn't go to the Dagon Hall he sold—an' fer a good price, a real good price they fetched. But they're all gone naow, all gone—an' the Order of Dagon's all done an' the Marshes ain't been seen hereabaouts ever since they dynamited the warehaouses. An' they wan't all arrested, neither—no, sir, they do say what was left o' them Marshes jist walked daown t' the shore an' aout into the water an' kilt themselves." At this point he cackled mirthlessly. "But nobuddy ain't seen a one o' them Marsh bodies, thar ain't been no corp' seen all up an' daown the shore."

He had reached this point in his narrative when something extremely odd took place. He suddenly fixed widening eyes on my companion, his jaw dropped, his hands began to shake; for a moment or two he was frozen in that position; then he shrugged himself up and off the bar-stool, turned, and in a stumbling run burst out of the building into the street, a long, despairing cry shuddering back through the wintry air.

To say that we were astonished is to put it mildly. Seth Akins's sudden turning from Corey was so totally unexpected that we gazed at each other in astonishment. It was not until later that it occurred to me that Akins's superstition-ridden mind must have been shaken by the sight of the curious corrugations on Corey's neck below his ears—for in the course of our conversation with the old man, Corey's thick scarf, which had protected his neck from the still-cold March air, had loosened and fallen to drape over his chest in a short loop, disclosing the indentations and rough skin which had always been a part of Jeffrey Corey's neck, that wattled area so suggestive of age and wear.

No other explanation offered itself, and I made no mention of it to Corey, lest I disturb him further, for he was visibly upset, and there was nothing to be gained by upsetting him further.

"What a rigmarole!" I cried, once we were again in Washington Street.

He nodded abstractedly, but I could see plainly that some aspects of the old fellow's account had made an impression of sorts—and a not entirely pleasant one—on my companion. He could smile, but ruefully, and at my further comments he only shrugged, as if he did not wish to speak of the things we had heard from Akins.

He was remarkably silent throughout that evening, and rather noticeably preoccupied, even more so than he had been previously. I recall resenting somewhat his unwillingness to share whatever burdened his thoughts, but of course this was his decision to make, not mine, and I suspect that what churned through his mind that evening must have seemed to him farfetched and outlandish enough to make him want to spare himself the ridicule he evidently expected from me. Therefore, after several probing questions which he turned off, I did not again return to the subject of Seth Akins and the Innsmouth legends.

I returned to New York in the morning.

Further excerpts from Jeffrey Corey's *Journal*.

"March 18. Woke this morning convinced that I had not slept alone last night. Impressions on pillow, in bed. Room and bed very *damp*, as if someone wet had got into bed beside me. I know intuitively it was a woman. But *how?* Some alarm at the thought that the Marsh madness may be beginning to show in me. *Footprints* on the floor."

"March 19. 'Sea Goddess' gone! The door open. Someone must have got in during the night and taken it. Its sale value could hardly be accounted as worth the risk! Nothing else taken."

"March 20. Dreamed all night about everything Seth Akins said. Saw Captain Obed Marsh under the sea! Very ancient. *Gilled!* Swam to far below the surface of the Atlantic off Devil Reef. Many others, both men and women. The queer Marsh look! Oh, the power and the glory!"

"March 21. Night of the equinox. My neck throbbed with pain all night. Could not sleep. Got up and walked down to the shore. How the sea draws me! I was never so aware of it before, but I remember now how as a child I used to fancy I *heard*—way off in mid-continent!—the sound of the sea, of the seas' drift and the windy waves! —A fearful sense of anticipation filled me all night long."

Under this same date—March 21—Corey's last letter to me was written. He said nothing in it of his dreams, but he did write about the soreness of his neck.

"It isn't my throat—that's clear. No difficulty swallowing. The pain seems to be in that disfigured area of skin— wattled or wartlike or fissured, whatever you prefer to call it—beneath my ears. I cannot describe it; it isn't the pain one associates with stiffness or friction or a bruise. It's as if the skin were about to break outward, and it goes deep. And at the same time I cannot rid myself of the conviction that something is about to happen—something I both dread and look forward to, and all manner of *ancestral awarenesses*—however badly I put it—obsess me!"

I replied, advising him to see a doctor, and promising to visit him early in April.

By that time Corey had vanished.

There was some evidence to show that he had gone down to the Atlantic and walked in—whether with the intention of swimming or of taking his life could not be ascertained. The prints of his bare feet were discovered in what remained of that odd clay thrown up by the sea in February, but there were no returning prints. There was no farewell message of any kind, but there were instructions left for me directing the disposal of his effects, and I was named administrator of his estate—which suggested that some apprehension did exist in his mind.

Some search—desultory at best—was made for Corey's body along the shore both above and below Innsmouth, but this was fruitless, and a coroner's inquest had no trouble in coming to the conclusion that Corey had met his death by misadventure.

No record of the facts that seemed pertinent to the mystery of his disappearance could possibly be left without a brief account of what I saw off Devil Reef in the twilight of the night of April 17th.

It was a tranquil evening; the sea was as of glass, and no wind stirred the evening air. I had been in the last stages of disposing of Corey's effects and had chosen to go out for a row off Innsmouth. What I had heard of Devil Reef drew me inevitably toward its remains—a few jagged and broken stones that jutted above the surface at low tide well over a mile off the village. The sun had gone down, a fine afterglow lay in the western sky, and the sea was a deep cobalt as far as the eye could reach.

I had only just reached the reef when there was a great disturbance of the water. The surface broke in many places; I paused and sat quite still, guessing that a school of dolphins might be surfacing and anticipating with some pleasure what I might see.

But it was not dolphins at all. It was some kind of sea-dweller of which I had no knowledge. Indeed, in the fading light, the swimmers looked both fishlike and squamously human. All but one pair of them remained well away from the boat in which I sat.

That pair—one clearly a female creature of an oddly claylike color, the other male—came quite close to the boat in which I sat, watching with mixed feelings not untinged with the kind of terror that takes its rise in a profound fear of the unknown. They swam past, surfacing and diving, and, having passed, the lighter-skinned of the two creatures turned and distinctly flashed me a glance, making a strange, guttural sound that was not unlike a half-strangled crying-out of my name: "Jack!" and left me with the clear and unmistakable conviction that the *gilled sea-thing wore the face of Jeffrey Corey!*

It haunts my dreams even now.

Robert E. Howard, who took his own life in 1936, was a Texan who is far and away best known for his creation Conan, a barbarian adventurer who roamed across a prehistoric fantasy world, broadsword never far from hand. But it would be a great mistake to limit Howard's important contributions to fantasy fiction to that series. He wrote a large number of excellent stories about other fascinating characters, notably Solomon Kane the Puritan adventurer, Bran Mak Morn the early Pict chieftan and King Kull the Atlantean. He also wrote a significant number of unrelated stories of horror and exotic adventure. This story, found among a group of papers after Howard's death, saw print only in 1969 and in a rather poorly distributed magazine called Spaceway. All the famous Howard qualities are here: the power and the emotional intensity, the colorful, image-ringing prose, and the violent warrior passions and uncompromising romanticism. Together they suggest what led to Howard's tragic end but also illustrate the unique nature of his genius.

PEOPLE OF THE BLACK COAST

by Robert E. Howard

THIS COMES of idle pleasure seeking and—now what prompted that thought? Some Puritanical atavism lurking in my crumbling brain, I suppose. Certainly, in my past life I never gave much heed to such teachings. At any rate, let me scribble down here my short and hideous history, before the red hour breaks and death shouts across the beaches.

There were two of us, at the start. Myself, of course, and Gloria, who was to have been my bride. Gloria had an airplane, and she loved to fly the thing—that was the beginning of the whole horror. I tried to dissuade her that day—I swear I did!—but she insisted, and we took off from Manila with Guam as our destination. Why? The whim of a reckless girl who feared nothing and always burned with the zest for some new adventure—some untried sport.

Of our coming to the Black Coast there is little to tell. One of those rare fogs rose; we soared above it and lost our way among thick billowing clouds. We struggled along, how far out of our course God alone knows, and finally fell into the sea just as we sighted land through the lifting fog.

We swam ashore from the sinking craft, unhurt, and found ourselves in a strange and forbidding land. Broad beaches sloped up from the lazy waves to end at the foot of vast cliffs. These cliffs seemed to be of solid rock and were—are—hundreds of feet high. The material was basalt or something similar. As we descended in the falling aircraft, I had had time for a quick glance shoreward, and it had seemed to me that beyond these cliffs, rose other, higher cliffs, as if in tiers, rampart above rampart. But of course, standing directly beneath the first, we could not

118

tell. As far as we looked in either direction, we could see the narrow strip of beach running along at the foot of the black cliffs, in silent monotony.

"Now that we're here," said Gloria, somewhat shaken by our recent experience, "what are we to do? Where are we?"

"There isn't any telling," I answered. "The Pacific is full of unexplored islands. We're probably on one. I only hope that we haven't a gang of cannibals for neighbors."

I wished then that I had not mentioned cannibals, but Gloria did not seem frightened—at that.

"I'm not afraid of natives," she said uneasily. "I don't think there are any here."

I smiled to myself, reflecting how women's opinions merely reflected their wishes. But there was something deeper, as I soon learned in a hideous manner, and I believe now in feminine intuition. Their brain fibers are more delicate than ours—more readily disturbed and reached by psychic influences. But I had no time to theorize.

"Let's stroll along the beach and see if we can find some way of getting up these cliffs and back on the island."

"But the island is all cliffs, isn't it?" she asked.

Somehow I was startled. "Why do you say that?"

"I don't know," she answered rather confusedly. "That was the impression I had, that this island is just a series of high cliffs, like stairs, one on top of the other, all bare black rock."

"If that's the case," said I, "we're out of luck, for we can't live on seaweed and crabs—"

"Oh!" Her exclamation was sharp and sudden.

I caught her in my arms, rather roughly in my alarm, I fear.

"Gloria! What is it?"

"I don't know." Her eyes stared at me rather bewilderedly, as if she were emerging from some sort of nightmare.

"Did you see or hear anything?"

"No." She seemed to be averse to leaving my sheltering arms. "It was something you said—no, that wasn't it. I don't know. People have daydreams. This must have been a nightmare."

God help me; I laughed in my masculine complacency and said:

"You girls are a queer lot in some ways. Let's go up the beach a way—"

"No!" she exclaimed emphatically.

"Then let's go down the beach—"

"No, no!"

I lost patience.

"Gloria, what's come over you? We can't stay here all day. We've got to find a way to go up those cliffs and find what's on the other side. Don't be so foolish; it isn't like you."

"Don't scold me," she returned with a meekness strange to her. "Something seems to keep clawing at the outer edge of my mind, something that I can't translate—do you believe in transmission of thought waves?"

I stared at her. I'd never heard her talk in this manner before.

"Do you think somebody's trying to signal you by sending thought waves?"

"No, they're not thoughts," she murmured absently. "Not as I know thoughts, at least."

Then, like a person suddenly coming out of a trance, she said:

"You go on and look for a place to go up the cliffs, while I wait here."

"Gloria, I don't like the idea. You come along—or else I'll wait until you feel like going."

"I don't think I'll ever feel that way," she answered forlornly. "You don't need to go out of sight; one can see a long way here. Did you ever see such black cliffs; this is a black coast, sure enough? Did you ever read Tevis Clyde Smith's poem—'The long black coasts of death—' something? I can't remember exactly."

I felt a vague uneasiness at hearing her talk in this manner, but sought to dismiss the feeling with a shrug of my shoulders.

"I'll find a trail up," I said, "and maybe get something for our meal—clams or a crab—"

She shuddered violently.

"Don't mention crabs. I've hated them all my life, but I didn't realize it until you spoke. They eat dead things, don't they? I know the Devil looks just like a monstrous crab."

"All right," said I, to humor her. "Stay right here; I won't be gone long."

120

"Kiss me before you go," she said with a wistfulness that caught at my heart, I knew not why. I drew her tenderly into my arms, joying in the feel of her slim young body so vibrant with life and loveliness. She closed her eyes as I kissed her, and I noted how strangely white she seemed.

"Don't go out of sight," she said as I released her. A number of rough boulders dotted the beach, fallen, no doubt, from the overhanging cliff face, and on one of these she sat down.

With some misgivings, I turned to go. I went along the beach close to the great black wall which rose into the blue like a monster against the sky, and at last came to a number of unusually large boulders. Before going among these I glanced back and saw Gloria sitting where I had left her. I know my eyes softened as I looked on that slim, brave little figure—for the last time.

I wandered in among the boulders and lost sight of the beach behind me. I often wonder why I so thoughtlessly ignored her last plea. A man's brain fabric is coarser than a woman's, not so susceptible to outer influences. Yet I wonder if even then, pressure was being brought to bear upon me—

At any rate, I wandered along, gazing up at the towering black mass until it seemed to have a sort of mesmeric effect upon me. One who has never seen these cliffs cannot possibly form any true conception of them, nor can I breathe into my description the invisible aura of malignity which seemed to emanate from them. I say, they rose so high above me that their edges seemed to cut through the sky—that I felt like an ant crawling beneath a Babylonian wall—that their monstrous serrated faces seemed like the breasts of dusty gods of unthinkable age—this I can say, this much I can impart to you. But if any man ever reads this, let him not think that I have given a true portrait of the Black Coast. The reality of the thing lay, not in sight and sense nor even in the thoughts which they induced; but in the things you know without thinking—the feelings and the stirrings of consciousness—the faint clawings at the outer edge of the mind which are not thoughts at all—

But these things I discovered later. At the moment, I walked along like a man in a daze, almost mesmerized by the stark monotony of the black ramparts above me. At times I shook myself, blinked and looked out to sea to get rid of this mazy feeling, but even the sea seemed shadowed by the great walls. The further I went, the more threatening they seemed. My reason told me that they could not fall, but the instinct at the back of my brain whispered that they would suddenly hurtle down and crush me.

Then suddenly I found some fragments of driftwood which had washed ashore. I could have shouted my elation. The mere sight of them proved that man at least *existed* and that there was a world far removed from these dark and sullen cliffs, which seemed to fill the whole universe. I found a long fragment of iron attached to a piece of the wood and tore it off; if the necessity arose, it would make a very serviceable iron bludgeon. Rather heavy for the ordinary man, it is true, but in size and strength, I am no ordinary man.

At this moment, too, I decided I had gone far enough. Gloria was long out of sight and I retraced my steps hurriedly. As I went I noted a few tracks in the sand and reflected with amusement that if a spider crab, something larger than a horse, had crossed the beach here, it would make just such a track. Then I came in sight of the place where I had left Gloria and gazed along a bare and silent beach.

I had heard no scream, no cry. Utter silence had reigned as it reigned now, when I stood beside the boulder where she had sat and looked in the sand of the beach. Something small and slim and white lay there, and I dropped to my knees beside it. It was a woman's hand, severed at the wrist, and as I saw upon the second finger the engagement ring I had placed there myself, my heart withered in my breast and the sky became a black ocean which drowned the sun.

How long I crouched over that pitiful fragment like a wounded beast, I do not know. Time ceased to be for me, and from its dying minutes was born Eternity. What are days, hours, years, to a shattered heart, to whose empty hurt each instant is an Everlasting Forever? But when I rose and reeled down to the sea edge, holding that little hand close to my hollow bosom, the sun had set and the moon had set and the hard white stars looked scornfully at me across the immensity of space.

There I pressed my lips again and again to that pitiful cold flesh and laid the slim little hand on the flowing tide which carried it out to the clean, deep sea, as I trust, merciful God, the white flame of her soul found rest in the Everlasting Sea. And the sad and ancient waves that know all the sorrows of men seemed to weep for me, for I could not weep. But since, many have shed tears, oh God, and the tears were of blood!

I staggered along the mocking whiteness of the beach like a drunken man or a lunatic. And from the time that I rose from the sighing tide to the time that I dropped exhausted and became unconscious seems centuries on countless centuries, during which I raved and screamed and staggered along huge black ramparts which frowned down on me in cold inhuman disdain—which brooded above the squeaking ant at their feet.

The sun was up when I awoke, and I found I was not alone. I sat up. On every hand I was ringed in by a strange and horrible throng. If you can imagine spider crabs larger than a horse—yet they were not true spider crabs, outside the difference in the size. Leaving that difference out, I should say that there was as much variation in these monsters and the true spider crab as there is between a highly developed European and an African bushman. These were more highly developed, if you understand me.

They sat up and looked at me. I remained motionless, uncertain just what to expect—and a cold fear began to steal over me. This was not caused by any especial fear of the brutes killing me, for I felt somehow that they would do that, and did not shrink from the thought. But their eyes bored in on me and turned my blood to ice. For in them I recognized an intelligence infinitely higher than mine, yet terribly different. This is hard to conceive, harder to explain. But as I looked into those frightful eyes, I knew that keen, powerful brains lurked behind them, brains which worked in a higher sphere, a different dimension than mine.

There was neither friendliness nor favor in those eyes, no sympathy or understanding—not even fear or hate. It is a terrible thing for a human being to be looked at in that manner. Even the eyes of a human enemy who is going to kill us have understanding in them, and a certain acceptance of kindred. But these fiends gazed upon me in something of the manner in which cold-hearted scientists might look at a worm about to be stuck on a specimen board. They did not—they could not—understand me. My thoughts, sorrows, joys, ambitions, they never could fathom, any more than I could fathom theirs. We were of different species! And no wars of human kind can ever equal in cruelty the constant warfare that is waged between living things of diverging order. Is it possible that all life came from one stem? I cannot now believe it.

There was intelligence and power in the cold eyes which were fixed on me, but not intelligence as I knew it. They had progressed much further than mankind in their ways, but they progressed along different lines. Further than this, I cannot say. Their minds and reasoning faculties are closed doors to me and most of their actions seem absolutely meaningless; yet I know that these actions are guided by definite, though inhuman, thoughts, which in turn are the results of a higher stage of development than the human race may ever reach in *their way*.

But as I sat there and these thoughts were borne in on me—as I felt the terrific force of their inhuman intellect crashing against my brain and will power, I leaped up, cold with fear; a wild unreasoning fear which wild beasts must feel when first confronted by men. I knew that these things were of a higher order than myself, and I feared to even threaten them, yet with all my soul I hated them.

The average man feels no compunction in his dealings with the insects underfoot. He does not feel, as he does in his dealings with his brother man, that the Higher Powers will call upon him for an accounting—of the worms on which he treads, nor the fowls he eats. Nor does a lion devour a lion, yet feasts nobly on buffalo or man. I tell you, Nature is most cruel when she sets the species against each other.

These thinking-crabs, then, looking upon me as God only knows what sort of prey or specimen, were intending me God only knows what sort of evil, when I broke the chain of terror which held me. The largest one, whom I faced, was now eying me with a sort of grim disapproval, a sort of anger, as if he haughtily resented my threatening actions—as a scientist might resent the writhing of a worm beneath the dissecting knife. At that, fury blazed in me and the flames were fanned by my fear. With one leap I reached the largest crab and with one desperate smash I crushed and killed him. Then bounding over his writhing form, I fled.

But I did not flee far. The thought came to me as I ran

124

that these were they whom I sought for vengeance. Gloria
—no wonder she started when I spoke the accursed name
of "crab" and conceived the Devil to be in the form of a
crab, when even then those fiends must have been stealing
about us, tingling her sensitive thoughts with the psychic
waves that flowed from their horrid brains. I turned, then,
and came back a few steps, my bludgeon lifted. But the
throng had bunched together, as cattle do upon the approach of a lion. Their claws were raised menacingly, and
their cruel thought emanations struck me so like a power
of physical force that I staggered backward and was unable to proceed against it. I knew then that in their way
they feared me, for they backed slowly away toward the
cliffs, ever fronting me.

My history is long, but I must shortly draw it to a close.
Since that hour I have waged a fierce and merciless warfare against a race I knew to be higher in culture and intellect than I. Scientists, they are, and in some horrid ex-
periment of theirs, Gloria must have perished. I cannot
say.

This I have learned. Their city is high up among those
lofty tiers of cliffs which I cannot see because of the
overhanging crags of the first tier. I suppose the whole
island is like that, a mere base of basaltic rock, rising to a
high flung pinnacle, no doubt, this pinnacle being the last
tier of innumerable tiers of rocky walls. The monsters
descend by a secret way which I have only just discovered.
They have hunted me, and I have hunted them.

I have found this, also: the one point in common between these beasts and the human is that the higher the
race develops mentally, the less acute become the physical faculties. I, who am as much lower than they mentally
as a gorilla is lower than a human professor, am as deadly
in single combat with them as a gorilla would be with an
unarmed professor. I am quicker, stronger, of keener
senses. I possess coordinations which they do not. In a
word, there is a strange reversion here—I am the wild
beast and they are the civilized and developed beings. I ask
no mercy and I give none. What are my wishes and desires
to them? I would never have molested them, any more
than an eagle molests men, had they not taken my mate.
But to satisfy some selfish hunger or to evolve some useless
scientific theory, they took her life and ruined mine.

And now I have been, and shall be, the wild beast with

a vengeance. A wolf may wipe out a herd, a man-eating lion has destroyed a whole village of men, and I am a wolf, a lion, to the people—if I may call them that—of the Black Coast. I have lived on such clams as I have found, for I have never been able to bring myself to eat of crab flesh. And I have hunted my foes, along the beaches, by sunlight and by starlight, among the boulders, and high up in the cliffs as far as I could climb. It has not been easy, and I must shortly admit defeat. They have fought me with psychic weapons against which I have no defense, and the constant crashing of their wills against mine has weakened me terribly, mentally and physically. I have lain in wait for single enemies and have even attacked and destroyed several, but the strain has been terrific.

Their power is mainly mental, and far, far exceeds human mesmerism. At first it was easy to plunge through the enveloping thought-waves of one crab-man and kill him, but they have found weak places in my brain.

This I do not understand, but I know that of late I have gone through Hell with each battle. Their thought-tides have seemed to flow into my skull in waves of molten metal, freezing, burning, withering my brain and my soul. I lie hidden and when one crab-man approaches, I leap and I must kill quickly, as a lion must kill a man with a rifle before the victim can aim and fire.

Nor have I always escaped physically unscathed, for only yesterday the desperate stroke of a dying crab-man's claws tore off my left arm at the elbow. This would have killed me at one time, but now I shall live long enough to consumate my vengeance. Up there, in the higher tiers, up among the clouds where the crab city of horror broods, I must carry doom. I am a dying man—the wounds of my enemies' strange weapons have shown me my Fate, but my left arm is bound so that I shall not bleed to death, my crumbling brain will hold together long enough, and I still have my right hand and my iron bludgeon. I have noted that at dawn the crab-people keep closer to their high cliffs, and such as I have found at that time are very easy to kill. Why, I do not know, but my lower reason tells me that these Masters are at a low ebb of vitality at dawn, for some reason.

I am writing this by the light of a low-hanging moon. Soon dawn will come, and in the darkness before dawn, I shall go up the secret trail I have found which leads to the clouds—and above. I shall find the demon city and as the east begins to redden, I shall begin the slaughter. Oh, it will be a great battle! I will crush and crash and kill, and my foes will lie in a great shattered heap, and at last I, too, shall die. Good enough. I shall be content. I have scattered death like a lion. I have littered the beaches with their corpses. Before I die I shall slay many more.

Gloria, the moon swings low. Dawn will be here soon. I do not know if you look in approval, from shadowland, on my red work of vengeance, but it has to some extent brought ease to my frozen soul. After all, these creatures and I are of different species, and it is Nature's cruel custom that the diverging orders may never live in peace with each other. They took my mate; I take their lives.

*Ramsey Campbell, born 1946, is an English writer of super-
natural stories, whose first book,* The Inhabitant of the Lake,
*was published when he was 18. Since then he has married,
written critically on books and comic art, reviewed films on
radio in his native Liverpool and produced many more horror
stories and an impressive second collection,* Demons By Daylight. *Slowly but distinctively he has evolved into one of the
most unusual and innovative practitioners in the genre. His
specialty is creepy happenings in familiar settings and using
the unexplained to powerful effect. In a variety of ways, as one
reviewer put it, Campbell turns the screws very tight. This
brief offering is no exception.*

CALL FIRST

by Ramsey Campbell

IT WAS the other porters who made Ned determined to find out who answered the phone in the old man's house.

Not that he hadn't wanted to know before. He'd felt it was his right almost as soon as the whole thing had begun, months ago. He'd been sitting behind his desk in the library entrance, waiting for someone to try to take a bag into the library so he could shout after them that they couldn't, when the reference librarian ushered the old man to Ned's desk and said, "Let this gentleman use your phone." Maybe he hadn't meant every time the old man came to the library, but then he should have said so. The old man used to talk to the librarian and tell him things about books even he didn't know, which was why he let him phone. All Ned could do was feel resentful. People weren't supposed to use his phone, and even he wasn't allowed to phone outside the building. And it wasn't as if the old man's calls were interesting. Ned wouldn't have minded if they'd been worth hearing.

"I'm coming home now." That was all he ever said; then he'd put down the receiver and hurry away. It was the way he said it that made Ned wonder. There was no feeling behind the words, they sounded as if he were saying them only because he had to, perhaps wishing he needn't. Ned knew people talked like that: his parents did in church, and most of the time at home. He wondered if the old man were calling his wife, because he wore a ring on his wedding finger, although in the claw where a stone should be was what looked like a piece of yellow fingernail. But Ned didn't think it could be his wife. Each day the old man left the library at the same time, so why would he bother to phone?

Then there was the way the old man looked at Ned

when he phoned: as if he didn't matter and couldn't understand the way most of the porters looked at him. That was the look that swelled up inside Ned one day and made him persuade one of the other porters to take charge of his desk while Ned waited to listen in on the old man's call. The girl who always smiled at Ned was on the switchboard, and they listened together. They heard the phone in the house ringing then lifted, and the old man's call and his receiver going down: nothing else, not even breathing apart from the old man's. "Who do you think it is?" the girl said, but Ned thought she'd laugh if he said he didn't know. He shrugged extravagantly and left.

Now he was determined. The next time the old man came to the library Ned phoned his house, having read what the old man dialed. When the ringing began, its pulse sounded deliberately slow, and Ned felt the pumping of his blood rushing ahead. Seven trills and the phone in the house opened with a violent click. Ned held his breath, but all he could hear was his blood thumping his ears. "Hello," he said and after a silence, clearing his throat, "Hello!" Perhaps it was one of those answering machines people in films used in their offices. He felt foolish and uneasy greeting the wide silent metal ear, and put down the receiver. He was in bed and falling asleep before he wondered why the old man should tell an answering machine that he was coming home.

The following day, in the bar where all the porters went at lunchtime, Ned told them about the silently listening phone. "He's weird, that old man," he said, but now the others had finished joking with him they didn't seem interested, and he had to make a grab for the conversation. "He reads weird books," he said. "All about witches and magic. Real ones, not stories."

"Now tell us something we didn't know," someone said, and the conversation turned its back on Ned. His attention began to wander, he lost his hold on what was being said, he had to smile and nod as usual when they looked at him, and he was thinking: they're looking at me like the old man does. I'll show them. I'll go in his house and see who's there. Maybe I'll take something that'll show I've been there. Then they'll have to listen.

But next day at lunchtime, when he arrived at the address he'd seen on the old man's library card, Ned felt more like knocking at the front door and running away.

The house was menacingly big, the end house of a street whose other windows were brightly bricked up. Exposed foundations like broken teeth protruded from the mud that surrounded the street, while hundreds of yards away stood a five-storey crescent of flats that looked as if it had been designed in sections to be fitted together by a two-year-old. Ned tried to keep the house between him and the flats as he peered in the windows.

All he could see through the grimy front window was bare floorboards; when he coaxed himself to look through the side window, the same. He dreaded being caught by the old man, even though he'd seen him sitting behind a pile of books ten minutes ago. It had taken Ned that long to walk here; the old man couldn't walk so fast, and there wasn't a bus he could catch. At last Ned dodged round the back and peered into the kitchen: a few plates in the sink, some tins of food, an old cooker. Nobody to be seen. He returned to the front, wondering what to do. Maybe he'd knock after all. He took hold of the bar of the knocker, trying to think what he'd say, and the door opened.

The hall leading back to the kitchen was long and dim. Ned stood shuffling indecisively on the step. He would have to decide soon, for his lunch-hour was dwindling. It was like one of the empty houses he'd used to play in with the other children, daring each other to go up the tottering stairs. Even the things in the kitchen didn't make it seem lived in. He'd show them all. He went in. Acknowledging a vague idea that the old man's companion was out, he closed the door to hear if they returned.

On his right was the front room; on his left, past the stairs and the phone, another of the bare rooms he'd seen. He tiptoed upstairs. The stairs creaked and swayed a little, perhaps unused to anyone of Ned's weight. He reached the landing, breathing heavily, feeling dust chafe his throat. Stairs led up to a closed attic door, but he looked in the rooms off the landing.

Two of the doors which he opened stealthily showed him nothing but boards and flurries of floating dust. The landing in front of the third looked cleaner, as if the door were often opened. He pulled it toward him, holding it up all the way so it didn't scrape the floor, and entered.

Most of it didn't seem to make sense. There was a single bed with faded sheets. Against the walls were tables and piles of old books. Even some of the books looked disused. There were black candles and racks of small cardboard boxes. On one of the tables lay a single book. Ned padded across the fragments of carpet and opened the book in a thin path of sunlight through the shutters.

Inside the sagging covers was a page which Ned slowly realized had been ripped from the Bible. It was the story of Lazarus. Scribbles that might be letters filled the margin, and at the bottom of the page: "p. 491". Suddenly inspired, Ned turned to that page in the book. It showed a drawing of a corpse sitting up in his coffin, but the book was all in the language they sometimes used in church: Latin. He thought of asking one of the librarians what it meant. Then he remembered that he needed proof he'd been in the house. He stuffed the page from the Bible into his pocket.

As he crept swiftly downstairs, something was troubling him. He reached the hall and thought he knew what it was. He still didn't know who lived in the house with the old man. If they lived in the back perhaps there'd be signs in the kitchen. Though if it were his wife, Ned thought as he hurried down the hall, she couldn't be like Ned's mother, who would never have left torn strips of wallpaper hanging at shoulder height from both walls. He'd reached the kitchen door when he realized what had been bothering him. When he'd emerged from the bedroom the attic door had been open.

He looked back involuntarily, and saw a woman walking away from him down the hall.

He was behind the closed kitchen door before he had time to feel fear. That came only when he saw that the back door was nailed rustily shut. Then he controlled himself. She was only a woman; she couldn't do much if she found him. He opened the door minutely. The hall was empty.

Halfway down the hall he had to slip into the side room, heart punching his chest, for she'd appeared again from between the stairs and the front door. He felt the beginnings of anger and recklessness, and they grew faster when he opened the door and had to flinch back as he saw her hand passing. The fingers looked famished, the colour of old lard, with long yellow cracked nails. There was no nail on her wedding finger, which wore a plain ring. She

133

was returning from the direction of the kitchen, which was why Ned hadn't expected her.

Through the opening of the door he heard her padding upstairs. She sounded barefoot. He waited until he couldn't hear her, then edged out into the hall. The door began to fall open with a faint creak, and he drew it stealthily closed. He paced toward the front door. If he hadn't seen her shadow creeping down the stairs he would have come face to face with her.

He was listening behind the kitchen door, and near to panic, when he realized she knew he was in the house. She was playing a game with him. At once he was furious. She was only an old woman, her body beneath the long white dress was sure to be as thin as her hands, she could only shout when she saw him, she couldn't stop him leaving. In a minute he'd be late for work. He threw open the kitchen door and swaggered down the hall.

The sight of her lifting the phone receiver broke his stride for a moment. Perhaps she was phoning the police. He hadn't done anything; she could have her Bible page back. But she had laid the receiver beside the phone. Why? Was she making sure the old man couldn't ring?

As she unbent from stooping to the phone she grasped two uprights of the banisters to support herself. They gave a loud splintering creak and bent together. Ned halted, confused. He was still struggling to react when she turned toward him, and he saw her face. Part of it was still on the bone.

He didn't back away until she began to advance on him, her nails tearing new strips from both walls. All he could see was her protruding eyes, unsupported by flesh. His mind was backing away faster than he was, but it had come up against a terrible insight. He even knew why she'd made sure the old man couldn't interrupt until she'd finished. His calls weren't like speaking to an answering machine at all. They were exactly like switching off a burglar alarm.

Richard L. Tierney, who holds a degree in entomology and has worked for the U.S. Forest Service in Alaska, is currently a resident of St. Paul, Minnesota. Formerly an editor of occult books, he has long been a devotee of the macabre and fantasy in fiction and has authored some highly intelligent and perceptive articles on the genre for the little magazines. He has also sculpted demons and monster gods in hard clay and created some extremely good fantastic and romantic verse of his own, collected in a volume entitled Dreams and Damnations. And now The Silver Scarab Press (500 Wellesley S.E., Albuquerque, New Mexico 87106) has made available his centuries-spanning novel The Winds of Zarr, which the author says has in it the influences of Dorothy Clarke Wilson, Emanuel Velikovsky and the epic dramatics of Cecil B. De Mille and Robert E. Howard. Tierney is strongly interested in the cosmic quality in fantastic art pioneered by writers such as H.G. Wells, Lord Dunsany, Clark Ashton Smith and H.P. Lovecraft and he touches on exactly that in this unnerving tale, set in his native Iowa.

FROM BEYOND THE STARS

by Richard L. Tierney

. . . Another place of supposedly supernatural importance in this region is Hunter's Hollow, which is held to be still actively haunted by strange forest demons. Indeed, upon seeing this place one is struck by its somber and lonely aspect. A dim hollow surrounded by hills whose steep sides rise up sharply to oak-forested crests, it seems the very type of spot likely to appeal darkly to the minds of the imaginative. A small stream trickles down into the hollow to feed a marsh which never seems to grow larger—a strange thing, considering that there is no outlet. Geologists speculate that the water drains out through cracks in the rock to underground passages—a reasonable possibility in view of the fact that the limestone hills in this part of the state are known to be honeycombed with caverns . . .

Gordon Huntington; *Iowa Folklore and Superstition*

I

IT WAS the unnatural *roundness* of the hollow that first struck Edgar Langton as he gazed down into its gloomy depths. The hills on every side followed a perfect circle about an eighth of a mile across, enclosing the hollow almost like the walls of a huge pit. In some places the cliffs were so sheer that they seemed to have been cut off smooth with a great knife. Langton wondered if it might be an ancient meteorite crater and wished he had supplemented his archaeological studies with more training in geology.

So far he had not found the Indian mounds which his friend, Dr. Harrister, had told him of, but across the hollow he noticed a black hole gaping in the base of a cliff. Perhaps an investigation of that cave would reveal some interesting relics. Descending the precipitous footpath down the hill, he skirted the edge of the stagnant marsh and picked his way among the blocky limestone fragments which thrust in ragged profusion above the ground. Then, clambering up a short, rocky draw, he arrived at the cave and went inside.

The cold draft that met him as he entered was a welcome relief from the hot August sun. He rested for a moment, wondering where the draft of cold air came from. After a few moments of fruitless searching for crevices with his small pen flashlight, he realized the cave went back only thirty feet or so. The icy air began to chill him, and he decided to stay no longer and risk possible ill effects.

His searchings in and around the cave uncovered a few broken arrowheads, some small bone fragments, and a rather good axehead of dark basalt. Recognizing this last item as being made of a stone not often found in the region, he pocketed it with some satisfaction. He then left the cave and, when the mist had cleared from his glasses, set out to find the mounds. Glancing at the sky, he realized he would have to hurry—the afternoon was nearly gone.

Half an hour later Langton had located three of the mounds in the dense woods on the ridge overlooking the hollow. All of them were overgrown and partly hidden by underbrush but he could tell, nevertheless, that they were mounds of the "effigy" type, that is, made in the shape of some animal or bird. In this case they were all of vaguely human configuration, the shape being that of a man with an exceptionally large, humped head, lying flat, with arms and legs outspread.

Langton set immediately to work digging one of the mounds open with a small trowel he had brought with him. In a few minutes he had unearthed a figure of bluish clay about six inches long and of roughly human shape. Its arms were folded across its broad chest and its large head rose like a tall hump from the shoulders, without an intervening neck. On brushing the dirt carefully away, Langton found that two hollow eyes had been punched into the head and that a vertical ridge ran between them from chest to cranium. No other features were present.

By this time the sun was almost down and Langton saw that he would have to start back immediately in order to reach the road before dark. Wrapping his find carefully in a handkerchief, he set out through the forest and soon regained the footpath. Here he paused to glance back into the hollow, and was surprised to see a man emerge from the distant cave and begin to pick his way toward him among the limestone boulders. As the figure approached, Langton saw that despite the man's agility he was aged and bent. Something about this lean figure scrambling among the rocks struck him unpleasantly, like watching a spider scuttle across a coal pile, and he decided to go on without waiting for the man. As he turned to leave he thought he glimpsed, from the corner of his eye, a dark figure standing in the far-off cave entrance. Focusing his eyes on the spot, however, he could not be sure, and decided it was his imagination playing tricks on him with one of the shadows of the dusk.

A short walk along the woodland path brought Langton to the gravel road. Across from him, at the base of a lowering, forested hillside, stood a gray, unkempt church with a small, weedy cemetery close by. Half a mile up the road was Dr. Harrister's house, and he set out for it briskly. At the top of the hill he paused and gazed back toward the west, where the last red glow of evening was slowly fading behind the black silhouette of hill and forest. A silver crescent moon and a few pale stars were already out and the night insects were beginning to hum, while frogs croaked stridently from hidden ponds and marshes. As Langton gazed silently at the overpowering beauty of the scene, a black shadow suddenly darted across the road from that path he had so recently followed. It vanished among the trees of the old cemetery behind the church, but not before he realized that it was the old man he had seen in the hollow.

Puzzled, Langton resumed his way down the lane. He made a mental note to ask Dr. Harrister about the man. Now he could see the lights of his friend's farmhouse, and found himself strangely relieved that he need not walk those woodland paths in the deepening shadows of night.

When supper was finished, Langton showed his archaeological finds to Dr. Harrister. This comfortable old country doctor, being a member of the Northeastern Iowa Historical Society, took a great interest in all things concerning the history of the region he had lived in all his life. He studied the artifacts with interest, turning them this way and that under the light of the shaded lamp.

"This is curious," he said presently. "I've never seen a figure like this clay image before. And the ax head—it's very dark and heavy. I don't remember ever having seen stone of this sort hereabouts."

"Exactly my impression," said Langton. "I think it's some kind of basalt. To have gotten into this area, it must have been traded from tribe to tribe from someplace fairly distant."

"Interesting." The doctor handed back the artifacts. "Are you about ready to write up your report for the Historical Society?"

"Not quite. First I want to visit the library again and do some more reading on the mound-builders. Also on the Fox and Sioux tribes who came later into this area. And I hope to finish excavating that mound I started on, too."

"Well, don't let old Charlie catch you digging up his mounds," said the doctor with a grin. "He'd probably try to put a hex on you."

"Old Charlie? Does he own the land?"

"No, he's just the caretaker of the old church down the road. But he's so fond of the mounds and the hollow that he acts almost as if he does own them."

Langton snapped his fingers as a thought struck him. "Is this Charlie an old man, bent, but rather spry?"

"That's right. Did you talk with him?"

"No, but I saw him come out of the cave in the hollow. I meant to ask you about him."

Again the doctor grinned slightly. "Why? Did he strike you as being somehow peculiar?"

"Yes, and rather unpleasantly so, though I don't know why."

"I'm not surprised," said Dr. Harrister. "Most people say the same thing about him. His name's Charlie Hinch, but everyone around here just calls him 'old Charlie.' He's been caretaker of that run-down church ever since it was abandoned thirty years ago. He just lives there, actually, on welfare."

"Why should he care if I examine the mounds?"

"I don't know, really, but he resents anyone going near the hollow. He's always poking around there himself, at night as well as in the daytime. Nobody knows why he does it, but, well—some of the country folk claim that he goes there to meet the Devil."

"Why, that's fascinating!" Aside from his archaeological studies, nothing intrigued Langton more than delving into regional folklore and superstition. "Is the hollow supposed to be haunted, then?"

"Not exactly haunted," replied the doctor thoughtfully. "At least not in the usual sense of the word—graveyard specters and all that. It's more in the line of strange goings-on about the countryside—things that people somehow connect with old Charlie and his doings in Hunter's Hollow. It's all rather vague, you understand . . ."

Dr. Harrister paused uncertainly. "Go on," said Langton, and the doctor, with perhaps a touch of embarrassment in his manner, continued . . .

Charlie Hinch had come to be caretaker of the church shortly after it was built in 1914 and continued in his job long after it was so abruptly abandoned. For some never-discussed reason, the church was without a congregation less than two years after its completion. Indeed, the minister had offered his resignation without explaining the reason and had departed from the region immediately thereafter. But old Charlie stayed on, and people began to maintain that he was in league with the Devil or something worse, though the tellers of these rumors were never specific. It was known that the old man frequently visited Hunter's Hollow at night, and he was occasionally seen poking around the Indian mounds on the ridges.

It was Adrian Hunter, the owner of the land which included the hollow, who claimed to have seen old Charlie enter the cave there one afternoon. Investigating, Hunter had entered the cave himself and was surprised to find it empty. There was no place where a man could hide, and the entire passage extended no more than twenty feet into the rock—yet Charlie was gone. Where he had vanished to, or how, none could guess and, as Adrian Hunter had put it, "Only the Devil could tell!"

As the years passed people came to regard the hollow and the church as haunted places. Charlie's nocturnal trips to the hollow continued, and there were those who claimed that he was not always alone in his wanderings. Sarah Tipford, a farm wife and former patient of Dr. Harrister's, attested to seeing Charlie one night in company with a "great tall man" whose aspect had filled her with dread. She had glimpsed them in the beams of her car headlights as they crossed the road ahead of her; they were going in the direction of the hollow and the large man was carrying some struggling thing under his arm. Before she had driven closely enough to see them clearly, the pair had vanished into the woods. The very next day Zeke Henshaw, a nearby farmer, found that one of his fullgrown pigs was missing while another had been killed in a singularly horrible manner; its chest cavity had been torn open and the blood drained from its body. Henshaw had found strange, large footprints in the mud around the slain pig and claimed they were the tracks of "neither man nor beast." For some unspecified reason he connected the atrocious deed with old Charlie Hinch.

All these suspicions about old Charlie could not be proved, of course, and Dr. Harrister had come to feel that they were only gossip inspired by the old man's manifest strangeness. This strangeness had on one occasion been brought directly to the doctor's attention. During the past few years old Charlie had written several papers on unusual topics, one of which he had sent to the Northeastern Iowa Historical Society. It described in detail the bloody sacrificial rites supposedly practiced by the prehistoric mound-builders of the region. Dr. Harrister himself had read the document, and found the rites which old Charlie described almost intolerably revolting. Yet the paper was obviously a fabrication, for only the barest amount of anthropological knowledge concerning these long-vanished Indians had yet been unearthed. Old Charlie's article was given no consideration save as a possible proof of his insanity.

Charlie's failure to get his document published did not discourage him, however, from turning out many other semiliterate writings on improbable subjects and sending them to various scientific organizations. None of them was ever published, needless to say. His last attempt went to an astronomical society, which rejected it as the sheerest

141

nonsense. It dealt with the Great Nebula of Andromeda and actually described in detail the creatures which supposedly inhabited the worlds of that far galaxy. Though obviously an invention of the wildest sort, it was written as though the author believed every word of his fantasy and was attempting to set down factual information on natural history.

"Since that last paper of his was rejected," concluded the doctor, "old Charlie seems to have abandoned his literary efforts. But I'm sure you'll agree now that he's a most unusual person."

"He certainly seems to be," said Langton. "He sounds to me like a 'Fortean'—you know, one of those people who believe the odd things you see in the newspapers occasionally about flying saucers and such. Still, one thing you told me *does* seem odd, now that I think of it . . ."

"And what's that?"

Langton lit his pipe and paused a long moment before he answered. "Something you said struck me as a coincidence. You mentioned that this Adrian Hunter, who owns the land, saw old Charlie go into the cave, but that he failed to find him inside."

"That's what Hunter told me," said the doctor. "He drinks a lot, though . . ."

"Perhaps so—but when you mentioned that incident I happened to remember something. I was in that cave this afternoon. As you said, there's no place where anyone could hide in there. Yet half an hour after I left, I saw old Charlie come out of that cave. Most of the time I was in sight of the path leading to it—*but I never saw him go in!*"

III

The next morning, when Langton drove to nearby Decorah, he had largely forgotten about Charlie Hinch and Hunter's Hollow. He soon found, however, while pursuing his studies in the libraries of Decorah and Luther College, that he was being reminded of these matters again and again.

Of the early mound-builders he learned little that he had not already known, but certain old and obscure pamphlets concerning the early history of the region gave him information about the comparatively recent Sioux

Indians—facts not to be found in the standard history texts. One of these documents—a yellowed translation of a report by Paul-Jacques Beauchamps, who came with the *voyageurs* shortly after Marquette—contained an account of Indian rituals in which human sacrifice played a part. A young man or woman—usually the bravest warrior or the fairest maiden from the tribe—was chosen to be given to the "Windmaker," a god or demon greatly feared by all the tribes in the area. First the tribe would gather at a certain round hollow in the forest, where appropriate rituals were enacted. The victim was then slain with a stone ax "made from a dense rock which the Indians say is brought up by the Daemons from that place where they dwell deep within the Earth." After this the demon himself would arrive, rip open the breast of the sacrifice and thrust its head within the chest cavity to feed on the blood directly from the heart. The writer avoided describing the demon, but ended his account with the statement: "Until now, I would not have believed that the fiends of Hell were allowed to walk the Earth; yet, having this day seen the Archdemon Himself, I can no longer doubt."

Langton felt a strange thrill. He remembered the stone axhead he had found the day before, and found himself wondering just what sort of dreadful event Beauchamps had actually witnessed in that "round hollow."

On impulse, he began to search the old pamphlets for a reference to Hunter's Hollow and, to his satisfaction, soon found a description of ". . . a place surrounded by hills and steep cliffs in a circle. A deep glen of evil aspect, it was called by the settlers 'Devil's Hollow,' as the heathen Indians were wont to come there to worship a daemon which they called the 'Maker of the Twisting Winds.'" Most of this account, however, concerned a church which had been built near the hollow shortly after 1860. To his surprise, Langton found that it had been situated near the site of the present church. It was said to have been presided over by a "mad" preacher named Jeremiah Potts who was "no true man of God" and who, it was claimed, "went often to the Hollow to hold meetings with the Devil." "Upon a certain holy Sunday," read the account, "this false preacher announced to his gathering that he had learned of Beings older and more powerful than Almighty God Himself. The people were greatly incensed at these words and cried out that he was a liar and a

143

blasphemer, whereat Jeremiah Potts raised up his arms and shouted in an awful voice: 'Behold, then, the proof of my words!' Whereupon a most monstrous blue fiend from Hell strode into the room and stood facing the congregation with evil round eyes. So fearsome was this being's aspect that the people were thrown into terror and fled hence in great haste." After this, according to the singular account, no one would go near the church and the minister was left to his own dubious doings. Then, in 1877, the church was destroyed during a tornado and Jeremiah Potts was found dead amid the wreckage, his chest torn open by flying debris. Yet there were some who attributed his death to less natural causes and expressed their belief that "the Devil had come for his own."

As Langton read, he found himself thinking of the similarites between this account of Jeremiah Potts and the present-day superstitions concerning old Charlie. It was strange that the past should hold such a close parallel. Stranger still were the Indian rites described in the aged document by the French explorer Beauchamps. He decided he would examine that basalt ax more closely when he returned to Dr. Harrister's.

That evening, as Langton drove back along the winding roads, he saw that it was too late to pay another visit to the mounds. He had used the entire day tracking down the material he needed. However, the mounds could wait another day; right now, it was enough merely to enjoy the beauty of the country around him. So lovely was the sunset-shadowed landscape of hill and forest limned against the yellowing sky that Langton doubted there could be a more beautiful spot in the Midwest. . . .

His mood changed to surprise as he drove past the old country church. Men were standing about in groups on the weed-grown lawn, seemingly in excited conversation. They looked like farmers for the most part, and some carried guns. A police car was parked alongside the road and a few uniformed men were standing among the crowd.

Langton drove on past and continued up the road to Dr. Harrister's farm. As he pulled into the drive he noticed that the doctor's car was there and wondered what his friend was doing home so early, since this was the night he usually attended the meeting of the historical society. Entering the house, he found Dr. Harrister reclining in his easy chair, looking tired and rather pale.

"What brings you home at this time of day?" asked Langton.

"I was called to examine a body down at the church." The doctor's voice trembled a little; he sounded weary. "A deputy was killed there today."

"I'll be damned! I *wondered* what all those people were doing down by the church. How did it happen?"

"It seems some of our farmers have been losing a lot of pigs and sheep for quite some time," said the doctor. "They've often claimed that old Charlie was somehow responsible and have pestered the sheriff a lot about it. He finally sent a deputy out this morning to investigate. When the deputy didn't return or call in, the sheriff came out himself with some men. They found what was left of the deputy inside the church, and they called me out to examine the remains." The doctor poured himself a shot of brandy and drank it down. "I must say I didn't enjoy the job."

Langton asked, rather hesitantly: "Why not?"

"It was a horrible thing," said the doctor, shuddering. "The man's chest had been torn wide open!"

Langton felt a strange chill as the fantastic thought at the back of his mind crystalized into shocking clarity. It was an effort for him to keep his voice steady as he queried: "What about old Charlie?"

"Gone without a trace. Some of the men are organizing a search party. Some think Charlie must have been keeping a vicious beast of some kind in the church, and letting it prey on farmers' livestock at night. It must have broken loose when the deputy came, killed him and then run away."

"Did they find any clue as to what it might have been?"

"No—except that it must have been big. Every bullet in the deputy's gun had been fired, but that hadn't stopped it, whatever it was."

Langton said nothing. His idea was fantastic—perhaps insane—yet there were too many coincidences for him to deny. He possessed information which no one else would have bothered to search out, and wondered if this might be a mystery beyond the law's power to solve . . .

He was jarred out of his thoughts as Dr. Harrister spoke again. "Here—you might be interested in seeing this."

Langton regarded the thick black folder in the doctor's hand. "What is it?"

"Old Charlie's papers—the ones I told you about. I found them after the sheriff had left, so I took them along. Read them if you're interested. I'll take them to town tomorrow and turn them over to the police."

Langton controlled his excitement with difficulty.

"Thanks," he said, taking the folder. "I'd like to read them—very much!"

IV

After Dr. Harrister had retired, Langton sat up and read all through the still night. And as he read, the chill he had felt earlier began to increase . . .

Though old Charlie was not highly literate, Langton found his writings fascinating and even terrifying in what they expressed. The article concerning tornadoes which had taken place in the region was particularly disturbing, and one could tell that the author believed every word he had written about the dark beings who lurked out beyond the stars.

At first Langton could make little sense out of the rambling accounts, for the scrawled longhand was hard to read and the ideas were difficult to apprehend and correlate. Some of the sentences seemed almost religiously esoteric and meaningless. What, for instance, could the writer mean by such phrases as "The World of the Blue Suns," "The Winds of Zarr" or "The Billion Thrones of Black Zathog" . . . ?

But gradually it grew clearer that all of old Charlie's writings, despite their diversity of subject matter, dwelt on the idea that a race of alien beings had come to earth long ago from a place "beyond the stars." This place Charlie termed the "Galaxy of the Zarr," and identified it from star charts as the Great Nebula of Andromeda. The Great Nebula's inhabitants—or "Zarrians," as old Charlie called them—had long ago conquered all the worlds of all the countless stars throughout their island universe, and in the last few hundred thousand years had sent their great ships out across space to the nearest other galaxies. There was evidence, the author claimed, that some of their enormous ships had come to earth at least once before the dawn of human history, and probably many times since. One had even crashed several thousand years ago in central North America—the author declined to say just where—and there had been *survivors*. These survivors, having knowledge and power far beyond that of man, had been looked upon as gods by the prehistoric Indians, who had built burial mounds and made clay images in their shape. The savages had referred to the Zarrians as "Wind Demons" due to their ability to artificially create tornadolike winds under any atmospheric conditions and send them against whatever tribe they wished to destroy. Since the Zarrians would feed on human or animal blood, the Indians sometimes offered them living sacrifices to stave off their wrath; in return, the Zarrians often gave them dark stones brought up from the interior of the earth—stones far better for toolmaking than any found in the surrounding hills.

In recent years, old Charlie claimed, the advance of civilization had forced these creatures to be more and more secretive, so that now they had few direct contacts with men and ventured abroad very infrequently and only at night. Not that they feared humanity—they could destroy all life on earth any time they so chose—but they were "waiting for something" and preferred to remain hidden until this vague event materialized.

Fantastic as these beings seemed, old Charlie wrote as if he had actually *seen* them. He described them as roughly humanoid creatures about eight feet in height and dark blue in color, with large, bullet-shaped heads rising directly from the shoulders. A crude drawing accompanied the description, and Langton noted uneasily the similarity it bore to the clay image he had unearthed.

Yet the thing which most surprised Langton was a worn and faded diary written in a hand quite different from old Charlie's; upon glancing over it, he found that it bore the signature of Jeremiah Potts, the "mad preacher" of a century before. How this manuscript had come into old Charlie's possession Langton could only wonder.

A certain passage from the old diary was especially disturbing. It read: "The gateway to the City of Satan lies in the chamber beneath Devil's Hollow. To reach it, one must move aside the great stone in the cave and follow the way which lies beyond. I have now visited this place many times and have learned wondrous secrets from the Daemons who dwell therein. They are wise beyond all the wisdom of men, learning my language even as I speak to them. Perhaps some day they will teach me the secret of the winds, or even greater secrets still. Only a few are active now, and will not harm me so long as I show them where to get the food they desire. The other thousands do naught but stare blankly from the tubes wherein they sleep, waiting for that time when their brothers shall come from some far place beyond the heavens. Perhaps they will spare me in that time, since I have been helpful to them . . ."

Here several pages had been torn away, and the subject matter that followed was irrelevant. Yet here, possibly, was the key to the whole mystery. If there were caverns beneath Hunter's Hollow, as Pott's writings seemed to indicate, then could the solution to the horror at the church lie somewhere in their dim recesses? Langton did not like to think so; the solution which suggested itself was so improbable, so wildly unheard-of, that he could not really bring himself to believe it. Suppose it was all a fabrication of old Charlie's disturbed mind, inspired by the mad ramblings in Jeremiah Pott's diary and the manuscript of the *voyageur* Beauchamps, and finally given authenticity by a deliberately gruesome murder?

He would have to make sure.

V

Early that morning, while Dr. Harrister was still asleep, Langton set out for the hollow. With him he took a knapsack containing a light lunch, some rope, a powerful flashlight and the black folder full of old Charlie's papers. In his hand he carried a long iron crowbar.

A half hour's hike brought him to the hollow. It looked less somber in the early morning sunlight. As Langton entered the cave, he unslung the packsack and drew out the black folder. Then, after reading something from one of the papers in the folder, he began to search along the base of a large limestone block in the back of the cave. Presently, finding a small crevice between the edge of this block and the cave wall, he inserted the crowbar and tugged on it heavily. The stone moved slightly along the floor of the cave, revealing a dark hole from which a draft of cold dank air blew upward.

After several minutes of strenuous effort, Langton had

moved the boulder over far enough to let him crawl through the hole. He peered in, and his flashlight showed a low tunnel stretching away before him, angling down into the rock beneath the hollow.

Tying one end of a ball of white cord to a rock, he began to crawl down the passage. After a short distance it widened enough so that he could go on hands and knees and eventually stand up. Evidently this was an underground watercourse—though here and there it appeared to have been artificially widened. Probably, thought Langton, the Indians who had used this cave had enlarged it. He knew now how old Charlie had vanished inside the cavern—and, as the thought crossed his mind, it was followed by another so disturbing that he stopped in his tracks. . . .

For, Langton realized, old Charlie could never have moved that great limestone slab by himself. He must have had *help!*

Langton shuddered. The thought of meeting something in that narrow passage filled him with a claustrophobic dread. It was a long moment before he could continue.

What urged him on after that moment even he could hardly understand. It had something to do with the burning thirst for knowledge and fame that had driven so many archaeologists along perilous jungle and desert trails in search of lost cities told of in elusive legends. The things Langton had read in old Charlie's papers had at least half convinced him that a great find awaited him here—perhaps the greatest find in anthropological history. . . .

The passage turned abruptly and opened into a wide cavern which stretched away into darkness. Langton's flashlight dimly showed the roof arching above him, like a great vault. It was composed of large, irregular blocks of limestone, split with innumerable fissures yet arched like a great dome, so regular in its overall contour as to suggest artificiality. To Langton it seemed as if it must come crashing down at any moment—he could not see how natural forces could hold it up—yet it had evidently been here for thousands of years. Thin stalactites hung down from the ragged ceiling like the needle-pointed teeth of some subterranean monster, and the water dripping from their tips convinced Langton that he was below the marsh in the hollow.

Slowly he advanced into the cavern, his footsteps echoing hollowly from the far walls. The floor, unlike the ceiling, was strangely smooth—the limestone seemed to have accumulated in a thick, concrete-like layer. The rock fragments jutting up from this smooth surface threw black, wavering shadows in Langton's path, confusing his vision.

The he saw something shining brightly in the distance, reflecting his light with nearly dazzling brilliance. Langton paused, puzzled and hesitant; then, advancing, he found that it was a rim of shining metal surrounding a vast pit. Perfectly circular, it rose from the cavern floor like a wall about four feet in height, and as Langton drew near he saw with amazement that the pit was a good hundred feet across.

Clearly it was artificial. Leaning over the edge, Langton gazed into its depths. The sides dropped off sheerly perpendicular and were of the same bright metal as the rim. He was looking down a mammoth cylinder, a shaft so deep that his flashlight could not pick out the bottom.

He began to circle the rim, speculating wildly on its nature and origin. The metal was certainly rustless, perhaps indestructable, for the floor all around it was of what appeared to be smooth, water-deposited limestone. How many ages this gigantic shaft had been here he could not imagine, but certainly it must date from ages long antedating man. . . .

Again Langton stopped, held in the grip of crawling fear as another thought struck him. For, he reasoned, if this shaft *had* been built before the age of man, then *who* had built it—or *what*?

Before he could speculate further his flashlight picked out an irregularity in the rim. Investigating, he found that it was a metal platform extending a few feet out over the pit. From this platform an inclined plane began a slow, spiraling descent that followed the wall of the cylinder.

Here was the way down. At the end of that ramp, Langton realized, he would find the answer to the mystery. Still, he hesitated. He had verified so many of the things in old Charlie's writings—what if the rest were true also? Suppose the demons worshipped by the ancient Indians *were* what old Charlie had claimed them to be? In that case, what might be lurking in the cold depths of that silent, unplumbed shaft . . . ?

Yet even as these things ran through his mind Langton

began to descend the incline. Did strange, unearthly beings indeed survive in these caverns, and were these vast cylinders of bright metal indeed traces of their alien civilization, then surely no archaeologist in all history had ever had such an opportunity as this! He had to probe this mystery further. Much as part of him longed to quit these cold, grinning caverns, he knew he would never forgive himself if he did not make the most of this fantastic opportunity. . . .

The ramp was made of tractionable metal much less smooth than the wall of the shaft to which it was roughly fused. Langton's footsteps rang out softly on the metal, evoking faint echos from below.

The descent seemed interminable, and there was no way to keep one's sense of direction, but at last Langton saw that he was nearing the bottom. The shaft began abruptly to widen out, like an inverted funnel—and soon after this the ramp ended at a vast floor of dark, solid metal.

The place in which Langton found himself was unlike anything he had ever seen. Huge objects of dark metal stood spaced geometrically about the immense, circular area—titanic cones and cylinders whose purposes he could not conceive. But most surprising of all was the large number of both human and animal skeletons which littered the floor. Examining some of these bones closely, Langton found that most of them were Indian remains. Almost all the skulls he saw were broken, and several basalt axheads were lying about. In many cases the skeletons and axheads were broken, as though they had fallen from a great height, and Langton realized that the Indians must have thrown their sacrifices over the rim rather than descend into that fearsome pit.

It was then that he discovered the trapdoor. It lay open in the very center of the great room—a huge, round disc of dark metal that leaned back on a single, massive hinge. It was evidently the cover to a gaping hole perhaps four yards in diameter. A faint blue light streamed up from this pit—a glow which the brilliance of his flashlight had prevented Langton from noticing sooner. Cautiously he advanced to the opening, wondering what could cause the light and why it should be of such an unearthly blue. . . .

Then he saw on the giant door of the hatch a strange

metal image that stood out in bold bas-relief—an image all too familiar in its general contours. Yet never had Langton seen the figure in such vivid detail. It was fully eight feet tall and must, he realized, be a life-sized image of—of what had fashioned it! He counted only four digits on the thing's hands. The ridge down the center of its face was segmented by many horizontal slits which perhaps were mouths or breathing orifices. . . . It seemed almost alive as it stood there, bathed in the blue light from the pit, and its eyes seemed to stare directly at him. . . .

He turned his gaze away uneasily. Advancing a step, he looked down into the glowing pit at his feet. Then a cry of amazement escaped him as he glimpsed level upon level of blue-lit floors lining a shaft that seemed to stretch down to infinity. He staggered back, fearful lest he should become giddy and fall—and in that moment full realization burst upon him. This structure could never have been built on earth, by man or anything else; *it was a ship from beyond the stars.*

A ship—but a ship surpassing anything he could ever have imagined. The bulk of it lay far beneath him, extending down to unthinkable depths. Just how vast it was he could not tell, but he could guess—for the mighty shaft in which he stood was probably only one of the many *propulsion tubes* which had blasted the colossal ship through normal space!

It must have come bursting out of hyperspace—for surely such cosmic distances could never have been crossed by living creatures at the mere speed of light—and struck the earth before realizing its proximity. The depth to which it had buried itself attested to its terrible velocity—and now Langton realized why Hunter's Hollow seemed so unnaturaly *round!*

But what sort of beings were these Zarrians who had managed to survive that frightful impact? Perhaps force fields of some kind had preserved them—for certainly some of them had lived on to originate the Indian legends that had crept down the centuries. And what sort of superscience had created a ship capable of generating a force-field enabling it to stand up under collision with a planet—machines that had continued to generate light over the millenia since that collision—techniques that might even have sustained life to this day in the ship's occupants . . . ?

Langton turned away, his curiosity quenched. Somehow he knew it would be dangerous to search farther for the answers to his questions—dangerous not only for himself but for all mankind.

As he stepped away from the yawning pit, he thought he glimpsed something lying in the wavering shadow of the open hatch, and he turned his light full upon it. Then, on seeing it directly, he cried aloud. It was the body of a man, the chest torn horribly open—and Langton recognized in the prostrate form the mangled remains of old Charlie Hinch.

VI

In the next instant he wished he had not cried out. Charlie and old Jeremiah Potts had formed alliances with things that were beyond man's understanding, things which had finally destroyed them, and Langton had no desire to arouse whatever might be lurking in those levels below. Silently he worked his way back to the foot of the incline, breathing softly, straining to listen for any unusual sound. He knew now that he should never have come this far, but it was not yet too late to turn back. . . .

The thing he had feared suddenly happened. The blood in his veins turned to ice as, from that dimly glowing pit, a sound issued—a sound unlike any he had ever heard. Soft and low-pitched, it nevertheless carried a suggestion of great power. It was not the sound of a machine, nor yet of any animal born on earth—and as its last echoes died away Langton realized that his presence had been discovered.

Swiftly he raced up the slippery incline, frantic in his attempts to gain speed and yet maintain silence. The echos of his footfalls seemed to his frightened mind to ring out like shots in the darkness. The upward slope made running seem like a nightmare wherein, no matter what efforts one made, one could not gain speed. The descent had seemed long to him, but the ascent seemed interminable. His heart pounded fiercely and his legs grew weak, yet he could not let himself stop and rest. He dared not think about what might have made that dreadful sound, for if he did he might go mad. . . .

Sheer fatigue forced him to stop at last. He saw that he was not far from the rim and gave a low, gasping cry of relief. For a moment he stood there, panting, trying to quiet his breathing, listening to the last echoes of his footsteps die away. . . .

But they did *not* die away, and he suddenly realized with cataclysmic horror that they were *other* footsteps, ascending the levels of the ramp below him. For a moment he could only listen with dread fascination as the sound drew nearer and nearer. . . . Then terror lent wings to his feet and he sped up the rest of the incline with desperate swiftness. Dashing over the rim, he stumbled onward across the rugged limestone floor of the cavern, the terrible footfalls of his pursuers ringing in his ears.

He must have relied on some instinct to follow the twisting cord back to the tunnel, for his mind was too shaken to guide him consciously. As he raced up the narrow passage a projecting rock dashed the flashlight from his hand, and he was suddenly in total darkness. He dared not stop, but dashed on, stumbling painfully against the rock walls in his haste. Luckily there were no side passages or he would have lost his way. Now he had arrived at that point in the passage where he could no longer stand. As swiftly as possible, he crawled forward, skinning his hands and knees and bumping his head in the process. Before he had gone far he heard, to his utter terror, something scrambling along the tunnel behind him, and a dim blue light began to filter down the passage. In the same instant he saw daylight ahead. He tried to go faster, but the passage was now so low that he had to crawl on his belly. The scrambling behind him was coming closer and he could hear something like regular breathing that followed no regular pattern.

The opening was only a few yards away now, and Langton redoubled his efforts to reach it. When it was only a yard from his face, something gripped his foot tightly. He screamed and jerked forward in a frenzy of fear, feeling his shoe come off as he did so. With a last violent effort he wriggled his way through the mouth of the tunnel —and then he was dashing out of the cave into the sunlight, screaming, dodging frantically among the blocky boulders of the hollow toward the footpath on the ridge. . . .

Some passersby found him lying half-conscious in the roadside ditch, his clothes torn and filthy with limestone dust. They were surprised to hear him babbling about such things as "the Blue Worlds beyond the stars" and "Black Zathog, god-king of the Zarr and ruler of a billion suns." After they had left him at Dr. Harrister's office in Decorah they discussed him in awed whispers, for in his eyes they had seen a terror beyond anything in their experience.

Under the doctor's excellent care, Langton soon recovered partially from his "nervous breakdown." He did not tell the doctor of his experience, however, or what had happened to old Charlie's manuscripts; and as soon as he was able he left the region forever. Later he explained to friends that he could not bear to stay on in that country of wooded hills and deep, twilit hollows, but no amount of prodding has ever caused him to be more explicit. Even now his mind is not entirely free from the things he experienced, for sometimes he cries out wildly in his sleep or mumbles of dynamiting a certain cave so that something cannot escape. During these recurrent nightmares he has often quoted a particular passage from the diary of a "mad preacher"—a passage describing "demons" who are waiting for others to come "from some far place beyond the heavens." And at certain times of the year he cannot bear to look at the night sky, when the Great Nebula of Andromeda shines down dimly from beyond the farthest stars.

along the ocean of the bottom.

"Yes," he said softly, "that is "there" the boy's breathing returned ...

a breath.

Although long a favorite author of horror stories and winner of the prized Hugo award for science fiction, Robert Bloch catapulted into the wider public eye when Alfred Hitchcock adapted his novel, Psycho, into a terrifying film. Since then he has written numerous screen and teleplays, produced further collections of stories and novels, American Gothic and Night-World being two of the most recent ones, and in the course of things given the world countless imaginatively strange and shivery moments. A Robert Bloch story is distinctive for its sharp strokes of ironic humor, skillful build-up of tension and vivid glimpses of the dark side of the mind. Bloch is in the very front rank in his field and why can be well understood in the reading of this story, from August Derleth's last hard-cover anthology, Dark Things.

THE FUNNY FARM

by Robert Bloch

IN ORDER to comprehend Joseph Satterlee's obsession with the comics one would have to be old enough to remember the 'Twenties. More than that, it would be necessary to remember the decade as Satterlee himself did, and such a subjective recall is impossible, even for a psychiatrist.

This isn't to say that a psychiatrist wouldn't have helped; indeed, it was a matter of more or less common knowledge around Redford that Joe Satterlee was a real weirdo, and inevitably his place of residence was dubbed "the funny farm." Because of the comics, naturally—the thousands upon thousands of comics Satterlee collected.

It was generally conceded that Satterlee would pay a ridiculously high price for any old piece of multicolored paper depicting the antics of *Little Jimmy, Salesman Sam,* or *Polly and Her Pals.* Obviously he must be some kind of a nut. Spending all that money on such foolishness was like—

The people who said such things generally paused here, because they didn't know *what* it was like.

Only Satterlee knew that. It was like buying a ticket to the past.

And that, of course, is exactly what Satterlee was doing. He was time-traveling. Returning, *via* the medium of comics, to the very best and most comfortable portion of that past—which, for him, was the 'Twenties.

Not the Roaring 'Twenties, mind you. The 'Twenties didn't roar for Satterlee or for anyone else who spent his childhood during that dim and distant decade. Actually it was a very quiet time, except for Fourth of July—there were less crowds, less traffic, even the movies were silent, and if one's family actually owned a superhetrodyne radio it was heard through the medium of earphones. Roaring

158

would have hurt Joe Satterlee's ears, for he had mastoiditis; even the earphones gave him trouble. As a result he was frequently absent from school and almost always away from the other children in the playgrounds and vacant lots. He was a shy youngster, a loner, a great reader.

Perhaps that's why the comics became so important to him. He'd actually learned to read from the funny papers and his most pleasant memories centered around those long, lonely afternoons in the attic with the collection of Sunday comic sections he'd started accumulating at the age of seven.

The funny papers were actually funny in those days. There were Happy Hooligan, with the tin can on his head, chinless Andy Gump and rich Uncle Bim from Australia, Barney Google and the faithful Spark Plug, Boob McNutt, Count Screwloose of Toulouse, cross-eyed Iggy in the Napoleon hat, lanky Mutt and dumpy bewhiskered Jeff. He knew them all, followed them faithfully throughout the week and reveled with them when they cut loose in full-page color on Sundays. When Jiggs took off his shoes and sneaked out on Maggie for a forbidden orgy of corned-beef and cabbage at Dinty Moore's, he tiptoed along at his heels. When Moon Mullins escorted Lord Plushbottom to the pool-hall, he went with them. When Krazy Kat cavorted across the lunar-like landscape of Never Never Land, he was there. Brickbats flew, grotesques capered and saw stars, animals spoke, balloon-encased lightbulbs signalled the origin of ideas in empty heads. Here was a world of fancy with a language and logic all its own—a world of escape and enchantment.

And somehow, because Joe Satterlee was largely cut off from the actual world beyond the rainstreaked or frostfogged attic windows, the funny pages served him as a guide to reality.

His Africa was the continent of Hans and Fritz—where *Katzenjammers* dwelt with a cannibal king who wore a top hat and a monocle, and the Herring Brothers pursued piratical careers to the point of idiocy. Later, it became the realm of Tarzan, of Tantor and Numa and Jad-bal-ja the Golden Lion. His ideas of higher education derived from *Harold Teen*, his notion of the business world from *Winnie Winkle* and *Tillie the Toiler*. Even in the early 'Thirties, his impression of life in the big city was based on the exploits of Dick Tracy or the vicissitudes of Apple Mary and Dixie Dugan. A psychiatrist might make a case for Satterlee's lifelong bachelorhood from the attitudes implanted by a faithful reading of *Mr. and Mrs.*, *Toots and Casper* and the tragicomedies enacted by George Bungle.

A psychiatrist might make quite a case indeed; pointing out that concentration on brightly colored figures in a darkened attic setting can serve to induce a form of auto-hypnosis, and a preoccupation with the idealized childhood of a Skeezix, a Skippy or even an Ella Cinders may make the reality pale by comparison. And certainly a psychiatrist might sense a peril in too great an identification with the dream-worlds of *Little Nemo, Buck Rogers, Flash Gordon, Prince Valiant, Mandrake the Magician,* and—at the very end of the cycle—*Superman.*

Not that Joe Satterlee emerged from comic-reading at the end of the 'Thirties as a Superman character himself. If anything, he was hardly the equal of a Clark Kent.

He became a bookkeeper, then an accountant, but was still—particularly after the death of his parents—more of a loner than ever.

And his collection grew. All through his years in the city he lived in a boardinghouse (without, needless to say, the amusing companionship of a Major Hoople) but he still retained the family home outside Redford. And it was here that he dispatched the comics he acquired through bookstore browsing and mail-order acquisition.

It was here, following his retirement in the late 'Sixties that he settled down to what could well be described as a second childhood. Premature senility might be the psychiatric diagnosis; as for Satterlee himself, he knew only that he felt safe and comfortable away from a world where everything had changed and even the comic strips weren't funny any more.

He didn't like that world. He didn't even like his own image in the mirror—it reminded him too much of Casper Milquetoast. But he did like sitting in the attic, where rack-lined walls housed his accumulation, and reading once again the adventures of *Little Orphan Annie, Joe Palooka,* or *Terry and the Pirates.*

Once a week he went into Redford for groceries, and more infrequently he ventured to the bank, the hardware store and the barber shop. People in town had a somewhat vague impression of him—and his impression of them was equally remote. Somehow, gradually, he seemed to withdraw into a realm of his own, where all problems were neatly compartmentalized in panel-strips; a world of bright colors and silently sensed messages, of easy laughter and innocent adventure which comforted him by satirizing the harsh reality of the wilderness outside his windows. He could laugh at that reality with *The Little King* or even *The Nebbs;* sometimes he laughed out loud, and when on occasion he did turn on his small-screen television set for the news he found himself watching the war footage and echoing Wimpy's ancient dictum of, "Let's you and him fight."

Joe Satterlee often dreamed about comics now, and at first it rather disconcerted him to encounter Abie Kabibble or Daddy Warbucks in the familiar surroundings of his own home. But after a time he became accustomed to it, and in fancy he could picture the dark halls of the rambling old house peopled with the colorful companions of his youthful imaginings. Again, a psychiatrist might have a field-day with a man whose erotic fantasies revolved around the earliest incarnation of Dixie Dugan, but then what would a psychiatrist know about the child who dwelt within the mind of an elderly, greying eccentric? The mind is merely an instrument of perception, and if it chooses to perceive the dream more vividly than the reality, who is to say that this is an error?

Satterlee loved his comic-strip companions, and he came to feel that they loved him. They lived together quite contentedly, and if Satterlee was indeed childish, he preferred the image to that of Caspar Milquetoast, the quite ineffectual man in the mirror whose empty daily routine protested both the comics collection and the child who retreated into its ageless domain in search of long-ago laughter. So what went on in Satterlee's house was really of no concern to a psychiatrist at all.

The only person who became concerned was Lenny Morgan. And Lenny Morgan was no psychiatrist—he was only a thief.

But a damned good one, Morgan told himself. If he hadn't been so good he wouldn't be hot, and if he wasn't hot, he wouldn't have come to this backwoods boondock to sit things out. Tall timber makes a good hiding-place, but Morgan figured it was a drag. He was just about ready to take his chances and cut back to town when he heard about this Joe Satterlee and his comics collection.

The first item of value that a good thief steals is information. And the information that Morgan obtained through listening to a chance conversation in the barber shop sounded valuable enough. He absorbed it the way a computer absorbs data.

An old man. Living alone. In a big house. On a back road three miles outside of town. No friends. Well-fixed for money. Spends it all for his collection. Must have thousands of comics out there.

Comics. That was the operative word, setting the circuits in motion, signaling all systems go.

Because Morgan's computerlike mind already had data stored away on comics. It was his business to know about hobbies and hobbyists.

Take your average stamp collection, now. Or better still, don't take it. No matter what the owner laid out for it over the years, chances are that a dealer will only offer one-tenth of the catalogue value, except for certain U.S. items. And if the collection contains rarities, you must peddle it around to the big operators who can afford to buy. This is as risky as trying to sell a Rembrandt to an art dealer—he'll know at once where it came from. And the big stamp merchants know who owns the scarce, valuable material. They'd spot Morgan as a ringer every time.

Coins are better, particularly gold and silver. But a good haul is bulky, heavy, hard to handle. You need the same amount of manpower it would take to rob a mint. So coins are out. Morgan never touched coins.

Paintings, sculpture, antiques—again, these items are too heavy, too awkward to load and too difficult to stash away until you dump them. Jewelry is good, but for that you need a fence, and a fence will steal you blind. Morgan didn't approve of anyone stealing from a fellow-professional, particularly if that fellow-professional was himself.

But comics; now you're with it! He'd seen the lists and the ads in collectors' magazines. At first he couldn't believe it—little kids, ten and twelve years old, paying a hundred and fifty bucks for some old *Batman* or *Wonder Woman* comic that sold for a dime when it first came out thirty years ago. It was big business, and getting bigger.

It was a big business, but the merchandise was small.

Portable, easy to handle. And easy to dispose of, with no way of tracing it, no questions asked—you could even peddle it by mail if you liked. One man could fill a station wagon with a load worth a fortune.

Morgan had a station wagon.

So there were no problems. But just to make sure, he checked everything out. It took him another week—cooped up in the crummy little motel with the red-jacketed yucks who came up to this godforsaken wilderness for the fall hunting season—but he stuck it out. Eating in the fry-joints, hanging around the barbershop, knocking off a few beers in the taverns, and always keeping his ears open. He found out what he needed to know.

Joe Satterlee didn't hunt. Probably meant he couldn't handle a gun—chances were he didn't even own one. And he wouldn't have any hunting dogs, either. Or any dogs at all. Which was important, for obvious reasons.

Another bit of good news turned up along the way. Old Satterlee was deaf. Wore a hearing aid, and it wasn't much good, either. When he came to town on Thursdays to stock up groceries for the week, he had trouble hearing the clerk.

Morgan got that word from a conversation he eavesdropped on in the store itself, but he didn't stop there. He waited until Thursday afternoon and planted himself across the street to wait. Sure enough, along about five o'clock, this beat-up old Plymouth rattled into a parking place and the skinny, gray-haired jigger climbed out. He wore a hearing aid all right, and when he headed into the store Morgan knew he'd spotted the clown. Morgan noticed he had trouble lugging his grocery bags when he came out, which meant he was pretty feeble, and that was good too; there'd be no trouble handling him.

So when Satterlee drove out of town, Morgan trailed him in the station wagon. He kept a good distance behind, but he followed him right to the dirt side-road where the Plymouth turned off into the woods. Morgan didn't go after him. Instead he drove on, checking the location of the nearest neighbors and discovering that the next farm-house was almost a mile away. Just past it was the junction with the main highway, so the setup was perfect.

And it was even more perfect by the time Friday night rolled around. Morgan checked out of the motel at noon, tipped the Indian broad who did the cleaning, and making sure that both she and the motel clerk knew he was anxious to get back to Duluth before dark. Then he cut out for the main highway, cruised thirty miles to a flyspeck on the map called Purdee, and took a room at the motel there. He timed the run at half an hour. He had a sandwich and coffee for dinner—no point eating a heavy meal just before going to work—and waited around until ten o'clock. Nobody noticed him pull out of the motel parking place and he barrelled back up the highway in plenty of time to get to Satterlee's place by eleven o'clock. And it was exactly eleven on the dot when he turned the station wagon onto the dirt road.

The night was dark and there was a feel of rain in the air. Which could be another break for Morgan; a good heavy fall rain would wash out tire tracks. And since the old jigger wouldn't be expected to show up in town again until next Thursday, that gave him six days clear. Maybe no one would get around to missing him for another four or five days after that, and by then the local fuzz wouldn't even remember Morgan. With all these hunters coming in, who kept track? It was the kind of caper Morgan always dreamed about.

Up in the old house Joe Satterlee was dreaming too. Sleeping in the big bed his parents occupied when he was a child. The bed he sometimes crawled into on Sunday mornings; little Joey, snuggling up in the warm, comfy-cosy place between Mama and Papa.

And Mama, laughing. *Oh, Joey—not again?*

Please, Papa promised he'd read them to me.

Papa shaking his head, but grinning as he reached for the papers. *All right. Which one do you want first?*

Hairbreadth Harry, Papa.

And the bright pages of the funny-papers unfurling across the bed, crispy-crinkly, smelling of ink, rattling and rustling—

Something was rattling and rustling *now*.

He awakened in darkness and he wasn't Joey any more, he was Joe, and it was half a century later, and he couldn't hear clearly and he couldn't see at all, but there was *something*.

Satterlee fumbled on the night-stand for his hearing aid, then threw back the covers and swung his feet to the floor. He fitted them into his slippers and stood up, moving towards the light-switch near the door.

164

Before he reached it the beam of the flashlight seared across his eyes and the voice buzzed in his ears.

"Don't move."

Satterlee didn't move. He stood stock-still, staring at the burly man holding the flashlight. Who was he? Why was he scowling so?

He didn't ask the questions aloud, and if he had, Morgan wouldn't have answered him. Because Morgan was uptight.

It was all going according to plan, and there were no hitches anywhere along the line. No dog. No trouble forcing the door downstairs. No trouble finding his way here to the bedroom. And sure as hell no trouble with this old futz in the nightgown. A nightgown, for Christ's sake—who wears them nowadays?

Maybe that's what was bugging him. This wasn't nowadays. This house. The damned furniture downstairs, like something out of a Sears Roebuck catalogue for 1920. The drapes and the rugs all mouldy, and everything smelling the way it did. Musty. Old. And dark as a tomb. He wanted no part of this place and the sooner he could split the better. So it was time to pop the question.

"Where are they?"

The old jerk blinked at him as if he hadn't heard. Morgan gave him a swipe across the side of his forehead with the heavy flashlight. "Where are they?" he repeated.

And this time he got complete attention. "Where are what?" the creep wanted to know.

"The comics," Morgan said. "I want to see the comics."

The jigger's mouth dropped open and for a moment he looked like a little kid—his lower lip wobbling as though he was getting ready to bawl.

But then Morgan lifted the flashlight again and old Satterlee got the message.

"Upstairs," he mumbled. "In the attic."

"Let's go," Morgan told him.

"What do you—?"

Morgan prodded him in the ribs with the flashlight and Satterlee shut up fast. He turned and shuffled out of the bedroom and down the hall. Morgan was right behind him, fanning the flash beam over the floorboards and the steps of the attic stairway.

The steps creaked loudly under their feet, and an answering echo came from above, but it didn't matter. There was no one else to hear. They were alone in the house, alone in the big, beamed room with the steeply slanted roof, alone in the darkness.

The beam of the flashlight sent shadows scurrying across the walls. Morgan saw the racks—row upon row of racks; the kind of thing he remembered seeing in the public library when he was a kid. Used them to store old newspapers or something.

He prodded Satterlee forward and turned the flash towards the nearest rack for a closer look. Then he shook his head. These *were* old newspapers. A whole damned attic filled with newspaper sheets—row on row of them, covered with cellophane, and the cellophane covered with dust. Peering down, he rubbed his fingers across the surface of a sheet and the color leaped forth. *Toonerville Folks, by Fontaine Fox.* One of those Sunday funny papers.

Morgan fanned the flashlight, *Dumb Dora. Petey Dink. Foxy Grandpa.* They were all funny papers.

He grabbed Satterlee's arm. "All right. Where you hiding the comics?"

Satterlee gestured at the racks. "These are the comics."

Morgan twisted his arm. "Not the newspapers. Comic books."

"Books? But I don't have any books—"

Morgan released his grip, staring at the rows of racks looming in the shadows.

It was the truth, and he knew it. Satterlee was too frightened to lie. *There were no books.* Because in the days when the old man was a kid, these newspaper strips were the only comics, and that's what he'd collected. Lousy old newspapers, not worth a dime even to a goddamn junk-dealer. *No books, it was all for nothing—*

Something was building inside Morgan, something that had to burst. He reached out blindly and ripped a paper from its frame, shredding the cellophane covering and tossing it to the floor. He tore another free, crumpled it.

"Please—don't—!" Satterlee quavered. But the man wasn't listening, nobody listened, nobody understood. These were all he had, his companions, his friends for fifty years, he'd preserved and protected them for their lifetimes, destroying his collection was like destroying his life—

Destroying his life. Satterlee felt the tug at the side of his head as the angry man jerked the cord of his hearing aid. He saw the livid, enraged face before him, saw the beefy hands rise gripping the ends of the cord to whip it around his neck, then felt the agonizing pressure against his throat.

And that, for Satterlee, was all.

But it wasn't all for Morgan. Only the rage died with his victim.

Now he stood over the body in the darkness; the body, crumpled on the floor like one of those old newspaper sheets. The attic was drafty and the night wind whispered through the papers in their racks.

The whispering wasn't real, of course, because there was no one here but himself. The real whispers would come later, when the body was discovered.

Morgan knew how to prevent that. The newspapers were the answer. A heap of old newspapers and a match—

He moved to the racks and started to tear the cellophane-covered sheets free with both hands. The paper rattled. And the wind rose all around him, making a rustling sound, a stirring sound, a whispering like the murmur of many voices. Cracked, brittle voices. Angry voices. Voices sounding from the shadows. Shadows that suddenly rose and moved.

Shadows do move, and when Morgan turned and saw them he was not alarmed. But shadows have no substance—they do not *creak*. And now there was a creaking of floorboards from the racks in the far corner.

Morgan started to glance in that direction, and as he did so he heard the attic door slam shut. Then he did panic for a moment, until he realized it must be the work of the wind. He dropped the wadded newspapers he'd clenched in his fists and spread them across the floor. Whispers whirled and shadows slithered, but Morgan ignored them, reaching for a match.

The light flared up, and then Morgan couldn't ignore them any longer—the shadows streaming forth from the racks, the shadows that surrounded and converged.

Morgan rose, then stepped back quickly as he saw the silhouette of the tall man in the top hat, the tall man carrying a cane that bore a curious resemblance to a magician's wand. He saw the outlines of the bald-headed figure with the tiny tin cup perched atop its bony head, the grotesque profile of a moustached man with a receding chin, a long-haired giant with a sword.

And then, from the moving mass of rustling, whispering shapes, an image emerged—the brightly colored, garish image of a small carrot-topped girl with eyes widened in a stare. Eyes that had no pupils.

She opened her mouth and the whisper came forth—a dry, paper-thin whisper.

"Get him, Sandy."

Something growled. Something crouched. Something sprang.

Morgan screamed once, and then the shadow was upon him and the other shadows watched and whispered as he died.

Then there was only silence in the attic.

A silence lasting for ten days, until the state police broke in and found Satterlee's body with the cord of the hearing aid still twisted around his neck. The verdict of death by strangulation was easy to arrive at.

Morgan's corpse presented a more difficult problem. He was sprawled amidst a pile of old comic strips—long-forgotten images of Mandrake the Magician, Happy Hooligan, Andy Gump, Prince Valiant, Little Orphan Annie. But there was no clue as to how he met his death.

All they could think of was that a timber wolf had bitten out his throat.

But then, they lacked Satterlee's imagination.

A lifelong Minnesotan and former newspaperman, Carl Jacobi has been writing notable supernatural fiction for more than four decades. He has a particular talent for deftly building up setting and atmosphere in an unpretentious manner that has much in common with the British traditionalist writers of the uncanny tale. He has published three collections of stories to date, Revelations in Black *(1947),* Portraits in Moonlight *(1964), and* Disclosures in Scarlet *(1972), the last two still being available from Arkham House and highly recommended. Here, played out to a marvelous finale, from Jacobi's rare first book, is a scary visitation called . . . .*

THE FACE IN THE WIND

by Carl Jacobi

TODAY IS Tuesday. For almost a week, or since the morning of last Wednesday when the dark significance of the strange affair was first publicly realized, my life and the quiet routine of Royalton Manor have been thrown into a miserable state of confusion. It was of course to be expected, all details considered, and I took it upon myself to answer carefully all questions and repeat again and again for each succeeding official the part I played in the prologue to the mystery. Doubtless the London press was justified in referring to the sequence of events as the Royalton Enigma; yet in so doing it aroused a morbid curiosity that has made my position even more bewildering. For the story which I told, and which I know to be true, has been termed impossible and merely the wanderings of a crazed brain.

Let me begin by saying that like my fathers before me, I have lived here at Royalton all the days of my life, and I have seen the manor dwindle from an imposing feudal estate to a few tottering buildings and a small plot of weed-choked ground. Time and times have gone hard with the house of Hampstead.

There are, or rather *were* until last Wednesday, but two of these buildings occupied. Both in a considerable state of disrepair, I had reserved the right lower wing of the one which in earlier years boasted the name, Cannon Tower, for myself and my books. The other, an ivy-covered cottage, formerly the gardener's quarters, I had given over to an old woman some four months before. Her name was Classilda Haven.

Classilda Haven was a curious individual. A hundred times I have sat at my desk watching her through the open window as she cultivated her patch of vegetables, and

I have racked my brain for a reasonable excuse to remove her from my property. The woman, according to her own statement, was nearly eighty; her body was bent and weazened, and her face witch-like and ugly with the mark of age. But it was her eyes that bothered me, drew my gaze every time she came within my vision. They were black, heavily browed, and sharp and clear as a young girl's.

At intervals when I have taken my morning walk through the old grounds, along the ruined frog wall, as I still prefer to call it, and on to the edge of Royalton Heath, I have felt those eyes staring after me. It was imagination, of course; nothing more. There has already been to my mind something grotesque in senility, something repelling in the gradual wasting away of all human qualities day by day.

Classilda Haven had stumped up to my door one evening late in April and inquired in a cracked voice if I wished to let the old gardener's cottage. She was a stranger to the district, I knew, and a woman of her age hobbling about unsheltered at that season is bound to be an object of pity. I asked casually if she had no relatives, no home; to which she replied that her son, her only means of support, had been killed in a motor lory accident in London a week before. She had taken her few savings and entrained for Royalton, where she seemed to remember a distant relative was living. Arriving in the village she had found no trace of him, and so, without money, had wandered aimlessly down the Gablewood Pike.

There was, of course, no refusing such a plea, and much as I disliked having my solitude interrupted, I had given her the key to the cottage, loaned her a few sticks of furniture, and tried to make her comfortable. In due time, I presumed, the relative would make his appearance and the woman would go on her way.

But as the spring gradually wore into summer and these things did not happen, I began to look upon the old crone as a fixture. Not until August did the horror begin, and then I had undying reason to regret my philanthropy.

It began with Peter Woodley. Woodley was a youth of twenty, a son of merchant villagers, in whom I had taken considerable interest. The boy aspired to paint. He had no unusual talent, it is true, yet his canvases had a certain simplicity in their likeness to surrounding landscapes that had caught my eye, and I had given him two or three art volumes that had found their way into the Hampstead library.

But on this morning as he stood in my study he appeared greatly excited and upset. His hair was clawed in wild disarray, and he was breathing hard, as if he had run to the manor all the way from Royalton:

"Mr. Hampstead," he gasped, "it isn't true, is it, the story I heard in the village? You're—you're not going to change the frog wall?"

I leaned back in my chair. "The frog wall?" I repeated. "Why yes, Woodley, I'm going to have it repaired. Repaired, that's all. It's badly in need of work, and the masons are coming tomorrow. But what on earth——"

Young Woodley dropped into the chair opposite me and spread his hands flat on the desk top.

"You mustn't do it, sir. You can't. You promised me I could use it for one of my pictures."

"Why, so I did," I said smiling. "I had forgotten. But I'm not changing the entire wall—just the two sections on either side of the gate. The stones have fallen almost entirely away, and I don't want the frogs to get through. That's the only reason for the wall being there, you know, Peter. The marsh on the other side is swarming with frogs. The wall was erected by my ancestors to keep the manor grounds free from the pests and permit the Hampsteads to sleep. . . . If it's rustic settings for your paintings you want, there are plenty of places——"

"But you don't understand, sir." Woodley in his earnestness was leaning far across the desk. "You don't understand. There's something on the other side of that wall besides frogs. There's something in that marsh that will get out, that will come into the grounds if you have the wall altered. I can't say what, sir. I really don't know what. But if you'd been out there at night in the moonlight, staring at the gate as I have, trying to see how I wanted to place my painting, you'd know."

I looked at him curiously there in the morning light of my study. "The wall is already down in those two places," I replied. "If there's anything in the marsh, and I'm quite sure there isn't, it certainly could get through now."

Woodley shook his head slowly, half in negative, half in perplexity.

"It's not the physical boundary I mean," he said. "It's

not the wall itself. It's the actual space and time that it's occupied all these years that you're changing. Mr. Hampstead, don't do it!"

Naturally, such vague innuendoes did not induce me to countermand my order to the masons. Yet as the hours passed, something in the memory of Woodley's disturbing attitude instilled in me an indefinable sense of nervousness. Several times I caught myself staring out of the window toward the decayed remnants of the old frog wall, wondering what the boy had meant.

I turned at length to the shelves of the Hampstead library and spent two hours among the ancient volumes there, trying to rest my curiosity. The diaries of each successive resident of the manor were still intact, and I knew they included all mention of wine-cellars, out-houses and rooms which had been added to Cannon Tower during the generations. Curiously enough, however, search as I would, I could find no allusion to the erection of the frog wall, save one and this in the last memoirs of one Lemuel Hampstead 1734, was most confusing. It read:

> The Frogg Wall, which I have ordered builded, will this day be finished, God willing, and I am now contente to departe from this world and bestowe my title and possessions upon my eldest son. There will be no more tragedyes like that which befelle my father, Charles Ulrich, and his wife, Lenore. The wall will be blessed by the church in the manner which I have planned, and there will be a Holie Bible sealed in each corner poste. I—

Here age had left its mark on the page and the writing became undecipherable. But vague and meaningless as it all was, it was enough to set me thinking hard.

I personally supervised the masons' work the following day. It was a prosaic affair. The two workers simply removed the crumbling bits of stone from the two sections of the wall flanking the gate and patched the aperture with modern bricks. But they were forced to move the gate forward a few feet because of the marshy condition of the ground.

Classilda Haven shambled up to me as I stood watching the men ply their trowels. She smiled a toothless, evil smile.

"Ye'll be changin' the frog wall, I see," she said in her rasping voice. "All of it?"

"No, just the two sections," I replied, viewing her presence with some irritation.

The aged woman nodded, and I found myself staring again into her strange eyes. They were young, those eyes, clear and piercing and they seemed oddly incongruous there in the wrinkled, leather-like face.

She turned abruptly, hobbled forward a few steps, and, head down like a bird, stared at one of the workmen as he carefully placed his bricks in position. Gingerly she ran a veined hand along the newly mortised surface then looked up and shrilled:

"Why don't you tear it all down?"

I forced a tolerant smile. "Don't be absurd, Classilda," I said. "If I did such a thing, the place would be overrun with frogs, your garden as well. You know that."

She made a queer reply, an answer which seemed to escape from her involuntarily.

"Frogs," she squeaked, her eyes gleaming queerly. "I like frogs. I like them better than anything in the world."

Peter Woodley came that afternoon with his easel and his box of paints. I saw him through the window of my study as he selected a position near the iron gate-door, opened his little folding camp-stool, and began to walk slowly back and forth along the side of the newly repaired wall.

His agitation, which had been so pronounced the day before, seemed to have left him, though I couldn't help feel that he looked upon the renovated stonework with resigned eyes. He moved about several times before he apparently found the angle he desired, then seated himself and began what I presumed were the charcoal outlines.

My book attracted my attention then, and I forgot the boy for perhaps an hour. But suddenly I was jerked out of my chair by an ear-splitting scream. With a lurch I was across the floor and staring through the open casement at the weed-tangled grounds.

Peter Woodley lay prone on his face by his easel, his body still as death!

I raced out of the house and across the intervening space with all the speed I could muster. A moment later, as I examined him, I breathed a sigh of relief. He was still alive, but his heart was fluttering weakly. Cold water applied to his forehead and smelling-salts administered to his nostrils brought him around five minutes later, but when his eyes blinked open and he looked up at me, a moan of terror came to his lips.

"Good God! Mr. Hampstead!" he whispered. "I saw it! It was beautiful, but it was horrible. I saw it!"

"Saw what?" I asked, chafing his wrists. "In heaven's name, Peter, what's the matter?"

He struggled to his feet then, swayed dizzily and stepped over to his easel. For a moment he stood there, staring down at the few charcoal outlines on the canvas. Then he slumped weakly into the camp-stool and buried his head in his hands.

"Mr. Hampstead," he said, looking up abruptly, "promise me you'll never let me come here again. Promise me you'll keep me away from the manor grounds, by force if necessary. I must never attempt to paint that wall again, do you understand? And you, sir, couldn't you lock this place up and move into the village? Couldn't you, sir?"

There was sincere anxiety written across his face, and his eyes were still gazing far out into space with a bewildered frightened expression that was foreign to the boy's usually calm nature.

"Nonsense, Peter," I replied. "You've been working too hard. You've let your imagination run away with you, that's all. Come into the Tower, and I'll give you a bit of brandy."

He shook his head, muttered something incoherently under his breath, and then, picking up his painting equipment, turned and strode quickly through the manor grounds toward the distant Gablewood Pike.

For a while I stood there, watching his figure grow smaller and smaller in the afternoon sunlight. I was puzzled more than I cared to admit by his strange attitude, and I was deeply disturbed by his allusions to "something which he had seen." For obviously as strapping a fellow as young Woodley does not faint dead away from sheer imagination. Neither does he babble queer warnings to a man twice his age without a reason.

And then as I turned and began to walk slowly toward the door of my study, my eyes suddenly took into focus a patch of ground near the old wall. The workmen repairing this section had, in order to aid their movements, torn up the weeds and rank underbrush, which grew unmolested in this part of the property.

And there in the freshly upturned earth was the imprint of a gigantic bird-like claw.

It was ten minutes past twelve that night when I found myself sitting up in bed staring at the radium dial of the taboret clock. Cannon Tower was still as death, and there was no sound from without save the distant mournful croaking of frogs beyond the wall. Even as I listened, that bass obbligato ceased abruptly, and the world lapsed into a heavy, ringing silence.

I got up, slid into a pair of slippers and moved across to the window. Curious. If there is one thing that is a certainty in my life, it is my profound manner of sleeping. Once retired I seldom if ever awake before my usual rising hour. And yet there I was, eyes wide open, heart thumping madly with the terror and bewilderment of one who has been jerked suddenly from the macabre fantasies of a nightmare.

But I had not been sleeping. Neither I was positive, had any unusual sound disturbed my slumbers. The manor grounds stretched below me, blue under the August moonlight like a motionless quilt, and beyond, vague and indistinct, I could see the flat, barren expanse of Royalton Heath.

A thin blanket of clouds slid over the moon then, darkening the shadows into a thick, brooding umbra and simultaneously it happened.

From the east, from somewhere deep in the recesses of the marsh that lay beyond the frog wall, there rose into the still air a horrible, soul-chilling cry. It was a cry I can never hope to forget, the scream of a bird of prey about to make its kill, a thousand times magnified, and ending in a high-pitched shriek that was strangely human.

Motionless I stood there, eyes riveted in the direction of the old wall, muscles tense as wire. For a moment I saw nothing, the blackness below me was thick and impenetrable. Then suddenly, with the quickness of a camera-shutter, the moon broke through that cloud mass once more, and the manor grounds returned to their blue silver.

The cry came again nearer. The echo thrown back from the walls of Cannon Tower passed on into the distance like the wail of a lost soul, and with a choking gasp I turned my eyes skyward.

High above me, outlined against the driven cloud, circling like a giant vulture in the night, was a bird of colossal size. Its wing-spread was enormous, a full twenty feet from tip to tip, and its head and body were curiously elongated and heavy. Even as I stood there, staring at it, my face wet with terror, it wheeled and swooped toward me.

Forward, straight toward the Tower it sped as if intent on dashing itself to pieces against the ancient masonry. Then it veered sharply and raced toward my window.

An instant I stood there, transfixed. Then, my subconscious mind had enough clarity to whip me around and send me lurching back into the room. There was a century-old percussion pistol on the right wall, mounted in its carved metal holster, and I knew it was always loaded, a feeble but comforting protection in my solitude.

In the half-darkness I seized it, pushed the hammer to full cock, leaped back to the window and fired.

There came an instantaneous violent flapping of those mighty wings, an over-powering stench of death and decay, and crashing into my ear-drums a repetition of that hideous cry. The spector disappeared.

Faintness seized me then. Spots and queer-colored lights swirled in my vision, and I sank backward to the floor. But even as I closed my eyes to unconsciousness I knew, as I know now, that what I had seen was no dream, no vagary of a sleep-drugged brain.

For gazing at me there, with its huge feathered wings and repulsive vulture body, had been the face of a beautiful woman!

A bad electrical storm came up next day after almost three weeks of sultry heat. I spent the morning pottering about my studio as usual. Outside, the thunder crashed and boomed ceaselessly.

But come afternoon I refused to be kept indoors any longer, and so, donning an old rain-jacket, I began my usual walk through the manor grounds. I was still weak and trembling from my unexplainable experience of the night before.

The rain was coming down hard from a thick, gray sky, and the weeds and undergrass flanking the little path were dripping with wet. Behind me the great vine-covered walls of Cannon Tower loomed grim and silent.

At the gate-door of the frog wall I suddenly stopped. The barrier, always locked with staple and bolt, stood wide open, revealing just beyond the wild, undulating expanse of the marsh. I moved to close it, but a moment later Classilda Haven appeared, working her way up the reed-covered incline toward me. And for some unknown reason I viewed her presence there with suspicion.

"Classilda," I snapped, "who gave you permission to go beyond the gate?"

Her clothes and her hair were dripping with rain, and the dishevelment gave to her, it seemed, a curiously repelling ornithoid appearance. It was odd, but never until that moment had I noticed how distinctly avian were the contours of her weazened body and her talon-like hands. She cocked her head to one side, looked at me, and laughed a squeaky laugh.

"I've been down in the marsh," she said. "I went to get some dirt for my garden. Those workmen, the careless fools, have trampled all over it."

I glanced at the orderly rows of lettuce and cabbages which in some places had been crushed and overturned by unobserving feet.

"Not workmen," I said. "I'm afraid it was young Woodley that did this. I shall have to tell him to be more careful. He comes here to paint, you know, at night sometimes in the moonlight, and I suppose he didn't notice where he walked. But," I added, remembering his words and firm decision which he had made following his fainting spell, "I don't think you'll be troubled with him any more. He's taken a dislike for the place, and he's staying away."

The old crone stood looking at me with those youthful, beady eyes. She smoothed some of the water from her black dress, shifted her basket of dirt to her other hand and smiled cryptically.

"Not too much of a dislike, Mr. Hampstead," she said, displaying her toothless gums. "He was here last night, painting. I spoke with him."

I stared at her. If both Classilda Haven and Peter Woodley had been awake and in the manor grounds during the night, then they too must have seen the hideous thing which had flown out of the marsh and looked in my bedchamber window. All the horror of what I had

178

been, all the terror of that nocturnal vision which the intervening hours had inclined to soften and pale in my memory, returned then, and I leaned weakly against the bole of a cypress tree.

"Classilda," I began slowly, "were you—did you see—"

But with a swish of her sodden skirts the old woman turned, laughed that mirthless falsetto laugh once more, and hobbled off toward her cottage.

Deeply troubled, I buttoned my jacket closer about the throat and continued my walk through the slanting rain. I was heading for the edge of Royalton Heath, where, as was my custom, I would stop a moment and gaze out over that somber stretch of wasteland which I had known for so many years. But this time my leisurely walk was destined to be interrupted.

Near the end of the manor grounds where the frog wall turned abruptly to the left and headed into the depths of the marsh, I came upon Peter Woodley. Hatless and without coat of any kind, he was sitting in the long, brown weeds, unmindful of the swirling rain and apparently oblivious of my approach. And in his hands were two impossible things.

For a full instant I stood there gazing at him, watching his hands as they worked diligently at their task. Then I cleared my throat and spoke:

"Peter," I said, "what on earth are you doing with that bow and arrow? I thought you were an artist, not a huntsman."

He started, leaped to his feet, and tried to conceal the two articles upon which he had been working. But as if through a telescope my eyes centered upon the arrow-shaft. It was the metallic arrow-head that held my gaze, a head long and slender, ending in a needle-point and made of silver.

Without answer Peter Woodley wrapped the two articles in a piece of canvas and seized a larger package from the ground, a package I had not noticed before.

"With your permission, sir," he said, "I'd like to walk back with you to the Tower. I finished my picture of the wall last night, and I'd like to hear what you think of it."

Fifteen minutes later, bent over the desk in my study, I stared down upon Woodley's newly painted canvas. The lowering clouds without had spread a premature darkness in the room, and I had lighted two of the candelabra.

But even with this added illumination I could not quite believe my eyes.

For a long time I stood there, looking down at the oily brush marks, examining the background and the objects in the center. Then with a gasp of incredulity I sank into a chair.

"Peter, my boy!" I exclaimed, "did you actually paint this? It's excellent—a masterpiece!"

He looked suddenly wan and haggard as he seated himself opposite me and began to run his fingers absently along the design of the table.

"Yes," he said dully, "I did it. There are a few remaining touches to be added before it is completed, but the painting as you see it is the work of a few hours. I worked last night in your grounds by moonlight. I—I wish to God I hadn't."

"What do you mean?" I asked.

He nervously lit a cigarette and leaned forward in his chair.

"Mr. Hampstead," he said, "that painting—I simply can't realize it came from my brush, done by my own hand. I meant to paint a simple likeness of the old frog wall with the iron gate in the center. But as I worked there in the moonlight, something seemed to take hold of me. I felt as if a will other than my own were controlling my thoughts. I painted as I have never painted before, worked at terrific speed in a nervous frenzy. And when I had finished I was in a state of complete exhaustion.

"I don't understand it, sir," he went on. "Sometimes I think I've been going mad the last few days. But there's something wrong with that picture, something terribly wrong. Every time I look at it I have a dreadful feeling it never should have been brought into creation."

"Nonsense, Peter," I said, looking across the desk at the propped-up canvas. "You've done an admirable piece of work. Frankly, I didn't think you had it in you. None of your earlier efforts have displayed such unusual talent as this."

Woodley left half an hour later, but not before I had persuaded him to leave the painting in my care.

"I'd like to study it if you don't mind," I told him. "I'm planning to go to London next month, and I may want to take this along. Perhaps I can place it in a contest for you, or if not, find someone who would like to buy it."

He seemed little affected by my words. Ordinarily any compliment I might bestow upon his work would have been received with boyish enthusiasm and appreciation of my interest. But now he stood there in the doorway, hands hanging at his sides, eyes lowered as if he were oppressed by some mental cloud.

When he had gone I carefully shut all the doors to my study, returned to my desk and moved the painting a few inches farther back where there was no chance of shadow impairing my view of it. Then I trundled the heavy arm-chair into the center of the room to a position about four feet directly before the desk, sat down, and deliberately fastened my eyes upon the canvas.

I confess that at the moment there was nothing positive in my mind which would account for my actions. But from the first moment I had gazed down upon the picture I had realized that young Woodley's strange speech was not the result of an overwrought imagination. Quite definitely there was something wrong with the painting. Something wrong, I say, and yet I was unable to see anything in the oil presentation beyond a simple and familiar scene.

That scene had been beautifully done, it is true. There was the old frog wall and the black bulk of the huge gate-door with the blur of the marsh in the background. The coloring and effect of the mellow moonlight had been accomplished with rare artistry, and it did not seem possible that so inexperienced and untrained a youth as Peter Woodley could have wielded a brush with such finesse. And yet more and more as I stared across at it there came the impression that I was looking upon something indescribably evil.

For perhaps ten minutes I remained there, studying each brush mark in the flickering glare of the two candelabra. Then abruptly, acting on impulse, I stepped across the room and unhooked the long framed mirror which adorned the farther wall.

I placed the painting now at an angle on the right corner of the desk. And at the opposite corner, lengthwise on a parallel, I set the mirror.

Returning to my chair, I adjusted my position slightly, then looked hard at the reflection in the mirror. Beyond the fact that the glass vision thus seen was the usual reverse of the original, there was no change.

But an instant later, with a choking cry I had leaped from the chair and, face down, had pressed my eyes to the looking-glass. In God's name, what I had seen could not possibly be true! It was a trick of my thoughts, a mental image projected into the droning solitude by a still persistent and bewildered memory. But no . . .

Clearly focused in the mirror was the reflection of Peter Woodley's painting in oil. But my eyes had caught a different angle to the lines now, the perspective had changed, and where before I had seen only the likeness of the frog wall and the iron gate-door, and the marsh—in place of that was—a woman's face!

It was incredible, and it was incredibly beautiful. A woman's face returning my gaze silently—with black lustrous hair, Grecian features, and lips that were curved in a slight mocking smile; an exquisite face painted with classic loveliness but with strange piercing eyes I seemed to remember having seen once and many times before.

Many moments I remained there, staring far into the glass. Then I reached for the decanter, poured myself a strong, undiluted portion of whisky and slumped dazedly into the chair. My brain was going round and round, my heart pounding like a trip-hammer.

It would have been a most curious enigma, this optical illusion, this accidental use of the double perspective, even had I looked upon a reflected object thus that was new and foreign. But when I stopped to realize that what I saw there was not only familiar but engraved in my brain in a hideous memory of the immediate past, the whole vision became alive with horrific possibilities.

For the woman's face which looked back at me from the reflection of the looking-glass was the same face I had seen in the head of that loathsome flying monster that had peered into my bed-chamber the night before!

I ate no dinner that evening. As dusk darkened into night and the thunder and rain dwindled off, I sat by the window of my study, staring out into the dripping grounds, drawing deeply on my old Hoxton pipe. The hours passed slowly. By ten o'clock the last remaining cloud had left the sky, and the moon rode high and clear.

I roused myself then, and still smoking furiously, let myself out of Cannon Tower and through the garden exit into the manor grounds. In contrast to the gloominess of the afternoon, the way before me now was brilliant under the blue light and tessellated with curious elliptical shadows from the overhanging verdure. Off in the marsh, the frogs, still unaware no doubt of the complete cessation of the storm, were silent.

I walked slowly, head down, immersed in my thoughts. When I reached the high gate-door in the wall, I paused a moment, reflecting how perfectly young Woodley had caught the moonlit scene in his painting. Then, knowing that sleep would be impossible under the circumstances, I crossed over to an old tree-stump, wiped the rainwater from its surface with my handkerchief, and sat down.

How long I remained there in the half-darkness I don't know. The moon moved high in the heavens and began to descend toward the west. I filled and lighted my pipe several times.

But suddenly the snappng of a twig whipped me out of my revery, and I turned to see Classilda Haven slowly advancing down the path. I watched her casually. Then I sat bolt upright, huddled farther back in the shadow, and stared with a rising feeling of perplexity.

What was the old crone doing in the grounds at this hour? And why was she skulking forward like a wary snake, looking back over her shoulder at each step to see if she were followed?

A moment later I was pressed close against the bole of a cypress tree, muscles stiffened to attention. With a final look behind her, Classilda Haven had stepped to the iron gate-door, unlatched the staple and pin, and was swinging the barrier slowly open. One instant she hesitated, head cocked to one side, listening. Then she passed through the aperture and disappeared in the direction of the marsh.

For a quarter of an hour I held my position, waiting for her to return. Far back in a corner of my brain a vague suspicion was beginning to grow, and I sought for an answer to the woman's strange actions.

Then it happened! The iron gate opened again—slowly, and a figure stepped into the shadows. It was not Classilda Haven. It was a woman who did not resemble the old crone in any way. She was young, tall, dressed in filmy white, with long raven hair that cascaded down her back. A moment she paused there, her hand on the latch.

Then she moved into the open moonlight, and I jerked electrified to attention.

That face again—divinely beautiful with a satin complexion, carmine lips, and eyes black and piercing! The same face I had seen once flying in the night and again in the changed perspective of Peter Woodley's painting! Was I going mad?

The woman seemed to glide slowly forward, to float down the path as though her feet were treading air. Presently she moved closer to the frog wall, raised one arm high over head and began to move it up and down, back and forth, in long sweeping arcs.

She was writing! Writing in chalk! I saw that as the moonlight streaming through the trees focused the crumbling masonry and the silent figure in blue relief. A foot high and carefully fashioned in curious stilted lines the characters took form.

The word completed, the woman stepped back and studied it carefully. I looked out from my hidden position behind the tree and read:

"CELAENO"

The chalk word seemed to gleam like white fire against the gray darkness of the old wall, and although I could not at the moment fathom its meaning, it touched a responsive chord somewhere in my memory. Celaeno. It seemed—

There was something weirdly impossible in it all. Standing there deep in the shadow of the huge cypress tree, my unlighted pipe clenched tightly between my teeth, I felt as if I were viewing the scene from the doorway of another world.

The woman moved farther down the wall to a position on the other side of the iron gate-door. Abruptly she stopped again, raised the chalk and scrawled in those same stilted letters:

"CELAENO"

I thought then I had unwittingly made my presence known, for the woman, upon completion of the last letter, whirled and turned those penetrating eyes straight in my direction. But it was another sound which she had heard, a sound of slow footsteps advancing down the path.

In measured pace they came on, louder and louder, like the rhythmic cadence of a muffled mallet. An instant later another figure came upon the scene, and a new wave of bewilderment swept over me.

It was Peter Woodley—Woodley clad in an old green dressing-robe, with his eyes closed and his arms stretched stiffly before him in the manner of a sleep-walker. Straight toward the woman in white he advanced, step by step.

"I'm coming, Celaeno," he whispered. "Celaeno . . . I love you, Celaeno."

As he drew nearer, a slight smile turned the woman's lips. I saw it in the moonlight. And she leaned forward, grasped the boy by the right arm and began to lead him toward the gate.

But there, as the iron door swung open of its own accord, a change came over Woodley. His eyes flickered open, his body stiffened, and a hoarse cry sounded deep in his throat. On the instant he seemed to realize what was happening. He wrenched his arm away from the woman's grasp, turned, and with a scream of terror began to run down the path toward the Gablewood Pike.

Transfixed, I stood there, looking after him. He fled like a deer, running wildly across the open patches of moonlight, the skirts of his green dressing-robe swirling after him. And when I again turned my eyes to the scene before me, three inexplicable things had happened.

The woman in white had disappeared; the iron gate-door was locked and pinioned from the outside; and the two chalk words scrawled upon the frog wall were no longer there!

Peter Woodley slammed open the door of my study next morning and strode into the room without knocking. I was thankful that he had come. There were a thousand questions I meant to ask, the whole fantastic mystery to discuss. It was time, I realized, to talk openly.

But Woodley brushed aside my preliminary remarks with a wave of his hand.

"My painting," he cried. "Where is it? I'm going to tear it apart bit by bit and throw the pieces in the fire! Give it to me!"

I stood up, walked across to the window, and answered him dully.

"It's gone," I said. "I had it locked here in the old wine cabinet. When I came down this morning I found the doors still locked but the picture gone."

He seemed on the verge of a complete collapse as he stood there swaying.

"Gone," he repeated in a far-away voice. "Gone." Then:

"It's that painting that's caused it all, Mr. Hampstead. It's a net, a spider-web that has entangled me and brought me under her power. Since I have finished it I can not help myself. I almost succumbed last night. She was beautiful. God, how beautiful! But when I think of the condition of my arm—"

"Your arm?" I repeated. "What do you mean?"

He stared at me a moment as if hesitant to say anything further. Then, abruptly, he slipped out of his coat and pulled back the sleeve of his shirt.

"I haven't been to a doctor yet," he said slowly. "But I know medicines won't be able to do anything for me. This—this is not a physical ailment."

I took a step closer and then suddenly recoiled.

"Good God!" I whispered. "Not a physical ailment? Are you mad?"

From the elbow down, the flesh of the right arm was a horrible blackened mass, with the veins standing in livid prominence and the hand shriveled as in the last stages of gangrene.

"But Peter—yesterday!" I began in a trembling voice.

He nodded lifelessly.

"Yesterday," he replied, "that arm was all right. I found it this way when I awoke in bed this morning. Mr. Hampstead, don't you realize what we're up against? Don't you realize what it all means?"

I reached for the brandy glass and drank a little with shaking lips.

"Am I going mad, Peter?" I asked finally. "Are we both mad? None of it seems possible—like some strange dream that has become a reality."

Woodley turned abruptly and strode across to the wall of bookshelves on the farther side of the room. There he ran his eyes slowly along the stacked array of ancient volumes. At length he chose one and returned with it to the desk.

"I was here yesterday morning when you were still in bed," he explained. "I knew I could find what I was looking for in your library, and I wanted to verify my suspicions. Mr. Hampstead, when you read this, you must believe. You must help me. Together perhaps we can free ourselves."

The volume he had laid on the desk before me was significant in itself. It was a copy of Richard Verstegan's *Restitution of Decayed Intelligence,* that evil work long ago banned by God-fearing people as being inspired by Satan. Up to that moment I had never been aware that it existed in my library, but from the signature on the flyleaf I saw it must have come into my ownership as part of the collection of Lemuel Hampstead, my ancestor of the Eighteenth Century. Woodley now opened it to a middle page, and bending lower, I read:

And Neptune and Terra had three daughters. And their names were Celaeno, Aello, and Ocypete. But theye were offspring accursed, for theye were winged monsters with the face of a woman and the bodys of vultures. Theye emitted an infectious smell and spoiled whatever theye touched bye their filth. Theye were harpies!

With a choking cry I kicked back my chair and leaped to my feet. "Harpies!" I screamed. "God in heaven!"

Harpies! Those fabulous monsters, creatures of evil who delighted in carrying mortals from this earth to hell and everlasting torture! Harpies, winged horrors of classic mythology, sometimes with the face of a hag, sometimes with the body and face of a beautiful woman! Was it possible such fantasies were more than the mental creations of Grecian philosophers and actually existed in our own mundane world?

In a swirl of confusion the pieces of the mystery were beginning to take position in my brain. One thing I saw. Alone among my ancestors, Lemuel Hampstead had sensed the hideous danger that lurked in that ancient marsh, and under guise of keeping the frogs out of the manor grounds had erected a protecting wall. I recalled the faded passage I had read in his memoirs:

The wall will be blessed by the church, and there will be a Holie Bible sealed in each corner poste . . .

Now I understood why the two manor residents previous to Lemuel Hampstead, Charles Ulrich and his wife,

187

Lenore, had come to such dark and horrible ends, the woman dying from "a strange maladie whiche caused her face and hands to blacken and rot away," and the body of the man "to be found in the depths of the slough with his eyes torn from their sockets and his head slashed with the mark of claws."

An idea struck me, and I whirled upon Peter Woodley. "Classilda Haven!" I cried. "Classilda Haven, it is she——"

He nodded. "I've suspected so for a long time," he said. "But there are two more. Always three. They are the spirit of the storm winds. Their homing-place is said to be in Crete, but they can move about the world with the speed of light. They are the personification of classic evil, created perhaps by mass mental imagery long ago and still existing, a throw-back from another age."

"Classilda!" I repeated dazedly. "I'm going to her cottage and——"

Woodley shook his head slowly. "You wouldn't find her now," he said. "But even if you did, nothing can harm them while in human form. No, we must wait." He turned on his heel, left the room a moment and returned with a long tube of rolled canvas. Opening it and removing its contents, I saw that he was holding the long bow and arrow which I had seen him working on in the grounds the day before.

"They're finished, sir," he said; "the only method I know of fighting them. A bow and an arrow with a silver head. I've made two arrows. What good they'd do even if they struck, I don't know. But we can try."

For a moment as the clock pounded its ticks through the silence of the room we sat staring at each other. Woodley's face was tight and drawn, his eyes were glassy, his hands shaking.

"Tonight," he said suddenly, "in a few hours the horror will begin. God help us!"

Midnight, and the wind was screaming over the grounds with the mournful whine of an Eolian harp. I lay stretched at full length in a clump of underbrush, waiting . . . waiting for I knew not what. At my side, within arm's reach, lay Woodley's bow and his two silver-headed arrows. In my pocket was a metal bottle with the crucifix emblazoned on its sides.

There was water in that bottle, holy water from the

little church in Royalton, obtained by Woodley early in the afternoon as part of our feeble and blind defense. What its Christian effect would be against these nightmares of another theology I did not know, but in case of any emergency I meant to use it.

We had made hurried plans there in my study before darkness closed in. Woodley was to remain in the Tower, all lights turned off, while I, armed with those strange weapons, kept watch near the wall. Not unless I called out for help was he to show himself, and then only with the utmost caution. I had argued hard before Woodley grudgingly consented to this arrangement.

"It's youth they want, Peter," I told him. "They want you because you're young. They care nothing about me. I'm a middle-aged man with a life half spent."

Time snailed by as I crouched there. Up above, the moon shone at intervals through rents in a flotilla of velvet clouds.

And then the garden door of the Tower creaked open, and I saw Peter Woodley step out and advance down the path. He had removed his hat and coat, and his face shone white as death.

Unable to understand his appearance, I hissed a warning at him there in the shadows.

"You fool!" I cried. "Go back! I didn't call."

My words had no effect. Slowly, stiffly, with the same mechanical sleep-walking pace that had marked his entrance to the grounds the night the harpy-woman wrote her name in chalk, he passed me and continued parallel to the wall. Straight to the iron gate-door he moved, then stopped motionless.

"Celaeno!" he called softly. "Where are you?"

For a moment there was silence, broken only by the moaning of the wind. Then mounting into the night air, wavering and hideous, came once again that wailing scream. From the other side of the frog wall it sounded, rushing nearer.

An instant later I had leaped to my feet and was staring above me. In the gloom, high over the manor grounds, circled that mighty shape—a giant, vulture-like bird with great pointed black wings *and the head and breast of a woman. A harpy!*

I watched it hover there, carried back and forth by the raging wind. Then my eyes turned farther to the left, and

I jerked back with a shriek of horror. There were two more of the loathsome creatures, and those two were swooping down straight toward me.

I caught a glimpse of female faces with exquisite features, long, streaming black hair and crimson, evil lips. Then a sharp claw ripped across my chest and tore my coat. I struck out madly, felt my fists pound deep into the feathery wings, struck again and went down, overwhelmed by their bodies.

I fought with every ounce of strength I possessed, with terror striking deep into my very soul. I rolled over and over, sought frantically to free my right hand and draw forth the bottle of holy water.

A stench of death and decay seared into my nostrils. My face and body were bleeding from a hundred places, and I was fast losing my strength. But suddenly one of those razor claws yielded to my frenzied blows and with a lunge I whipped my hand sideward, grasped the bottle, uncorked its spout and showered the water out before me.

The harpies leaped back and stood gazing at me, women faces twisted in expressions of stark hate. Again I whirled the bottle, this time spilling part of the contents into their eyes.

There was a double shriek of rage. The monsters ran clumsily backward, then swooped into the air and fled.

I leaned gasping against the trunk of a tree. Then as the realization that the horror still was not finished filtered into my bewildered senses, I turned, seized the bow and silver-headed arrows and ran on into the grounds.

Near the end of the property, far beyond the gate, I saw them again. They were flying high above me, three huge shapes etched black against the moonlit sky. And in the claws of one of them, held by his hair dangled the body of Peter Woodley.

With shaking hands I fitted an arrow to the bow-string and pointed it upward. Back until the bow was bent almost double I pulled, then released it. It whined upward, shot past one of the monsters—and missed.

Panting, mumbling a prayer aloud, I seized the second shaft and made ready to fire again. But the harpies had sensed their danger, ceased their circling and with enraged cries were heading high toward the frog wall and the distant marsh.

I gave a last frenzied look above me, took quick aim and let fly that last arrow. Upward it sped, a gleaming streak in the moonlight.

And suddenly the night was hideous with the cries and shrieks of the wounded monster. The creature fluttered and spun like a top. It opened its claws as it wobbled off toward the marsh, and the body of Woodley, released, dropped downward, fell like a meteor straight onto the jagged top of the frog wall.

An instant later I was at the boy's side, bending over his broken and blood-covered body. He rose up as I lifted his head in my arms.

"Thanks, Mr. Hampstead," he whispered. "It was—it was the only way."

He fell back with a sigh, and I was alone with the corpse of Peter Woodley.

There is little more to tell. No one believes me. The villagers stare curiously at my whitened hair and shrink away shuddering as I meet their gaze. The district doctor feels of my pulse, looks into the cornea of my eye and shakes his head perplexedly. And the police continue to search the countryside for some trace of Classilda Haven.

Fools! I have taken them to the gardener's cottage and shown them the empty black silk dress, nailed as it is to the center of the floor by a silver-headed arrow. I have led them to that section of the frog wall near the iron gate-door and traced slowly, letter for letter, the faint, almost obliterated lines that one moonlight night spelt so clearly the word "Celaeno." And I have placed on the table the wall mirror and Woodley's painting, which had been found somewhere in the depths of the marsh— placed them at their proper angles and pointed out the strange woman face that looked back silently from the changed perspective.

But in each case they only look at me sadly and murmur: "Poor man, there is nothing there."

Manly Wade Wellman is perhaps best known for his stories of the wandering ballad singer John, who encounters and tells of strange happenings in the Southern mountain country. The mountain people of the Southern Appalachians are special to Wellman and he evokes them in his stories as an easy-going, self-reliant and determined breed, wisely uncomplicated in their ways. His country folk seem to have something in common with those seen in certain paintings of Thomas Hart Benton and Grant Wood. He's been traveling about their country and recording them on paper for over forty years, very much with the eye of a poet and the ear of a regionalist. Indeed, it may well be that Wellman will win a dual place in American letters, both as a regionalist and as an extraordinary author of supernatural stories. And Wellman seems to get better and better as the years go by, as this recent effort testifies.

GOODMAN'S PLACE

by Manly Wade Wellman

WHEN Doc Ferro came to these mountains, folks asked him to cure what ailed them. He said he was a doctor of philosophy, not medicine, but he whispered over Lottie Burden's sore jaw and put flower dust to Sam Taber's lame arm and they got well. He fetched his stuff to board at the Uttiger house. He was a smooth, middling tall man, maybe thirty-five, with dark hair. His brows made one line above his eyes, and he wore black pants and a wide black hat, and under his long black coat a white shirt and tie. His square teeth showed when he smiled.

He asked to buy Goodman's Place that old Mrs. Sue Lovatt owned, other side of Darkscrabble Creek. She took his offer, but felt bound to tell him what she'd heard when she was young; how five-six men and women rented from her grandsire to build on, how whatever they were up to made the neighbors burn them out, and maybe not all of them came clear of the fire. Goodman's Place didn't much tempt hunters or gadabouts. Trees shut off the daylight there, and sometimes rain fell and lightning skippered when it was fair other places. Beasts and birds stayed off, too, except things folks weren't sure of and hated to guess at. And how if you passed there towards evening, sometimes you heard a singing or mumbling.

Doc Ferro smiled with his square teeth. "Let me worry about those old notions, Ma'am," he said. "I've walked there, and things seemed quiet. Anyway, isn't Goodman's Place a good name for a home? Here's half the money. I'll pay the rest the day I finish my cabin."

Glenn and Becky Uttiger and their daughter Grace liked Doc in their home. He was neat and clever. Some nights he read stories to them from his books. The only one he could hire to cut trees and set up a cabin at Goodman's Place was Sue Lovatt's grandson Hode, twenty that summer and fresh back out of the army. Hode was more than common tall and ganted everywhere but across the shoulders and hands, like his grandsire and daddy, both dead and gone. His yellow hair was thick behind his ears and on his forehead. "You're not scared of Goodman's Place, are you?" Doc Ferro inquired him.

"Not till I see something to scare me," said Hode.

"We'll work from nine in the morning till three," Doc told him. "I'll pay a dollar an hour."

"That sounds fine," Hode agreed him. But he'd really taken the job to be round and watch. He didn't relish how Doc smiled and sweet-talked Grace Uttiger.

Two years back when Hode enlisted, Grace had been just a girl. Now she'd come on to be a slim, well-grown young woman, with big blue eyes and hair as black as a yard up a chimney. Hode had already bluffed out two fellows who wanted to talk to her. But the Uttigers liked Doc better.

"Your daughter's intelligent," Doc told them. "I'll lend her books to read. She'd ornament a bigger, more gracious society then this—not that I find fault with the good friends I've made here."

And Grace said to Hode, "I'll go with you to the Whippard's party tomorrow night, but tonight I want to read in this book Dr. Ferro lent me. All about knights of old and ladies fair."

"It looks too dry for me," said Hode, though he'd have loved to read in it if it wasn't Doc Ferro's book.

"He's traveled in lands beyond the sea."

"So have I," Hode reminded her.

"But all you did was fight."

"That's a right much to do, most times," Hode said.

When he and Doc waded Darkscrabble and went up to Goodman's Place, he felt the trees standing mightily close to him in gray air. Doc shed his coat and turned up his shirt sleeves, and chopped as well as Hode while they cleared a yard. Big black stones showed there, laid out oblong for a foundation.

"A house stood here, and a house will stand here again," Doc said. "This log will make our first sill."

Hode trimmed branches off. "I hear singing," he said. "Humming."

"Your imagination," said Doc. "Let's flatten the sill log's bottom side, and notch the top for the sleepers."

They shaped two sill logs, laid them both solid on the stones, and fitted two more logs across the ends for the first sleepers. That made a start, about sixteen feet by twenty. They ranged on more sleepers, two feet apart, flat sides up to bear the floor.

"We'll split floor slabs later," said Doc. "First, more wall logs. Let's cut them here in front for the door."

"Just one door?" Hode asked.

"I won't need a back door to run out of when a visitor knocks at the front," smiled Doc, tinny-eyed. "We'll center that door here at the east. Where's our saw?"

It got shadowier while they put up more logs, and it was sort of smokey amongst the trees when Doc said, "Noon. Let's have this good lunch Mrs. Uttiger put up for us."

Eating the sandwiches, Hode thought again he heard that soft song, with words he didn't quite catch. Back at work, he tried to chop loud enough to shut the song away. He was glad when Doc took out his watch and said, "Three o'clock. We'll come back again tomorrow. Here's six dollars, Hode. I'll pay you at the end of each day."

But it was dark in those woods for just three o'clock. Picking up the tools, Hode heard a flutter in branches above him, like wings. But birds stayed out of Goodman's Place. If that was a bat, it would be as big as a dog. He was glad to go with Doc across Darkscrabble and to the Uttiger place. Grace was sweeping off the front stoop. She smiled at Hode, then smiled bigger at Doc Ferro. "Good evening," Hode bade her, and headed off to his grandmother's cabin.

After supper, he got out the banjo his daddy had left him. He tuned it and picked and sang a song he recollected from his grandsire:

> "Them things up there
>   at Goodman's
> At Goodman's where
>   they dwell,
> For one drop of a
>   virgin's blood
> They'd wade the fords
>   of hell."

Singing and picking, he wondered what that song meant. Next day, they cut and laid up more logs and marked window places at the back wall and ends and both sides of the door in front. That night, half a moon shone over the mountains. Hode called for Grace and took her to the dancing at the Whippards' new barn. But Doc Ferro was there and played the fiddle for the dances. Old folks said he outdid the playing of champion fiddlers in past years, like Os Deaver and Mitch Wallin. Nothing would do Doc but that Hode go fetch his banjo to play along with him. Hode picked his possible best, but he couldn't dance with Grace while he picked. The praise Doc spoke him wasn't enough comfort for that.

More wall logs to hike up next day, with the door hole and the window holes held square by chunks between the logs. Before three o'clock, they muscled up two twenty-foot logs for plates and two sixteen-footers top of the side walls, and jammed them into their notches. By now, Hode didn't hear the singing so much, and wondered if maybe he was getting used to it. Doc paid him six dollars as usual and said, "You're earning more than your wages, Hode."

The day after that, Saturday, they strung lap-jointed joist logs across the plates, and at midpoint of these set up four-foot pieces to hold the ridgepole above all. Then they notched six-inch poles for rafters and slanted them up, spiking them to plates and ridgepole. "Tomorrow, Sunday, we rest," said Doc when they quit. "We'll get back Monday to do the floors and shingling and so on."

Hode polished his boots that night, and after noon dinner Sunday he headed for the Uttiger place. Mrs. Uttiger said, "Grace and Dr. Ferro made themselves a picnic and went out." Not a short answer, but not a very long one either. Hode headed back down the path, following the prints of Grace's little shoes and Doc's narrow ones to where they turned off toward Darkscrabble.

Those tracks led to where a tree lay across the creek. Hode pinched a frown, imagining Doc holding Grace's hand to help her over. He didn't cross there, he went up to where he could wade, polished boots and all. Then back to follow the tracks. He moved like the hunter he was, from behind one tree to another. As he got close, sure enough he heard voices, plainer than the other times.

But that was Grace talking and Doc replying her. Hode moved without showing himself, to where he could see.

"Goodman's is a good name all right," Doc was saying. "It was meant to be particularly good, long ago in England."

Grace sat on a log in front of where Doc sat in the door hole of the cabin, and poured from a jug into Doc's cup—buttermilk, likely. The Uttigers were proud for their churning.

"Goodman's Field, or Goodman's Grove," Doc went on. "Many places called that, to mean land set aside for the one they called Goodman because they never dared call him Satan."

"Does Goodman's Place mean Satan's Place?" Grace asked, and she sounded a mite scared.

"Those who built here must have thought so, before they were driven away," said Doc. "But I don't think so, and you needn't."

"Don't you believe in Satan?" asked Grace.

"Not especially." Doc's teeth smiled. "I've studied that belief for years, belief in what comes out of nowhere to frighten you. But my theory might sound silly."

"No," she said back, "nothing you say sounds silly."

Hode made a face. Grace talked like a little girl instead of a big one; though sometimes big girls flatter a fellow like that.

"You've a good, trusting soul, Grace." Doc's voice was gentle. "Now, to explain, I have to talk about astronomy."

"The sun and moon and planets and stars." Grace was proud to know what astronomy was.

"Suns and moons and planets make up systems," said Doc. "Systems make up galaxies—too big in space to comprehend, at least for you and me. And many galaxies make up our universe."

"Isn't the universe everything?" Grace added in. "No end to it, no end to space?"

"Not everything, child," Doc Ferro said gently. "The astronomers say that the universe is like the film of a soap bubble, only unthinkably great. And in the film, our worlds and suns and galaxies—in the film itself, not inside or outside."

Harking to him, Hode almost forgot to be jealous of him.

"But what's inside or outside?" Grace asked.

"We can only guess at that," said Doc. "Maybe inside the universe bubble is all that happened in the past, while

198

it grew. Outside may be waiting all that will happen when the bubble swells to it. But you wonder what all this has to do with Goodman's Place."

"Yes, sir," Grace agreed him.

"Think, my child, what if other universes are bubbling all around ours? What if one touches our universe, at some solid point?"

Hode could see Grace smile. "That's hard to think about."

"What if men found that happening, all through history?" Doc said. "A Goodman's Place, where another universe looks into ours?"

Grace hiked her pretty shoulders. "That scares me."

"People fear what's strange," Doc nodded. "But maybe people have met unknown things from other universes, gave them gifts and got gifts in exchange. I've been studying that."

Grace got up. "I hope I don't have bad dreams tonight."

"Don't fear dreams, Grace. But those old charms and incantations to call up Satan at strange places—what if they really let creatures from other universes through? Would you fear that?"

"Not if you were there, Dr. Ferro, but I don't know what to say."

"Then say nothing for the time being. To nobody."

Hode backed off, got across Darkscrabble and home. He felt low in his mind about spying on Doc and Grace. That night at supper, he asked his grandmother if she'd ever heard tell of calling up Satan at Goodman's Place. She named it that she'd heard some rumor tale, but not just what. "Recollect," she said, "that Satan hasn't nair power over a pure heart."

Hode didn't feel comforted. He didn't reckon his heart was all that pure. He ate some cornpone and chicken and went to bed, but he didn't sleep air wink for hours.

He felt jumpy working with Doc on Monday. If Goodman's Place was Satan's Place, it was next door to hell, which had been a scare word when he was a boy. He'd never dared say it for fear God would get mad and put him there.

They spiked lathing slabs on the rafters. Then Hode sawed oak logs into bolts, while Doc split them into shingles with a mallet and froe. Hode had trouble sawing bolts enough to keep up with him. He heard voices singing a moany song just past reach of his ear. He looked over his shoulder, time and time again, but saw only misty shadows.

Nailing the shingles Tuesday, Hode mentioned to Doc about the singing, and Doc laughed him out of it again. After that, the singing died down till you hardly knew it was there, but it was there all right. At three o'clock, Hode allowed it might could rain.

"No," Doc smiled. "That's the shade of the branches."

Hode looked up as he took his six dollars. No clouds in the sky; just that grubby mist amongst the trees. Hode almost quit the job, but for two reasons he didn't. First, he wasn't coward enough to quit just for being nervish; second, he wanted to study out what Doc was up to with Grace Uttiger.

Shingling the balance of the roof and the gable ends took most of Wednesday. "We'll be done by day after tomorrow," said Doc, with nails in his mouth. "Friday, in time for the full moon."

"You sound as if you work by the signs," said Hode, on the ground riving slabs for door and window frames. "I've heard tell if you start something of a Friday, you never finish the job. But what if you finish of a Friday?"

Doc swung down and looked sharp at Hode. "Do you credit such beliefs?"

Hode started nailing a plank in for the side frame of the door. "I just note beliefs and try to find out the truth of them. Truth comes along in strange places."

Doc fitted a shorter piece to a window hole. "Hode," he said, "you show sense in the things you say. What would you call the biggest, best thing in the world a man could have?"

Hode drove a nail. "Offhand, I'd say true love."

"True love," Doc repeated him. "Is that better than wisdom and power?"

"I reckon wisdom and power come with true love, Dr. Ferro."

Doc fitted another piece of window frame. "We're doing well," he changed the subject. "We still have the floor slabs to lay, and the side logs to chink."

"And a door and windows to hang in," Hode added to that. "And how about a fireplace?"

"Those things can wait in this good weather," said Doc. "I'll be moved in before they're needed."

It put an end to the talk, the way Doc could make an end come.

On Thursday morning they fetched four big buckets to Darkscrabble Creek. Doc shoveled clay into them and mixed in trickle by trickle of water. "It must be sticky and tough at the same time," he said, stirring. "Help me get these buckets up to the cabin. I'll chink the logs while you split some floor slabs."

Hode watched Doc work while he himself rived slabs. Chinking with clay was old-timey; Hode never recollected seeing it done before. Doc wadded the stuff between the logs with his hands and shaped it with a whittled stick. "Never let it bulge out, or the rain will wash it," he lectured Hode. "Recess it solidly between the logs."

Hode made the floor slabs flat on both sides, and when he had enough to start with he went inside and began to spike them to the sleepers. Out yonder, Doc chinked away like an expert. He stood on a piece of oak log to put the clay to the chinks. The cabin began to darken inside as he sealed out the light. When Hode used up his slabs, he went out to rive more. The flooring job took care, as much as Doc's chinking, and they still had plenty of both to do when Doc said, "We'll go down to the creek, I must wash up. After we eat, we'll get more buckets of clay."

Something moved at the creekside as they got there, and Hode felt his hair crawl. But it was Grace, coming through the trees. She'd fetched their noon dinner, enough for her to eat with them. There were sausage biscuits and a steaming pot of cornfield beans and bacon, and a cold jug of buttermilk. Grace said. "How you come on, Hode, how's your grandma?", very sweetly, but mostly she talked to Doc as they ate. She'd been reading one of his books, called *Magick, its Theory and Practice,* by Aleister Crowley, and she wondered Doc why Mr. Crowley spelled *Magick* with a k. Doc grinned his teeth and said Mr. Crowley had spent long years studying old, old things, including the spellings. When they'd done eating, Grace wanted to help mix the clay in the buckets, but Doc said not to dirty her hands. So she goodbyed them and headed home.

"Do you hold by magic?" Hode asked Doc as they carried the buckets.

"Only when it helps explain something sensible," said

201

Doc. "Many modern sciences started with magic. Alchemy helped develop chemistry. Astrology helped develop astronomy, and modern medicine began with conjuring. We'll talk about it sometime."

Hode went on splitting and nailing down the floor slabs, Doc chinking the logs. When it was three o'clock, Doc said, "I should be able to move in by noon tomorrow."

"You don't have a bed or a chair, even," said Hode.

"I'll more or less camp here tomorrow night," Doc replied. "The night of the full moon."

Again he'd named it about the full moon.

Back home that night, Hode dug out the almanac. It said the full moon rose the next night about half-past seven, less than an hour after sunset. He recollected old tales of the full moon, how some folks turned into wolves that time, how the tides of the sea rose their highest. That was another night when Hode nair slept much, wondering if there was aught he could do about this that would be right.

When Hode got to Uttiger's next morning, Doc asked him to help carry stuff. There was a blanket roll and some pots and pans and a bag of food, and some of Doc's books. "This will do to start with," Doc allowed. "I'll fetch up the rest of my things later."

They dumped their loads on the half of the floor that was already down, and split slabs to finish the other half. While Hode split the logs, Doc spiked them to the sleepers. He was good at fitting them close and even. But as Hode fetched in a stack of slabs, he saw Doc beside the wall logs at the back. His knife was out and open, and he was cutting something on a log.

"I'm just marking the date of this house," Doc grinned. "Now, those slabs will just about finish the floor."

He bent to pick up the saw. Hode looked across him at what was cut on the wall. It didn't look like figures of a date, didn't look to be figures at all, nor either to be air letters Hode could read. Other places on the logs, Doc had carved more strange signs. Hode headed for the door, and as he went he saw that one of Doc's books lay open on the blanket, in the light of a window hole. He said nair word. He couldn't think of aught to say, not then. He split a few last slabs for Doc to put down, and then cleaned up the truck in the yard. When Doc came out again, Hode spoke.

"I fetched something for the new house," he said, and dug it out of his back pocket. "A horseshoe. Folks put them over their doors, you know."

Doc took the shoe and laughed. "I don't think I'll put it up there," he said. "A horseshoe is to keep away witches, and I don't believe in them."

"What if a witch came and made you believe?" Hode asked, and Doc gave him a quick, sharp look.

"Maybe she and I could learn something from each other," he answered. "But thanks, Hode, for bringing this. I tell you what, let's both spit on it for luck and I'll throw it in Darkscrabble Creek."

They spit, and Doc trotted away toward Darkscrabble. Hode watched him go among the trees, then quick headed inside the cabin to where that book lay open.

It wasn't a printed book. It had words written in red ink, in what looked like a right old-timey hand:

Hail our Father, which WERT in heaven!

But afterwards; see your temple finished on Friday of the full moon; at moonrise, make on the earth before the door a circle ten feet across, and within that a pentacle in which you may stand. At each point of the pentacle, a word of these: ALPHA, OMEGA, BELPHEGOR, GOETULA, TETRAGRAMMATON.

See you stand within pentacle and circle, and with you a virgin you have selected. Build there a fire of manner previously described above. Then say boldly the words you have learned for the summoning. When those come who are called, they will grant what you ask, in exchange for the blood of the virgin . . .

"Hode! Hode!" Doc was calling outside, and Hode came out.

"What were you doing in there?" Doc growled.

"Walking the floor to test it."

"I've already done that." Out came Doc's watch. "It's noon, and we're finished. But here," and he fumbled for money. "I'll pay you your full six dollars, you've worked so well. Goodbye, and thanks."

Leaving, Hode wondered if Doc hung back to finish the house sure enough, without him.

Alone, he tried to study out some sense of things. Our Father which WERT in heaven—that wasn't the Lord's prayer he knew. What might could it have to do with Satan falling out of heaven? One thing he didn't like, that about the virgin's blood. That had to mean Grace Uttiger's blood, whose else? Other things, those marks on the walls inside, the names in the book, they were past and beyond Hode's thinking. At home he asked his grandmother. "What's a pentacle?"

"Oh, just lines crisscrossed to make a star shape, this-away." She traced with her finger on the table. "It goes into a quilt pattern, the one they call Witch Blazing Star."

"Witch Blazing Star," he repeated her. "Is that a witch spell?"

"I heard tell, when I was a little girl, that make of quilt would keep off witches from the bed. What you got in mind, Hode?"

"Just bothering," he said. "Can't rightly decide what to say or do."

"Hode Lovatt," said his grandmother, "you're a good man, like what your grandsire and your daddy were before you. Nor I don't mean a good man like what Goodman's Place got named for. I'm glad you're through working there."

"Maybe I'm not through working there," was all he could say.

"Then bear in mind that goodness lays over badness," she told him. "Lays over it air time."

Not much comfort, but it was something. Hode wished he was as good as his old grandmother thought. Trying to fit sense together was another sight harder than fitting up logs and shakes and slabs to make Doc Ferro's house. One thing was sure; whatever happened was set to happen when the full moon came up, not long past sundown.

He pretended to eat his supper, and went out into the last gray of the light, heading for Darkscrabble Creek and Goodman's Place just beyond.

For the first time in his life, Hode Lovatt felt thankful for training in army night maneuvers. He got across Dark-scrabble Creek without making air sound, then waited a breath or two to figure on the trees. They were crammed so full of dark mist he wondered if he could brush it away like a curtain. He moved on, setting his heels down and then his toes, to keep from rustling leaves or weeds. He caught branches and eased past them to keep them quiet. Up ahead he saw light. The rising moon, and something besides the moon.

He heard, too. That singing he'd learned to expect, but

not quite the same. It had a tune different from in the daytime, high and low together, like harmony. And suddenly, Grace Uttiger's voice:

"I'm afraid, Dr. Ferro!"

As Hode slid forward amongst the trees, he heard Doc reply her, "Fear nothing, Grace. We're here to find such power as this world doesn't know. Here, inside this diagram, we're safe."

Hode crawled on his hands and knees to where he could see into the clearing in front of the cabin, bright with the light of the rising moon and of a fire that burned blue and green.

Doc and Grace were there beside the fire. Around them were marks in the earth amongst the stumps, a circle, and a star inside that. Doc's book had mentioned such markings. Grace cowered in her gingham dress. Doc stood straight in his black coat, his hat off, his left hand up above his head, his right holding something at his side.

But they weren't alone in the yard. Things, blurred and gloomy black, humped over in a ring all around them, seeming to look at Doc and Grace inside the circle. First look, Hode reckoned they were folks, a bunch come out to see what was up. Second look, he knew he'd nair seen the like of them.

They had crouched-down bodies, and heads, but the shoulders didn't shape up like shoulders. The heads themselves had here and there a horn, or two horns, or things sticking out like horns. Doc moved his left hand over his head like a signal. One of the things signaled back. But its arm, if that was an arm, wiggled in the air like a long black snake, and its hand seemed to have a heap of extra fingers. The singing rose louder. Doc said a word Hode couldn't understand, maybe it was a name. He said another, louder than the first. Then a third, shouting it. The crooning hum seemed to stir the dark mist in the trees where Hode rose on one knee. All sorts of arms and hands lifted up.

"Now, Grace," and Doc brought down his left hand and took hold of her arm. Hode saw his right hand, with a knife as bright as the moon.

"Don't!" she screamed. "You promised I wouldn't be hurt!"

"I lied to you, Grace," Doc said patiently, the way

you talk to a baby child. "I had to get you here. I needed you, I needed your blood to buy—"

"Stop right there!" Hode yelled his loudest, jumping to his feet, and Doc looked round to see who was speaking.

Hode ran straight at the fire, amongst humped backs turned toward him. Heads lifted, no faces to them, just rotten-bright eyes. The singing rose to a roar, and Hode choked as if the air had been shut off. He took a big leap, clear in over that blue-green fire, and he got both hands on Grace and he yanked her away from Doc.

"You'll kill us all, you fool," he heard Doc gurgle.

Doc slashed at Hode, but already Hode had dragged Grace clear out of that star-and-circle diagram. The voices yapped and bawled round him, and shapes came stumbling toward him.

"You can't take her," Doc was gabbling. Here came Doc, the knife up again. The shapes crowded round them all three, and the air was breathless tight in there.

As Doc came close, Hode let go Grace with one hand and fisted it to fling like a chunk of stone. Smash into Doc's face it drove. Hode felt the nose and teeth break as it slammed in. Doc went over backward like a cornstalk in a high wind. As he struggled to get up, the light showed blood all shiny over his face. The things turned quick toward Doc. Hode didn't tarry longer. He made for the trees, fetching Grace along in a flutter.

Nothing followed him. Hode looked around once. The shapes bunched and stooped round where Doc had gone down. Hode and Grace ran between the trees, bumping into them hard. Back there rose Doc's voice:

"Help!"

More jumps amongst the trees, as fast as Hode could go and make Grace hurry along with him. Again Doc yelled out:

"Help!"

Up ahead, the moon made splashes of bright light on Darkscrabble's waters. Hode floundered right in. He slipped and almost went down, but he got his feet back under him. He dragged Grace to the far side, and they both fell down there. Once more Doc's cry:

"Oh, help!"

Not a sound more, the singing or anything. Just the fall of Hode's feet and Grace's feet and their gasping for breath as they ran through the night, ran for where they knew about things, where would be folks' houses.

Back home, Grace stammered to her folks that she and Hode would be married, she loved him more than all this world, and they goggled but said all right. Next day, Mrs. Sue Lovatt called in neighbors to hear Hode and Grace tell their tale. It called out all those recollections of what had happened at Goodman's Place long before. Some reckoned that Doc Ferro had found the books and spells of that other bunch that once, maybe, had tried to call up strange creatures to turn stones to gold for them or set them on the thrones of the world. Old Sam Taber allowed that whether or not Doc was a virgin, the blood Hode fetched out on his face must have satisfied whatever that called-up bunch of things were, since they hadn't tried to come after Grace's blood.

Nobody felt brash enough, then or later, to go look for what might could have happened to Doc in his own front yard. Not long ago a fellow came visiting and mentioned someone named Charles Fort, who wrote books about how things can come to this world from other worlds and bring all manner of strange happenings, and how it's no good pushing them too close if you can help it.

Some vow there's still a singing hum round Goodman's Place, and if you go to where you can see, there's the cabin Doc and Hode built, all falling in, with strange-looking vines snaked all over it and strange-looking flowers bunched at the door. So I hear tell. But, gentlemen, don't ask me to go there and find out for a fact.

Mary Elizabeth Counselman is a Southern lady, a native Alabaman whose stories, articles and poems have been appearing in a wide variety of magazines since the mid-1930s. She burst onto the supernatural scene with "The Three Marked Pennies", one of the most popular stories ever to appear in Weird Tales and which has gone on to dozens of reprintings all over the world. Another exceptional story, "The Tree's Wife", has been anthologized numerous times as well. To date she has one book to her credit, Half in Shadow, published in England in 1964. Presently Ms. Counselman resides in Gadsden, Alabama, with her husband and a large number of cats, planning another collection of stories and thinking out new ways to scare people. As in this recent story. . . .

KELLERMAN'S EYEPIECE

by Mary Elizabeth Counselman

Cruikshank Scientific Co.
706 Sci-Co. Bldg.
Eddington, New Jersey 08903

Gentlemen:

I should like to order one 12.5mm orthoscopic eyepiece, 96-power, for my Bardou refractor telescope (200-power). The stock number, as listed in your catalog, is #30,405.

Enclosed please find a money order for $19.00 (plus tax) to cover cost and mailing. Thanking you, I am,

> Very truly yours,
> Cyrus Kellerman
> Route #2
> Jethro, Alabama 35860

Mr. Cyrus Kellerman
Route #2
Jethro, Alabama 35860

Dear Mr. Kellerman:

I regret to inform you that our 12.5mm eyepiece is a discontinued item. However, we have in stock a very good 18mm, 67-power eyepiece (Stock No. 30,406), at $21.00.

As we feel this will suit your needs for magnification with a wide, flat field, greater eye-relief, and freedom from ghosts and scattered light, we are sending the item along (postpaid). This eyepiece also has a 4-element design, coated lens, standard 1-¼ O.D., with chrome-plated brass mount. I trust you will find it satisfactory. Our customers are finding it especially good for observing the planets and the moon craters.

> Sincerely yours,
> Peter Cruikshank, Jr.
> Vice-pres., Cruikshank Scientific Co.

P.S. Please remit an additional $2.00 for difference in price.

Mr. Peter Cruikshank, Jr.
Cruikshank Scientific Co.

Dear Sir:

Thank you for sending along (for trial) the 18mm, 67-power eyepiece, in lieu of the one I ordered. I am returning it under separate cover, as the features you mentioned in your letter do not seem to be borne out in the product, and I am sure you would not want the reputation of sending out a product that is not up to the usual Cruikshank standard.

For instance, in observing the moon craters from my rooftop home-observatory last night, there was a most definite display of ghosts and scattered light, particularly in the area of the Sea of Tranquillity. Also, I noticed a peculiar difference in *color*—almost a prismatic effect. Swarms of gnats (which at times interfere with seeing on my rooftop) seemed to be coming out of the larger craters, with a translucent quality that made accurate observation of the craters almost impossible.

Please check your stock again and send me the 96-power eyepiece which I ordered. If you do not have one in stock, please have the courtesy to return my check.

> Very truly yours,
> Cyrus Kellerman

Mr. Reginald Maugham
Complaint Dept.
Cruikshank Scientific Co.

Dear Mr. Maugham:

I have repeatedly written to your company demanding the return of my money ($19.00) for the 96-power eyepiece which I ordered, and for which I received a defective 67-power eyepiece (with additional charge of $2). When I returned the item (Stock No. 30,406), "another 67-power eyepiece" was mailed to me from your shipping department—ostensibly. However, I was simply sent back the *same* defective eyepiece (with charges for reshipping).

Since I have done business with your company for a number of years, after my retirement in 1946 (at which time I started my hobby of amateur astronomy), I feel that I am not being fairly treated. Will you please see that this situation is corrected?

Last night, and the night before last, I again observed what seemed to be translucent swarms of gnats boiling up out of the moon craters in a kind of spiral. What was most disturbing, they seemed to have *human faces*— undoubtedly a trick of reflection caused by your defective eyepiece picking up images of people passing my house. But what alarmed me most—indeed, almost caused me to have another nervous attack; a condition which forced my retirement in '46—was the fact that I *recognized* one of the faces. It was Neil Armstrong, first of our astronauts to make the moon landing. Another seemed to resemble Carpenter. Since I was only mildly interested in watching the space program telecasts, it is highly improbable that this effect was the result of any obsession of mine. The resemblances were quite distinct; so much so that I have considered writing the Space Center about it—with, of course, full details of how I was treated in regard to the 96-power eyepiece I ordered. May I hear from you soon?

Very truly yours,
Cyrus Kellerman

Mr. Cyrus Kellerman
Route #2
Jethro, Alabama

Dear Mr. Kellerman:

It has been brought to my attention by our Mr. Maugham of the Complaint Dept. that you are not happy over an 18mm, 67-power eyepiece that you received as a substitute for an out-of-stock item. I am grieved to hear that you even contemplate passing along this complaint to the Space Center, our largest stockholder. In view of the rather odd (to say the least) story that you saw "faces of our astronauts on the heads of *gnats,*" I wonder if you have considered, first, seeing your family physician? I hope you will not be affronted, but I feel that you do need professional help. When you receive it, perhaps you will no longer bear this grudge against our company in the matter of the defective eyepiece.

I am herewith returning your money ($19.00) in full. We are also sending out calls to our various retailers for a possible 96-power eyepiece, as you originally ordered, which will be sent to you (at catalog price) if one can be found.

Hoping this clears up our little misunderstanding, I am,

> Cordially yours,
> Peter B. Cruikshank, Sr.
> Pres., Cruikshank Scientific Co.

Mr. Peter B. Cruikshank
Cruikshank Scientific Co.

Dear Sir:

Thank you very much for your courteous response in regard to the matter of my defective eyepiece. Since I have continued to use the item, and since it has become rather badly scratched from being inserted in the adapter I made in my home shop, I do not feel right in accepting your company check for the $19.00. I am therefore returning it herewith.

In regard to your friendly suggestion that I see a doctor about my supposed "mental quirk," I have already done just that. A very old friend, Dr. Amos Peabody (himself an amateur astronomer), dropped by last night, and I let him look at the moon craters through the 67-power eyepiece in question. For some reason (probably his new contact lenses), he was unable to see the giant insects I described to him. There were hundreds of the creatures —very large, quite gigantic beings, with gossamer wings, eight hairlike legs, and translucent bodies like wasps— boiling up out of several craters. I had previously sprayed my rooftop area with bug-repellent, so there were *no* gnats flying around the large end of my 200-power refractor. We were both, therefore, at a loss to explain the effect—or that of the faces, human faces, on the heads of the wasplike creatures. Have any of your other customers ever observed so weird an effect? I do wish Amos Peabody—or some other witness—could confirm my findings! Thanking you for your personal attention,

Cordially yours,
Cyrus Kellerman

Mr. Cyrus Kellerman
Route #2
Jethro, Alabama

Dear Mr. Kellerman:

A very odd letter has come to my attention from a young Japanese astronomer, one Hideo Nagashima, of Tokyo, who is experiencing the same strange effects described in your letter. He, too, observed "transparent insects" curling out of the craters around the Sea of Tranquility and the crater Clavius.

Most disturbing of all was his report that the "insects" appeared to have "features, human features" recognizable as those of *two more astronauts*—the last crew landing in March of this year. If this is not a hoax, engineered by both of you as a practical joke, I must request that you return that 67-power eyepiece to our laboratory for study. I have requested that Mr. Nagashima also return the eyepiece he ordered from our company at about the same time you received yours. I believe they were two out of a gross of eyepieces in our stockroom which were subjected to extreme heat during a chemical fire in that area. In some way, the glass of the lenses must have been affected by the heat, thus producing this weird effect. Our scientists in residence would like very much to study the phenomenon, if you would be so kind as to cooperate. It seems the rest of the gross were thrown out, having been damaged by the explosion.

Meanwhile, I have located a 96-power eyepiece in Racine, Wisconsin, at one of our branch labs. They are sending it to you, free of charge, in exchange for the 67-power eyepiece, which I trust you will return to us in the next mail. Thanking you, I am,

Mr. Peter B. Cruikshank, Sr.
Cruikshank Scientific Co.

Dear Mr. Cruikshank:

Thank you for your friendly offer and interest in my experiences with the 67-power eyepiece. The 96-power eyepiece arrived safely, and I am therefore enclosing my check for $19.00 (plus tax) for the item as ordered.

However, I am afraid I must decline your request to return the 67-power defective eyepiece. I am in correspondence with Mr. Nagashima, whose Tokyo address I obtained from an amateur "ham" radio club here (one of the members contacted a Tokyo "ham," who simply looked up Mr. Nagashima's address in the phone book). We exchanged letters, and feel that Cruikshank Scientific Company is seeking to take the credit for our discovery of a matter that may be of worldwide importance to the space program.

If such insectlike creatures were observed in two parts of the world, it stands to reason that there must be *something to see*. That other telescopes have not picked up the "phenomenon," as you choose to call it, is probably due to the special effect on those eyepieces subjected to the chemical fire. It may, as you suggest, have warped or coated the lenses in such a way as to make "invisible" creatures visible through 'scopes using these particular eyepieces. If, as you say, there was a whole gross, there may have been others sent out by mistake to customers ordering them. If you hear from any more "dissatisfied" buyers, please let me know so that we can compare our findings. The Japanese boy would like to know, too, in case what we both saw might be a bizarre kind of optical illusion.

Mr. Nagashima has a strange theory—one which I consider most thought-provoking. He mentioned especially the similarity to Armstrong's features and those of Carpenter, and suggested that these beings may be *adapting themselves* in such a way that an invasion of Earth would not be detected until their "mission" (whatever it may be) is accomplished. They assumed the features of our astronauts, of course, because they were the only humans near enough to contact and . . . shall we say, *become like?* They may have only imitated, as a chameleon imitates by color change. Again, they may have stolen or exchanged some vital atomic structure of the bodies of these men in our space program, who obligingly supplied physical contact with these insect-creatures by landing and walking about on the moon.

As the general public is well aware, all returning astronauts are checked medically for "contaminations" of any kind. But these mammoth-sized insects may have affected —or infected—them in ways that our science is not yet aware exist. If the effects are at all contagious, we may be in for some new "virus" that could wipe out the whole human race. Whether the creatures are native to the moon, or were transferred there by a meteor fragment and hatched in the craters (ant beds?), I dare not surmise.

But I must therefore decline your request for the 67-power eyepiece, which I have duly paid for and which is now legally my property.

Sincerely yours,
Cyrus Kellerman

Mr. Cyrus Kellerman
Route # 2
Jethro, Alabama

Dear Mr. Kellerman:

It has been brought to our attention by the Cruikshank Science Co. of Eddington, N.J., that you have in your possession a 67-power eyepiece through which you, as an amateur astronomer, have observed some startling effects on the moon; perhaps an optical illusion, and perhaps something of danger to our continuing space probe.

As a responsible citizen of the United States—which I am sure you are, Mr. Kellerman—you must realize the impact on the public if such a "menace" as you describe were announced prematurely in your local newspaper. I trust that you will keep this matter to yourself until our representative calls to investigate. I am sure you are aware of the "panic-potential"—as evidenced by recent scares caused by irresponsible citizens making public announcements of the sighting of a UFO (Unidentified Flying Object) in your area. All such reports are, of course, duly investigated by the Federal Bureau, and as many of the *proven facts* made public as we deem advisable for the national welfare.

Our Mr. Lyle will call on you in the next few days. Please cooperate with him in turning over your 67-power eyepiece for proper examination in our space labs at Huntsville. If you have indeed made an important (and alarming) discovery, rest assured that all credit will be given you by the government when the matter can safely be made public in the various news media.

> Thanking you, I am
> H. D. Smith, Co-director
> Federal Bureau of Investigation

News Item: *Tokyo Times,* September 6, 1973
YOUNG ASTRONOMER KILLED IN FALL

A young amateur astronomer, Hideo Nagashima, 16, fell to his death from his rooftop observatory in the Tokyo tenement district at about midnight last night. Nagashima was a resident of the tenement building, where he shared a flat with another youth, who was briefly out of town.

Passersby heard the youth cry out, possibly when he lost his balance atop the stepladder from which he was observing the stars through a 20-inch homemade reflecting telescope of the mirror variety. The body was discovered by a night watchman about dawn, and police were called. Nagashima was clutching an American-made eyepiece. The plastic casing was shattered, and bits of glass were driven into the youth's hands. But death was instantaneous, caused by concussion and a broken neck. . . .

> Hawashi Apts.
> Tokyo, Japan
> Sept. 4, 1973

Mr. Cyrus Kellerman
Route #2
Jethro, Alabama, U.S.A. Zip 35860

Dear Mr. Kellerman, sir:

I write again for telling you what I see. I think now these creatures on moon hatch in crater. They from some

217

star, may be Betelgeuse, where all matter is gaseous. They not solid, like we. But they make self solid. Like they *condense*, the way vapor condense to make water. To human-size they condense. And they assume faces they come near—Armstrong's, Carpenter's, or other. May learn to adopt whole body of human man. Maybe they have already done this thing, and are *now on earth*. We think is astronaut but is *not*. One of them. May be more. You believe is possible? What if they change place with astronaut? If they of high intellect, could fool even doctors.

I asking you, Mr. Kellerman, sir, what should we do? I am *most frighten*, I tell you this. Please to answer and to advise me. I am only a boy, sixteen. You are man, much older, and you will know what we should doing with such knowledge.

> I await your reply, Mr. Kellerman, sir.
> Faithful yours,
> Hideo Nagashima

Director
Riverview Sanatorium
Pleasantboro, Alabama 35972

Dear Sir:

I trust that my old friend, Cyrus Kellerman, has been settled in his quarters with you, and is now improving. It was with deep regret that I was forced to certify him dangerously insane, in compliance with a request from the FBI in connection with his hallucination about "seeing winged creatures on the Moon with the faces of the astronauts." This is not an unusual delusion, perhaps, considering Mr. Kellerman's absorbed interest in astronomy during the years since his retirement. I saw the delusion coming on, but was unable to help him.

When you consider him sufficiently rational for company, I should like to visit him at the sanatorium some weekend, when my practice of medicine permits an absence. We have been very close friends for many years, and as you know, Mr. Kellerman has no family.

> Sincerely yours,
> Amos Peabody, M.D.

P.S. Did you happen to find on Mr. Kellerman's person a 67-power telescope eyepiece, which he may have secreted in some pocket before your attendants strapped him on the stretcher? In listing his personal effects for his estate (which he has kindly left to me), I discovered the eyepiece to be missing. A Mr. Cruikshank of the Cruikshank Scientific Company has offered $1,000 for its return —for some reason not clear to me. This sum could clear up a great many of Mr. Kellerman's outstanding debts, which I, as the executor of his will, must attend to myself. If he mentions the eyepiece during some lucid interval, I would be most obliged if you would ask him where I can find the item. It is my opinion, however, that some sort of paranoid obsession over the purchase of this "defective" item may have brought on Mr. Kellerman's breakdown, so I advise extreme caution when questioning him about it . . .

Karl Edward Wagner, born 1945, is one of the most promising young American fantasists. By training as a medical doctor, he is now working as a psychiatrist in a North Carolina state mental hospital near Chapel Hill, a town he makes his home in with his wife Barbara. He is the editor and main force behind Carcosa, a small, quality publisher of books devoted to weird fiction. His two most recent books are Bloodstone *and* Death Angel's Shadow, *both in the heroic fantasy vein and both concerning an immortal wanderer named Kane, whose continuing saga is breathing new vitality into a sometimes jaded genre. Here, however, Wagner turns his interest to things strange and more modern, with superior results.*

STICKS

by Karl Edward Wagner

I

THE LASHED-TOGETHER framework of sticks jutted from a small cairn alongside the stream. Colin Leverett studied it in perplexment—half a dozen odd lengths of branch, wired together at cross angles for no fathomable purpose. It reminded him unpleasantly of some bizarre crucifix, and he wondered what might lie beneath the cairn.

It was the spring of 1942—the kind of day to make the war seem distant and unreal, although the draft notice waited on his desk. In a few days Leverett would lock his rural studio, wonder if he would see it again—be able to use its pens and brushes and carving tools when he did return. It was goodby to the woods and streams of upstate New York, too. No fly rods, no tramps through the countryside in Hitler's Europe. No point in putting off fishing that troutstream he had driven past once, exploring back roads of the Otselic Valley.

Mann Brook—so it was marked on the old geological survey map—ran southeast of DeRuyter. The unfrequented country road crossed over a stone bridge old before the first horseless carriage, but Leverett's Ford eased across and onto the shoulder. Taking fly rod and tackle, he included pocket flask and tied an iron skillet to his belt. He'd work his way downstream a few miles. By afternoon he'd lunch on fresh trout, maybe some bullfrog legs.

It was a fine, clear stream, though difficult to fish as dense bushes hung out from the bank, broken with stretches of open water hard to work without being seen. But the trout rose boldly to his fly, and Leverett was in fine spirits.

From the bridge the valley along Mann Brook began as

222

fairly open pasture, but half a mile downstream the land had fallen into disuse and was thick with second-growth evergreens and scrub-apple trees. Another mile, and the scrub merged with dense forest, which continued unbroken. The land here, he had learned, had been taken over by the state many years back.

As Leverett followed the stream he noted the remains of an old railroad embankment. No vestige of tracks or ties —only the embankment itself, overgrown with large trees. The artist rejoiced in the beautiful dry-wall culverts spanning the stream as it wound through the valley. To his mind it seemed eerie, this forgotten railroad running straight and true through virtual wilderness.

He could imagine an old wood-burner with its conical stack, steaming along through the valley dragging two or three wooden coaches. It must be a branch of the old Oswego Midland Rail Road, he decided, abandoned rather suddenly in the 1870s. Leverett, who had a memory for detail, knew of it from a story his grandfather told of riding the line in 1871 from Otselic to DeRuyter on his honeymoon. The engine had so labored up the steep grade over Crumb Hill that he got off to walk alongside. Probably that sharp grade was the reason for the line's abandonment.

When he came across a scrap of board nailed to several sticks set into a stone wall, his darkest thought was that it might read "No Trespassing." Curiously, though the board was weathered featureless, the nails seemed quite new. Leverett scarcely gave it much thought, until a short distance beyond he came upon another such contrivance. And another.

Now he scratched at the day's stubble on his long jaw. This didn't make sense. A prank? But on whom? A child's game? No, the arrangement was far too sophisticated. As an artist, Leverett appreciated the craftsmanship of the work—the calculated angles and lengths, the designed intricacy of the maddeningly inexplicable devices. There was something distinctly uncomfortable about their effect.

Leverett reminded himself that he had come here to fish and continued downstream. But as he worked around a thicket he again stopped in puzzlement.

Here was a small open space with more of the stick latices and an arrangement of flat stones laid out on the ground. The stones—likely taken from one of the many

223

dry-wall culverts—made a pattern maybe twenty by fifteen feet, that at first glance resembled a ground plan for a house. Intrigued, Leverett quickly saw that this was not so. If the ground plan for anything, it would have to be for a small maze.

The bizarre lattice structures were all around. Sticks from trees and bits of board nailed together in fantastic array. They defied description; no two seemed alike. Some were only one or two sticks lashed together in parallel or at angles. Others were worked into complicated lattices of dozens of sticks and boards. One could have been a child's tree house—it was built in three planes, but was so abstract and useless that it could be nothing more than an insane conglomeration of sticks and wire. Sometimes the contrivances were stuck in a pile of stones or a wall, maybe thrust into the railroad embankment or nailed to a tree.

It should have been ridiculous. It wasn't. Instead it seemed somehow sinister—these utterly inexplicable, meticulously constructed stick lattices spread through a wilderness where only a tree-grown embankment or a forgotten stone wall gave evidence that man had ever passed through. Leverett forgot about trout and frog legs, instead dug into his pockets for a notebook and stub of pencil. Busily he began to sketch the more intricate structures. Perhaps someone could explain them; perhaps there was something to their insane complexity that warranted closer study for his own work.

Leverett was roughly two miles from the bridge when he came upon the ruins of a house. It was an unlovely colonial farmhouse, box-shaped and gambrel-roofed, fast falling into the ground. Windows were dark and empty; the chimneys on either end looked ready to topple. Rafters showed through open spaces in the roof, and the weathered boards of the walls had in places rotted away to reveal hewn timber beams. The foundation was stone and disproportionately massive. From the size of the unmortared stone blocks, its builder had intended the foundation to stand forever.

The house was nearly swallowed up by undergrowth and rampant lilac bushes, but Leverett could distinguish what had been a lawn with imposing shade trees. Farther back were gnarled and sickly apple trees and an overgrown garden where a few lost flowers still bloomed—wan and serpentine from years in the wild. The stick lattices were everywhere—the lawn, the trees, even the house were covered with the uncanny structures. They reminded Leverett of a hundred misshapen spider webs—grouped so closely together as to almost ensnare the entire house and clearing. Wondering, he sketched page on page of them, as he cautiously approached the abandoned house.

He wasn't certain just what he expected to find inside. The aspect of the farmhouse was frankly menacing, standing as it did in gloomy desolation where the forest had devoured the works of man—where the only sign that man had been here in this century were these insanely wrought latticeworks of sticks and board. Some might have turned back at this point. Leverett, whose fascination for the macabre was evident in his art, instead was intrigued. He drew a rough sketch of the farmhouse and the grounds, overrun with the enigmatic devices, with thickets of hedges and distorted flowers. He regretted that it might be years before he could capture the eeriness of this place on scratchboard or canvas.

The door was off its hinges, and Leverett gingerly stepped within, hoping that the flooring remained sound enough to bear even his sparse frame. The afternoon sun pierced the empty windows, mottling the decaying floorboards with great blotches of light. Dust drifted in the sunlight. The house was empty—stripped of furnishings other than indistinct tangles of rubble mounded over with decay and the drifted leaves of many seasons.

Someone had been here, and recently. Someone who had literally covered the mildewed walls with diagrams of the mysterious lattice structures. The drawings were applied directly to the walls, crisscrossing the rotting wallpaper and crumbling plaster in bold black lines. Some of vertiginous complexity covered an entire wall like a mad mural. Others were small, only a few crossed lines, and reminded Leverett of cuneiform glyphics.

His pencil hurried over the pages of his notebook. Leverett noted with fascination that a number of the drawings were recognizable as schematics of lattices he had earlier sketched. Was this then the planning room for the madman or educated idiot who had built these structures? The gouges etched by the charcoal into the soft plaster appeared fresh—done days or months ago, perhaps.

A darkened doorway opened into the cellar. Were there drawings there as well? And what else? Leverett wondered if he should dare it. Except for streamers of light that crept through cracks in the flooring, the cellar was in darkness.

"Hello?" he called. "Anyone here?" It didn't seem silly just then. These stick lattices hardly seemed the work of a rational mind. Leverett wasn't enthusiastic with the prospect of encountering such a person in this dark cellar. It occurred to him that virtually anything might transpire here, and no one in the world of 1942 would ever know.

And that in itself was too great a fascination for one of Leverett's temperament. Carefully he started down the cellar stairs. They were stone and thus solid, but treacherous with moss and debris.

The cellar was enormous—even more so in the darkness. Leverett reached the foot of the steps and paused for his eyes to adjust to the damp gloom. An earlier impression recurred to him. The cellar was too big for the house. Had another dwelling stood here originally—perhaps destroyed and rebuilt by one of lesser fortune? He examined the stonework. Here were great blocks of gneiss that might support a castle. On closer look they reminded him of a fortress—for the dry-wall technique was startlingly Mycenaean.

Like the house above, the cellar appeared to be empty, although without light Leverett could not be certain what the shadows hid. There seemed to be darker areas of shadow along sections of the foundation wall, suggesting openings to chambers beyond. Leverett began to feel uneasy in spite of himself.

There was something here—a large tablelike bulk in the center of the cellar. Where a few ghosts of sunlight drifted down to touch its edges, it seemed to be of stone. Cautiously he crossed the stone paving to where it loomed —waist-high, maybe eight feet long and less wide. A roughly shaped slab of gneiss, he judged, and supported by pillars of unmortared stone. In the darkness he could only get a vague conception of the object. He ran his hand along the slab. It seemed to have a groove along its edge.

His groping fingers encountered fabric, something cold and leathery and yielding. Mildewed harness, he guessed in distaste.

Something closed on his wrist, set icy nails into his flesh.

Leverett screamed and lunged away with frantic

strength. He was held fast, but the object on the stone slab pulled upward.

A sickly beam of sunlight came down to touch one end of the slab. It was enough. As Leverett struggled backward and the thing that held him heaved up from the stone table, its face passed through the beam of light.

It was a lich's face—desicated flesh tight over its skull. Filthy strands of hair were matted over its scalp, tattered lips were drawn away from broken yellowed teeth, and sunken in their sockets, eyes that should be dead were bright with hideous life.

Leverett screamed again, desperate with fear. His free hand clawed the iron skillet tied to his belt. Ripping it loose, he smashed at the nightmarish face with all his strength.

For one frozen instant of horror the sunlight let him see the skillet crush through the mold-eaten forehead like an ax—cleaving the dry flesh and brittle bone. The grip on his wrist failed. The cadaverous face fell away, and the sight of its caved-in forehead and unblinking eyes from between which thick blood had begun to ooze would awaken Leverett from nightmare on countless nights.

But now Leverett tore free and fled. And when his aching legs faltered as he plunged headlong through the scrub-growth, he was spurred to desperate energy by the memory of the footsteps that had stumbled up the cellar stairs behind him.

II

When Colin Leverett returned from the war, his friends marked him a changed man. He had aged. There were streaks of grey in his hair; his springy step had slowed. The athletic leanness of his body had withered to an unhealthy gauntness. There were indelible lines to his face, and his eyes were haunted.

More disturbing was an alteration of temperament. A mordant cynicism had eroded his earlier air of whimsical asceticism. His fascination with the macabre had assumed a darker mood, a morbid obsession that his old acquaintances found disquieting. But it had been that kind of a war, especially for those who had fought through the Apennines.

Leverett might have told them otherwise, had he cared

227

to discuss his nightmarish experience on Mann Brook. But Leverett kept his own counsel, and when he grimly recalled that creature he had struggled with in the abandoned cellar, he usually convinced himself it had only been a derelict—a crazy hermit whose appearance had been distorted by the poor light and his own imagination. Nor had his blow more than glanced off the man's forehead, he reasoned, since the other had recovered quickly enough to give chase. It was best not to dwell upon such matters, and this rational explanation helped restore sanity when he awoke from nightmares of that face.

Thus Colin Leverett returned to his studio, and once more plied his pens and brushes and carving knives. The pulp magazines, where fans had acclaimed his work before the war, welcomed him back with long lists of assignments. There were commissions from galleries and collectors, unfinished sculptures and wooden models. Leverett busied himself.

There were problems now. *Short Stories* returned a cover painting as "too grotesque." The publishers of a new anthology of horror stories sent back a pair of his interior drawings—"too gruesome, especially the rotted, bloated faces of those hanged men." A customer returned a silver figurine, complaining that the martyred saint was too thoroughly martyred. Even *Weird Tales,* after heralding his return to its ghoul-haunted pages, began returning illustrations they considered "too strong, even for our readers."

Leverett tried halfheartedly to tone things down, found the results vapid and uninspired. Eventually the assignments stopped trickling in. Leverett, becoming more the recluse as years went by, dismissed the pulp days from his mind. Working quietly in his isolated studio, he found a living doing occasional commissioned pieces and gallery work, from time to time selling a painting or sculpture to major museums. Critics had much praise for his bizarre abstract sculptures.

III

The war was twenty-five-year history when Colin Leverett received a letter from a good friend of the pulp days—Prescott Brandon, now editor-publisher of Gothic House, a small press that specialized in books of the weird-fantasy genre. Despite a lapse in correspondence of many years, Brandon's letter began in his typically direct style:

The Eyrie/Salem, Mass./Aug. 2

To the Macabre Hermit of the Midlands:

Colin, I'm putting together a deluxe 3-volume collection of H. Kenneth Allard's horror stories. I well recall that Kent's stories were personal favorites of yours. How about shambling forth from retirement and illustrating these for me? Will need 2-color jackets and a dozen line interiors each. Would hope that you can startle fandom with some especially ghastly drawings for these—something different from the hackneyed skulls and bats and werewolves carting off half-dressed ladies.

Interested? I'll send you the materials and details, and you can have a free hand. Let us hear—Scotty

Leverett was delighted. He felt some nostalgia for the pulp days, and he had always admired Allard's genius in transforming visions of cosmic horror into convincing prose. He wrote Brandon an enthusiastic reply.

He spent hours rereading the stories for inclusion, making notes and preliminary sketches. No squeamish subeditors to offend here; Scotty meant what he said. Leverett bent to his task with maniacal relish.

Something different, Scotty had asked. A free hand. Leverett studied his pencil sketches critically. The figures seemed headed in the right direction, but the drawings needed something more—something that would inject the mood of sinister evil that pervaded Allard's work. Grinning skulls and leathery bats? Trite. Allard demanded more.

The idea had inexorably taken hold of him. Perhaps because Allard's tales evoked that same sense of horror; perhaps because Allard's visions of crumbling Yankee farmhouses and their depraved secrets so reminded him of that spring afternoon at Mann Brook . . .

Although he had refused to look at it since the day he had staggered in, half-dead from terror and exhaustion, Leverett perfectly recalled where he had flung his notebook. He retrieved it from the back of a seldom used file, thumbed through the wrinkled pages thoughtfully. These hasty sketches reawakened the sense of foreboding evil, the charnel horror of that day. Studying the bizarre lattice patterns, it seemed impossible to Leverett that others would not share his feeling of horror that the stick structures evoked in him.

He began to sketch bits of stick latticework into his pencil roughs. The sneering faces of Allard's degenerate creatures took on an added shadow of menace. Leverett nodded, pleased with the effect.

IV

Some months afterward a letter from Brandon informed Leverett he had received the last of the Allard drawings and was enormously pleased with the work. Brandon added a postscript:

"For God's sake Colin—*What is it* with these insane sticks you've got poking up everywhere in the illos! The damn things get really creepy after a while. How on earth did you get onto this?"

Leverett supposed he owed Brandon some explanation. Dutifully he wrote a lengthy letter, setting down the circumstances of his experience at Mann Brook—omitting only the horror that had seized his wrist in the cellar. Let Brandon think him eccentric, but not madman and murderer.

Brandon's reply was immediate:

"Colin—Your account of the Mann Brook episode is fascinating—and incredible! It reads like the start of one of Allard's stories! I have taken the liberty of forwarding your letter to Alexander Stefroi in Pelham. Dr. Stefroi is an earnest scholar of this region's history—as you may already know. I'm certain your account will interest him, and he may have some light to shed on the uncanny affair.

Expect 1st volume, *Voices from the Shadow*, to be ready from the binder next month. The proofs looked great. Best—Scotty"

The following week brought a letter postmarked Pelham, Massachusetts:

"A mutual friend, Prescott Brandon, forwarded your fascinating account of discovering curious sticks and stone artifacts on an abandoned farm in upstate New York. I found this most intriguing, and wonder if you recall further details? Can you relocate the exact site after 30 years? If possible, I'd like to examine the foundations this spring, as they call to mind similar megalithic sites of this region. Several of us are interested in locating what we believe are remains of megalithic construction dating back to the Bronze Age, and to determine their possible use in rituals of black magic in colonial days.

Present archeological evidence indicates that ca. 1700–2000 BC there was an influx of Bronze Age peoples into the Northeast from Europe. We know that the Bronze Age saw the rise of an extremely advanced culture, and that as seafarers they were to have no peers until the Vikings. Remains of a megalithic culture originating in the Mediterranean can be seen in the Lion Gate in Mycenae, in Stonehenge, and in dolmens, passage graves and barrow mounds throughout Europe. Moreover, this seems to have represented far more than a style of architecture peculiar to the era. Rather, it appears to have been a religious cult whose adherents worshipped a sort of earth-mother, served her with fertility rituals and sacrifices, and believed that immortality of the soul could be secured through interment in megalithic tombs.

That this culture came to America cannot be doubted from the hundreds of megalithic remnants found—and now recognized—in our region. The most important site to date is Mystery Hill in N.H., comprising a great many walls and dolmens of megalithic construction—most notably the Y Cavern barrow mound and the Sacrificial Table (see postcard). Less spectacular megalithic sites include the group of cairns and carved stones at Mineral Mt., subterranean chambers with stone passageways such as at Petersham and Shutesbury, and uncounted shaped megaliths and buried 'monk's cells' throughout this region.

Of further interest, these sites seem to have retained their mystic aura for the early colonials, and numerous megalithic sites show evidence of having been used for sinister purposes by colonial sorcerers and alchemists. This became particularly true after the witchcraft persecutions drove many practitioners into the western wilderness—explaining why upstate New York and western Mass. have seen the emergence of so many cultist groups in later years.

Of particular interest here is Shadrack Ireland's 'Brethren of the New Light,' who believed that the world was soon to be destroyed by sinister 'Powers from Outside' and that they, the elect, would then attain physical immortality. The elect who died beforehand were to have their bodies preserved on tables of stone until the 'Old Ones' came forth to return them to life. We have definitely linked the megalithic sites at Shutesbury to later unwholesome practices of the New Light cult. They were absorbed in 1781 by Mother Ann Lee's Shakers, and Ireland's putrescent corpse was hauled from the stone table in his cellar and buried.

Thus I think it probable that your farmhouse may have figured in similar hidden practices. At Mystery Hill a farmhouse was built in 1826 that incorporated one dolmen in its foundations. The house burned down ca. 1848–55, and there were some unsavory local stories as to what took place there. My guess is that your farmhouse had been built over or incorporated a similar megalithic site—and that your 'sticks' indicate some unknown cult still survived there. I can recall certain vague references to lattice devices figuring in secret ceremonies, but can pinpoint nothing definite. Possibly they represent a development of occult symbols to be used in certain conjurations, but this is just a guess. I suggest you consult Waite's *Ceremonial Magic* or such to see if you can recognize similar magical symbols.

Hope this is of some use to you. Please let me hear back.

Sincerely, Alexander Stefroi"

There was a postcard enclosed—a photograph of a 4½ ton granite slab, ringed by a deep groove with a spout, identified as the Sacrificial Table at Mystery Hill. On the back Stefroi had written:

"You must have found something similar to this. They are not rare—we have one in Pelham removed from a site now beneath Quabbin Reservoir. They were used for sacrifice—animal and human—and the groove is to channel blood into a bowl, presumably."

Leverett dropped the card and shuddered. Stefroi's letter reawakened the old horror, and he wished now he had let the matter lie forgotten in his files. Of course, it couldn't be forgotten—even after thirty years.

He wrote Stefroi a careful letter, thanking him for his information and adding a few minor details to his account. This spring, he promised, wondering if he would keep that promise, he would try to relocate the farmhouse on Mann Brook.

V

Spring was late that year, and it was not until early June that Colin Leverett found time to return to Mann Brook. On the surface, very little had changed in three decades. The ancient stone bridge yet stood, nor had the country lane been paved. Leverett wondered whether anyone had driven past since his terror-sped flight.

He found the old railroad grade easily as he started down-stream. Thirty years, he told himself—but the chill inside him only tightened. The going was far more difficult than before. The day was unbearably hot and humid. Wading through the rank underbrush raised clouds of black flies that savagely bit him.

Evidently the stream had seen severe flooding in the past years, judging from piled logs and debris that blocked his path. Stretches were scooped out to barren rocks and gravel. Elsewhere gigantic barriers of uprooted trees and debris looked like ancient and moldering fortifications. As he worked his way down the valley, he realized that his search would yield nothing. So intense had been the force of the long-ago flood that even the course of the stream had changed. Many of the dry-wall culverts no longer spanned the brook, but sat lost and alone far back from its present banks. Others had been knocked flat and swept away, or were buried beneath tons of rotting logs.

At one point Leverett found remnants of an apple orchard groping through weeds and bushes. He thought that the house must be close by, but here the flooding had been particularly severe, and evidently even those ponderous stone foundations had been toppled over and buried beneath debris.

Leverett finally turned back to his car. His step was lighter.

A few weeks later he received a response from Stefroi to his reported failure:

"Forgive my tardy reply to your letter of 13 June. I have recently been pursuing inquiries which may, I hope, lead to the discovery of a previously unreported megalithic site of major significance. Naturally I am disappointed that no traces remained of the Mann Brook site. While I tried not to get my hopes up, it did seem likely that the foundations would have survived. In searching through regional data, I note that there were particularly severe flash floods in the Otselic area in July 1942 and again in May 1946. Very probably your old farmhouse with its enigmatic devices was utterly destroyed not very long after your discovery of the site. This is weird and wild country, and doubtless there is much we shall never know.

I write this with a profound sense of personal loss over the death two nights ago of Prescott Brandon. This was a severe blow to me—as I am sure it was to you and to all who knew him. I only hope the police will catch the vicious killers who did this senseless act—evidently thieves surprised while ransacking his office. Police believe the killers were high on drugs from the mindless brutality of their crime.

I had just received a copy of the third Allard volume, *Unhallowed Places*. A superbly designed book, and this tragedy becomes all the more insuperable with the realization that Scotty will give the world no more such treasures. In Sorrow, Alexander Stefroi"

Leverett stared at the letter in shock. He had not received news of Brandon's death—had only a few days before opened a parcel from the publisher containing a first copy of *Unhallowed Places*. A line in Brandon's last letter recurred to him—a line that seemed amusing to him at the time:

"Your sticks have bewildered a good many fans, Colin, and I've worn out a ribbon answering inquiries. One fellow in particular—a Major George Leonard—has pressed me for details, and I'm afraid that I told him too much. He has written several times for your address, but knowing how you value your privacy I told him simply to permit me to forward any correspondence. He wants to see your original sketches, I gather, but these overbearing occult-types give me a pain. Frankly, I wouldn't care to meet the man myself."

VI

"Mr. Colin Leverett?"

Leverett studied the tall lean man who stood smiling at the doorway of his studio. The sports car he had driven up in was black and looked expensive. The same held for the turtleneck and leather slacks he wore, and the sleek briefcase he carried. The blackness made his thin face deathly pale. Leverett guessed his age to be late forty by the thinning of his hair. Dark glasses hid his eyes, black driving gloves his hands.

"Scotty Brandon told me where to find you," the stranger said.

"Scotty?" Leverett's voice was wary.

"Yes, we lost a mutual friend, I regret to say. I'd been talking with him just before . . . But I see by your expression that Scotty never had time to write."

He fumbled awkwardly. "I'm Dana Allard."

"Allard?"

His visitor seemed embarrassed. "Yes—H. Kenneth Allard was my uncle."

"I hadn't realized Allard left a family," mused Leverett, shaking the extended hand. He had never met the writer personally, but there was a strong resemblance to the few photographs he had seen. And Scotty had been paying royalty checks to an estate of some sort, he recalled.

"My father was Kent's half-brother. He later took his father's name, but there was no marriage, if you follow."

"Of course." Leverett was abashed. "Please find a place to sit down. And what brings you here?"

Dana Allard tapped his briefcase. "Something I'd been discussing with Scotty. Just recently I turned up a stack of my uncle's unpublished manuscripts." He unlatched the briefcase and handed Leverett a sheaf of yellowed paper. "Father collected Kent's personal effects from the state hospital as next-of-kin. He never thought much of my uncle, or his writing. He stuffed this away in our attic and forgot about it. Scotty was quite excited when I told him of my discovery."

Leverett was glancing through the manuscript—page on page of cramped handwriting, with revisions pieced throughout like an indecipherable puzzle. He had seen photographs of Allard manuscripts. There was no mistaking this.

Or the prose. Leverett read a few passages with rapt absorption. It was authentic—and brilliant.

"Uncle's mind seems to have taken an especially morbid turn as his illness drew on," Dana hazarded. "I admire his work very greatly but I find these last few pieces . . . Well, a bit *too* horrible. Especially his translation of his mythical *Book of Elders*."

It appealed to Leverett perfectly. He barely noticed his guest as he pored over the brittle pages. Allard was describing a megalithic structure his doomed narrator had encountered in the crypts beneath an ancient churchyard. There were references to "elder glyphics" that resembled his lattice devices.

"Look here," pointed Dana. "These incantations he records here from Alorri-Zrokros's forbidden tome: 'Yogth-Yugth-Sut-Hyrath-Yogng—Hell, I can't pronounce them. And he has pages of them."

"This is incredible!" Leverett protested. He tried to mouth the alien syllables. It could be done. He even detected a rhythm.

"Well, I'm relieved that you approve. I'd feared these last few stories and fragments might prove a little too much for Kent's fans."

"Then you're going to have them published?"

Dana nodded. "Scotty was going to. I just hope those thieves weren't searching for this—a collector would pay a fortune. But Scotty said he was going to keep this

236

secret until he was ready for announcement." His thin face was sad.

"So now I'm going to publish it myself—in a deluxe edition. And I want you to illustrate it."

"I'd feel honored!" vowed Leverett, unable to believe it.

"I really liked those drawings you did for the trilogy. I'd like to see more like those—as many as you feel like doing. I mean to spare no expense in publishing this. And those stick things . . ."

"Yes?"

"Scotty told me the story on those. Fascinating! And you have a whole notebook of them? May I see it?"

Leverett hurriedly dug the notebook from his file, returned to the manuscript.

Dana paged through the book in awe. "These things are totally bizarre—and there are references to such things in the manuscript, to make it even more fantastic. Can you reproduce them all for the book?"

"All I can remember," Leverett assured him. "And I have a good memory. But won't that be overdoing it?"

"Not at all! They fit into the book. And they're utterly unique. No, put everything you've got into this book. I'm going to entitle it *Dwellers in the Earth,* after the longest piece. I've already arranged for its printing, so we begin as soon as you can have the art ready. And I know you'll give it your all."

VII

He was floating in space. Objects drifted past him. Stars, he first thought. The objects drifted closer.

Sticks. Stick lattices of all configurations. And then he was drifting among them, and he saw that they were not sticks—not of wood. The lattice designs were of dead-pale substance, like streaks of frozen starlight. They reminded him of glyphics of some unearthly alphabet—complex, enigmatic symbols arranged to spell . . . what? And there *was* an arrangement—a three-dimensional pattern. A maze of utterly baffling intricacy . . . .

Then somehow he was in a tunnel. A cramped, stone-lined tunnel through which he must crawl on his belly. The dank, moss-slimed stones pressed close about his wriggling form, evoking shrill whispers of claustrophobic dread.

And after an indefinite space of crawling through this and other stone-lined burrows, and sometimes through passages whose angles hurt his eyes, he would creep forth into a subterranean chamber. Great slabs of granite a dozen feet across formed the walls and ceiling of this buried chamber, and between the slabs other burrows pierced the earth. Altarlike, a gigantic slab of gneiss waited in the center of the chamber. A spring welled darkly between the stone pillars that supported the table. Its outer edge was encircled by a groove, sickeningly stained by the substance that clotted in the stone bowl beneath its collecting spout.

Others were emerging from the darkened burrows that ringed the chamber—slouched figures only dimly glimpsed and vaguely human. And a figure in a tattered cloak came toward him from the shadow—stretched out a claw-like hand to seize his wrist and draw him toward the sacrificial table. He followed unresistingly, knowing that something was expected of him.

They reached the altar and in the glow from the cuneiform lattices chiseled into the gneiss slab he could see the guide's face. A moldering corpse-face, the rotted bone of its forehead smashed inward upon the foulness that oozed forth. . . .

And Leverett would awaken to the echo of his screams. . . .

He'd been working too hard, he told himself, stumbling about in the darkness, getting dressed because he was too shaken to return to sleep. The nightmares had been coming every night. No wonder he was exhausted.

But in his studio his work awaited him. Almost fifty drawings finished now, and he planned another score. No wonder the nightmares.

It was a grueling pace, but Dana Allard was ecstatic with the work he had done. And *Dwellers in the Earth* was waiting. Despite problems with typesetting, with getting the special paper Dana wanted—the book only waited on him.

Though his bones ached with fatigue, Leverett determinedly trudged through the greying night. Certain features of the nightmare would be interesting to portray.

VIII

The last of the drawings had gone off to Dana Allard in Petersham, and Leverett, fifteen pounds lighter and gut-weary, converted part of the bonus check into a case of good whiskey. Dana had the offset presses rolling as soon as the plates were shot from the drawings. Despite his precise planning, presses had broken down, one printer quit for reasons not stated, there had been a bad accident at the new printer—seemingly innumerable problems, and Dana had been furious at each delay. But the production pushed along quickly for all that. Leverett wrote that the book was cursed, but Dana responded that a week would see it ready.

Leverett amused himself in his studio constructing stick lattices and trying to catch up on his sleep. He was expecting a copy of the book when he received a letter from Stefroi:

"Have tried to reach you by phone last few days, but no answer at your house. I'm pushed for time just now, so must be brief. I have indeed uncovered an unsuspected megalithic site of enormous importance. It's located on the estate of a long-prominent Mass. family—and as I cannot receive authorization to visit it, I will not say where. Have investigated secretly (and quite illegally) for a short time one night and was nearly caught. Came across reference to the place in collection of 17th-century letters and papers in a divinity school library. Writer denouncing the family as a breed of sorcerers and witches, references to alchemical activities and other less savory rumors—and describes underground stone chambers, megalithic artifacts, etc., which are put to 'foul usage and diabolic praktise.' Just got a quick glimpse but his description was not exaggerated. And Colin—in creeping through the weeds to get to the site, I came across dozens of your mysterious 'sticks!' Brought a small one back and have it here to show you. Recently constructed and exactly like your drawings. With luck, I'll gain admittance and find out their significance—undoubtedly they have significance— though these cultists can be stubborn about sharing their secrets. Will explain my interest is scientific, no exposure to ridicule—and see what they say. Will get a closer look one way or another. And so—I'm off! Sincerely, Alexander Stefroi"

Leverett's bushy brows rose. Allard had intimated certain dark rituals in which the stick lattices figured. But Allard had written over thirty years ago, and Leverett assumed the writer had stumbled onto something similar to the Mann Brook site. Stefroi was writing about something current.

He rather hoped Stefroi would discover nothing more than an inane hoax.

The nightmares haunted him still—familiar now, for all that its scenes and phantasms were visited by him only in dream. Familiar. The terror that they evoked was undiminished.

Now he was walking through forest—a section of hills that seemed to be close by. A huge slab of granite had been dragged aside, and a pit yawned where it had lain. He entered the pit without hesitation, and the rounded steps that led downward were known to his tread. A buried stone chamber, and leading from it stone-lined burrows. He knew which one to crawl into.

And again the underground room with its sacrificial altar and its dark spring beneath, and the gathering circle of poorly glimpsed figures. A knot of them clustered about the stone table, and as he stepped toward them he saw they pinned a frantically writhing man.

It was a stoutly built man, white hair disheveled, flesh gouged and filthy. Recognition seemed to burst over the contorted features, and he wondered he if should know the man. But now the lich with the caved-in skull was whispering in his ear, and he tried not to think of the unclean things that peered from that cloven brow, and instead took the bronze knife from the skeletal hand, and raised the knife high, and because he could not scream and awaken, did with the knife as the tattered priest had whispered . . .

And when after an interval of unholy madness, he at last did awaken, the stickiness that covered him was not cold sweat, nor was it nightmare the half-devoured heart he clutched in one fist.

IX

Leverett somehow found sanity enough to dispose of the shredded lump of flesh. He stood under the shower all morning, scrubbing his skin raw. He wished he could vomit.

There was a news item on the radio. The crushed body of noted archeologist, Dr. Alexander Stefroi, had been discovered beneath a fallen granite slab near Whately. Police speculated the gigantic slab had shifted with the scientist's excavations at its base. Identification was made through personal effects.

When his hands stopped shaking enough to drive, Leverett fled to Petersham—reaching Dana Allard's old stone house about dark. Allard was slow to answer his frantic knock.

"Why, good evening, Colin! What a coincidence your coming here just now! The books are ready. The bindery just delivered them."

Leverett brushed past him. "We've got to destroy them!" he blurted. He'd thought a lot since morning.

"Destroy them?"

"There's something none of us figured on. Those stick lattices—there's a cult, some damnable cult. The lattices have some significance in their rituals. Stefroi hinted once they might be glyphics of some sort, I don't know. But the cult is still alive. They killed Scotty . . . they killed Stefroi. They're onto me—I don't know what they intend. They'll kill you to stop you from releasing this book!"

Dana's frown was worried, but Leverett knew he hadn't impressed him the right way. "Colin, this sounds insane. You really have been overextending yourself, you know. Look, I'll show you the books. They're in the cellar."

Leverett let his host lead him downstairs. The cellar was quite large, flagstoned and dry. A mountain of brown-wrapped bundles awaited them.

"Put them down here where they wouldn't knock the floor out," Dana explained. "They start going out to distributors tomorrow. Here, I'll sign your copy."

Distractedly Leverett opened a copy of *Dwellers in the Earth*. He gazed at his lovingly rendered drawings of rotting creatures and buried stone chambers and stained altars—and everywhere the enigmatic latticework structures. He shuddered.

"Here." Dana Allard handed Leverett the book he had signed. "And to answer your question, they *are* elder glyphics."

But Leverett was staring at the inscription in its unmistakable handwriting: "For Colin Leverett, Without whom this work could not have seen completion—H. Kenneth Allard."

Allard was speaking. Leverett saw places where the hastily applied flesh-toned makeup didn't quite conceal what lay beneath. "Glyphics symbolic of alien dimensions —inexplicable to the human mind, but essential fragments of an evocation so unthinkably vast that the 'pentagram' (if you will) is miles across. Once before we tried —but your iron weapon destroyed part of Althol's brain. He erred at the last instant—almost annihilating us all. Althol had been formulating the evocation since he fled the advance of iron four millennia past.

"Then you reappeared, Colin Leverett—you with your artist's knowledge and diagrams of Althol's symbols. And now a thousand new minds will read the evocation you have returned to us, unite with our minds as we stand in the Hidden Places. And the Great Old Ones will come forth from the earth, and we, the dead who have steadfastly served them, shall be masters of the living."

Leverett turned to run, but now they were creeping forth from the shadows of the cellar, as massive flagstones slid back to reveal the tunnels beyond. He began to scream as Althol came to lead him away, but he could not awaken, could only follow.

The late Marjorie Bowen is overdue for recognition as one of the foremost authors of supernatural stories in the 20th century. "Marjorie Bowen" is the best known of the pen-names employed by the versatile and incredible Gabrielle Margaret Vere Campbell Long, who died in 1952 at the age of 67 and left behind more than 150 books, many under the pseudonyms of Joseph Shearing and George Preedy. Mainly an author of historical novels—The Viper of Milan, The Burning Glass, The Veil'd Delight and scores of others—Mrs. Long excelled in the recreation of the past and its drama and the passions that drive men and women. Of her terror tales, Michael Sadleir wrote: "This mastery of descriptive detail and sureness in period expression, combined with a curiously inexorable reading of human nature, give to Marjorie Bowen's best stories a sinister force both realistic and alarming. . . . Under the bitter fascinated realization of love turned to loathing, under the relentless evocation of gloom, decay and tarnished grandeur, Marjorie Bowen has a capacity for anguished pity."

THE SIGN-PAINTER AND THE CRYSTAL FISHES

by Marjorie Bowen

I

THE RIVER AND THE HOUSE

THE HOUSE was built beside a river. In the evening the sun would lie reflected in the dark water, a stain of dirty red in between the thick shadows cast by the buildings. It was twilight now, and there was the long ripple of dull crimson, shifting as the water rippled sullenly between the high houses.

Beneath this house was an old stake, hung at the bottom with stagnant green, white and dry at the top. A rotting boat that fluttered the tattered remains of faded crimson cushions was affixed to the stake by a fraying rope. Sometimes the boat was thrown against the post by the strong evil ripples, and there was a dismal creaking noise.

Opposite this house was a garden—a narrow strip of ground closed round by the blank, dark houses, and led up to from the water by a flight of crumbling steps.

Nothing grew in this garden but tall, bright, rank grass and a small tree that bore white flowers. The house it belonged to was empty and shuttered; so was every house along the canal except this one, at the top window of which Lucius Cranfield sat shivering in his mean red coat. He was biting his finger and looking out across the water at the tree with pale flowers knocking at the closed shutter beside it.

The room was bare and falling to decay. Cobwebs swung from the great beam in the roof, and in every corner a spider's web was spun across the dirty plaster walls.

There was no glass in the window, and the shutters swung loose on broken hinges. Now and again they creaked against the flat brick front of the house, and then Lucius Cranfield winced.

He held a round, clear mirror in his hand, and sometimes he looked away from the solitary tree to glance into it. When he did so he beheld a pallid face surrounded with straight brown hair, lips that had once been beautiful, and blurred eyes veined with red like some curious stone.

As the red sunlight began to grow fainter in the water a step sounded on the rotting stairway, the useless splitting door was pushed open, and Lord James Fontaine entered.

Slowly, and with a mincing step, he came across the dusty floor. He wore a dress of bright violet watered silk, his hair was rolled fantastically, and powdered such a pure white that his face looked sallow by contrast. To remedy this he had painted his cheeks and his lips, and powdered his forehead and chin. But the impression made was not of a pink and fresh complexion, but of a yellow countenance rouged. There were long pearls in his ears and under his left eye an enormous patch. His eyes slanted towards his nose, his nostrils curved upwards, and his thin lips were smiling.

He carried a cane hung with blood-coloured tassels, and his waistcoat was embroidered with green flowers, the hue of an emerald, and green flowers the tint of a pale sea.

"You paint signs, do you not?" he said, and nodded.

"Yes, I paint signs," answered the other. He looked away from Lord James and across the darkening water at the lonely tree opposite. The sky above the deserted houses was turning a cold wet grey. A flight of crows went past, clung for a moment round the black chimney-pots, and flew on again.

"Will you design *me* a sign-board?" asked Lord James, smiling. "Something noble and gay, for I have taken a new house in town."

"My workshop is downstairs," said Lucius Cranfield, without looking round. "Why did you come up?" He laid down the mirror and rubbed his cold fingers together.

"I rang and there was no answer, I knocked and there was no answer, so I pushed open the door and came up; why not?" Lord James regarded the sign-painter keenly, and smiled again, and pressed the knob of his clouded cane against his chin.

"Oh, why not?" echoed Lucius Cranfield. "Only this is a poor place to come to for a gay and noble sign."

He turned his head now, and there was a curious twist on his colourless lips.

"But you have a very splendid painting swinging outside your own door," said Lord James suavely. "Never did I see fairer drawing nor brighter hues. Is it your work?" he questioned.

"Mine, yes," assented the sign-painter drearily.

"Fashion me a sign-board such as that," said Lord James.

Lucius Cranfield left off rubbing his hands together.

"The same subjects?" he asked.

The other lowered his lids.

"The subjects are curious," he replied. "Where did you get them?"

"From life," said the sign-painter, staring at the tattered veils of cobwebs fluttering on the broken window-frame. "From my life."

The bright dark eyes of the visitor flickered from right to left. He moved a little nearer the window, where, despite the thickening twilight, his violet silk coat gleamed like the light on a sheet of water.

"You have had a strange life," he remarked, sneering, "to cull from it such incidents."

"What did you behold that was so extraordinary?" asked Lucius Cranfield.

"On one side there is depicted a gallows, a man in a gay habit hanging on it, and his face has some semblance to your own; the reverse bears the image of a fish, white, yet shot with all the colours . . . . it is so skilfully executed that it looks as if it moved through the water. . . ."

An expression of faint and troubled interest came over the sign-painter's face.

"Have you ever seen such a fish?" he asked.

Lord James's features seemed to contract and sharpen.

"Never," he said hastily.

Lucius Cranfield rose slowly and stiffly.

"There are two in the world," he said, half to himself; "and before the end I shall find the other, and then everything will be mended and put straight."

"Unless you lose your own token first," remarked Lord James harshly.

"How did you know I had one?" asked the sign-painter sharply.

Lord James laughed.

"Oh, you're going mad, my fine friend! Do you not feel that you must be, living alone in such fashion in this old house?"

Lucius Cranfield dragged himself to a cupboard in the wall.

"How my limbs ache!" he muttered. "Mad?" A look of cunning spread over his features. "No, I shall not go mad while I have the one crystal fish, nor before I find the owner of the other."

It was so dark they could barely see each other; but the nobleman's dress still shone bright and cold in the gloom.

"Yet it is enough to make a man go mad," he remarked suavely—"to reflect how rich and handsome you were once, with what fine clothes and furniture, and friends . . . and then to remember how your father was hanged, and you were ruined, and all through the lies of your enemy. . . ."

"But my enemy died, too," said Lucius Cranfield. He took a thick candle and a rusty tinderbox out of the cupboard.

"His son is alive," replied Lord James.

A coarse yellow flame spurted across the dust.

"I wish I had killed them both," said the sign-painter; "but I could never find the son. . . . How badly the candle burns! . . ."

He held the tinder to the cold wax, and only a small tongue of feeble fire sprang up.

"You are quite mad!" smiled Lord James. "You never killed either . . . and now that your blood is chilled with misery and weakened with evil days, you never will."

The candle-flame strengthened and illumined the chamber. It showed Lord James holding his sharp chin in a long white hand, and woke his diamonds into stars.

"Will you come downstairs and choose your design?" said Lucius Cranfield, shivering. "Take care of the stairs. They are rather dusty."

He shuffled to the door and held aloft the light. It revealed the twisting stairway where the plaster hung cracked and dry on the walls, or bulged damp and green in patches as the damp had come through. The rafters were warped and bending, and in one spot a fan-shaped fungus had spread in a blotch of mottled orange.

Lord James came softly up behind the sign-painter, and peered over the stairs.

"This is a mean place," he said, smiling, "for a great gentleman to live in . . . and you were a great gentleman once, Mr. Cranfield."

The other gave him a cunning look over his shoulder.

"When I find the owner of the fish," he answered, "I shall be a great gentleman again or kill my enemy—that is in the spell."

They went downstairs slowly because of the rotting steps and uncertain light. Lord James rested his long fingers lightly on the dusty balustrade.

"Do you not find the days very long and dull here?" he asked.

The reply came unsteadily from the bowed red figure of the sign-painter.

"No . . . I paint . . . and then I make umbrellas."

"Umbrellas!" Lord James laughed unpleasantly.

"And parasols. Would you not like a parasol for your wife, James Fontaine?"

"Ah, you know me, it seems."

"I know what you call yourself," said Lucius Cranfield. "And here is my studio. Will you look at the designs upon the wall?"

Lord James grinned and stepped delicately along the dark passage to the door indicated. It opened into a low chamber the entire depth of the house. There were windows on either side: one way looking on to the river, the other on to the street.

Lucius Cranfield set the candle in a green bottle on the table, and pointed round the walls where all manner of drawings on canvas, wood, and paper hung. They depicted horrible and fantastic things—mandrakes, dragons, curious shells and plants, monsters, and distorted flowers. In one corner were a number of parasols of silk and brocade, ruffled and frilled, having carved handles and ribboned sticks.

Lord James put up his glass and looked about him.

"So you know who I am?" he said, speaking in an absorbed way, and keeping his back to Lucius Cranfield, who stood huddled together on the other side of the table, staring before him with dead-seeming eyes.

There was no answer, and Lord James laughed softly.

"You paint very well, Mr. Cranfield, but I must have something more cheerful than any of these"—he pointed his elegant cane at the designs. "That fish, now, that you have on your own sign, that is a beautiful thing."

The sign-painter groaned and thrust his fingers into his untidy brown hair.

"I cannot paint that again," he said.

"Sell me the sign, then." Lord James spoke quickly.

"I cannot . . . it is hanging there that it may be seen . . . that whosoever holds the other fish may see it . . . and then. . . ."

"How mad you are!" cried Lord James. "What then, even should one come who has the other fish?" His black eyes blinked sharply, and his lips twitched back from his teeth.

"Then I shall find my enemy. The witch said so. . . ."

"But you may die first."

"I cannot die till the spell is accomplished," shivered Lucius Cranfield. "Nor can I lose the fish."

Lord James put his hand to his waistcoat-pocket.

"Your light is very dim," he remarked. "I do not see clearly, but I think I observe a violet-coloured parasol—"

The other lifted his head.

"They are very interesting to make."

"Will you show me that one?"

Lucius Cranfield turned slowly towards the far corner of the room.

"I began to work on that the night my father was hanged . . . as I sewed on the frills I thought of my enemies and how I hated them; and the night I killed one of them I finished it, carving the handle into the likeness of an ivory rose."

"You have sinned also," said Lord James, through his teeth. He took his hand from his pocket and put it behind his back.

"I have been a great sinner," answered the sign-painter.

He took the purple parasol from the corner and shook out its shimmering silk furbelows.

"I will buy that." Lord James leant against the table, close to the candle flaring in the green bottle. In its yellow light the brilliant colour of his coat shone like a jewel.

"The parasol is not for sale," said Lucius Cranfield sourly, gazing down on it. "Why do you not choose your design and go?"

Now it was quite dark, both outside, beyond the windows, and in the corners of the long room. The waters sounded insistently as they lapped against the house. There was no moon; but through a rift in the thick, murky sky one star flickered, and the sign-painter lifted his dimmed eyes from the candle-flame and looked at it.

"What do you see?" asked Lord James curiously. He came softly up behind the other.

"A star," was the reply. "It is shining above the lonely white tree that is always knocking at the closed shutters. . . ."

Lord James's hand came round from behind his back.

"But one can never see them both at the same time," continued the sign-painter. "When the star comes out, the tree is hidden; and only when the star sets. . . ."

Lord James's fine hand rose slowly and fell swiftly. . . .

Lucius Cranfield sank on his face silently, and the flaring light of the unsnuffed candle glistened on the wet dagger as it was withdrawn from between his shoulders.

Lord James stepped back and gazed with a long smile at his victim, who writhed an instant and then lay still on the dusty floor.

The sound of the water without seemed to increase in strength. The secretive yet turbulent noise of it filled the chamber like a presence as Lord James turned over the body of the sign-painter and opened his red coat.

In an inner pocket he found it, wrapped in a piece of blue satin.

The crystal fish. It was of all colours yet of no colour; translucent as water, holding, like a bubble, all hues, finely wrought with fins and scales, light and cold to the hand, shining with a pure light of its own to the eye.

Lord James rose from his knees and put out the candle.

The river sounded so loud that he paused to listen to it. He thought he could distinguish the swish of oars and the clatter of them in the rowlocks.

He went to the window and looked out. By the glimmer of the star and the radiance cast by the fish in his hand he could discern that there was nobody on the river, only the deserted boat fastened to the rotting stake.

He smiled; the faint light was caught in his ribbons, his diamonds, his dark, evil eyes. As he stared up and down the black road of water, the crystal fish began to writhe in his hand. It pulsed and struggled, then leapt through his fingers and plunged into the blackness of the river.

Lord James peered savagely after it, his smile changing

to a grin of anger. But the fish had sunk like a bolt of iron, and thinking of the depth of the river Lord James was comforted.

He came back to the table. It was quite dark, but his eyes served him equally well day or night. He picked up his clouded cane with the crimson tassels, his black hat laced with gold, his vivid green cloak, he kissed his hand to the prone body of the sign-painter, and left the room. In a leisurely fashion he walked down the passage, pushed open the crazy front door, and stepped into the lonely street.

He looked up at the sign on which were painted the crystal fish and the man on the gallows; then he began to put on his gloves.

As he did so the violet parasol came to his mind. He turned back.

Softly he re-entered the long studio. The noise of the water had subsided to a mere murmur. Rats were running about the room and sitting on the body of Lucius Cranfield. He could see them despite the intense darkness, and he stepped delicately to avoid their tails.

The violet parasol was on the floor near the dead man. He stooped to pick it up, and the rats squealed and showed their teeth.

Lord James nodded to them and left the house again with the parasol under his arm.

II

THE RIVER AND THE GARDEN

The garden sloped down to the straight high-road upon the side to which the house faced, and at the back ran the river dividing the pleasaunce from the meadows.

Separating the garden from the road was a prim box hedge, very high, very wide, and very old. Behind this grew the neat garden flowers, and beneath it the tangled weeds that edged the road.

Here sat Lord James on a milestone, playing Faro with a one-eyed gipsy.

The summer sunset sparkled on the red gables of the

house and in the clothes of Lord James, which were of crimson and blue sarcenet branched with gold and silver.

The gipsy was young and ugly; he wore a green patch over his eyeless socket, and now and then listened, keenly, to the sound of the church-bells that came up from the valley, for the village ringers were practising for Lord James's wedding.

The two played silently. The red and black cards scattered over the close green grass shaded by the large wild-parsley flowers. Beside the milestone lay Lord James's hat, stick, and cloak. His horse was fastened by its bridle to a stout branch of a laurel-tree that bent over from the garden.

"You always win," said the gipsy.

Lord James smiled, then coughed till he shook the powder off his face on to his cravat.

"Another game," he said, and shuffled the cards.

At this a lady looked over the box hedge, and gave them both a bitter frown.

Little bright pink and blue ribbons were threaded through her high-piled white curls, round her neck was a diamond necklace, and on the front of her black velvet bodice a long trail of jasmine was pinned. Her painted lips curled scornfully, and her azure eyes darkened as she stared across and over the box hedge at Lord James.

He looked up at her, waved his hand, and rose.

"You are late," she remarked stiffly.

"I have been playing cards," he answered. "May I present you to my friend?" He pointed to the gipsy.

"No," she said, and turned her back.

The gipsy laughed silently. The sound of the bells swelled and receded in the golden evening.

"Take my horse round to the stables." Lord James grinned at the gipsy, and gathered up his hat and cloak from the grass.

"I hate those bells!" cried the lady pettishly.

"They will ring no more after to-morrow, my dear."

Lord James came round to the gate as he spoke, and entered the garden.

She gave him a side-glance and pouted. Her enormous pink silk hoop, draped with festoons of white roses, overspread the narrow garden-path, and crushed the southernwood that edged it. Her hands rested on her black velvet panniers embroidered with garlands of crimson carnations.

There was a moonshaped patch on her bare throat, and one like a star on her roughed cheek; beneath her short skirts showed her black buckle shoes and immensely high red heels. Her name was Serena Thornton.

"I have broken my parasol," she said, looking at the gables of her house where the red-gold sunset rested. "The violet one you brought me."

"It can be mended," answered Lord James.

He came up to her, and they kissed.

"Yes," assented Serena. "I sent it to be mended to-day," she added.

He laughed.

"There is no one here can mend a parasol like that. You must give it to me, Serena, and I will take it to town."

They moved slowly along the gravel walk, he in front of her, since her hoop did not allow him to be by her side.

It was a very pleasant garden. There were beds of pinks, of stocks, of roses, bushes of laurel, yew, and box, all intersected with little paths that crossed one another and led towards the house.

"There is a man in the village," said Lady Serena, "who is a maker of umbrellas. He came here yesterday."

"Ah?" questioned Lord James. He glanced back over his shoulder.

"I heard he was painting a new sign for 'The Goat and Compasses,' and that he had made a beautiful blue umbrella for the host, so I sent down my parasol."

A slight greenish tinge, visible through the paint and powder, overspread Lord James's handsome face.

"It was careless of you to break it," he said softly.

Lady Serena lifted her shoulders.

"I could not help it. Shall I tell you how it happened?"

They had reached a square plot of close grass round which ran the box hedge and a low stone coping. In the centre stood a prim fountain, and in its clear water swam the golden and ruby carp.

"Yes, tell me how it happened," said Lord James. He pressed his handkerchief to his thin lips and looked up at the sunset.

"I wish they would stop those bells!" cried Lady Serena.

"They are practising for our wedding to-morrow, my dear," he smiled.

They could walk now side by side, she looking in front of her, and he gazing at the sunset that was pale and

253

bright, the colour of soft gold, of pink coral, and of a dove's wings above the gables of her house.

"I was walking by the river two days ago," said Lady Serena, "and I had in my hand the crystal fish. Do you remember, Lord James, that I showed it to you just before you left for town?"

"Yes; a foolish toy," he answered.

"How pleasant the box smells!" murmured Lady Serena, in a softer tone. "Well, I walked along the bank, thinking of you, and as I looked into the water I saw another fish—it floated just as if it were swimming—and oh, it was like the one I held in my hand! Just as it neared me it became entangled in the water weeds. . . ."

"This does not explain how you broke your parasol," remarked Lord James.

"I drew the fish to land with it—my new parasol that your little black boy had just brought me—and broke the handle."

Lord James turned his pallid face towards her.

"Did you get the fish?"

"Yes. It is just like the one I have." She pulled out a green ribbon from the white velvet bag that hung on her arm, and at the end of it dangled two crystal fishes, cut and carved finely, holding a clear light, and filled with changing colours.

Lady Serena touched one with her scented forefinger. "That is the one I found. See, it has a bright bloodlike stain across the side."

"So it has," said Lord James, putting up his glass. "It is curious you should have found it. A witch gave you the other, did you not say?"

"Yes," she answered half sullenly. "And she told me that the other was owned by my lover, and that he must live in misery till he found me." She turned the blue light of her eyes on her companion. "*You* should have had it," she said, and slipped the fishes back into her bag.

The afterglow was fading from the sky, and they turned towards the house.

"I won three thousand pounds at Faro last night," said Lord James, "and I have brought you some presents."

And he thrust his hand into his pocket and drew out a string of amethysts.

"I dislike the colour," said Lady Serena, and put it aside.

"It is the colour you wear," he answered.

She took the necklace at this with a sudden laugh, and fastened it round her long, pale throat.

They reached the three shallow steps that led to the open door of the house, and passed side by side out of the sunset glow into the soft-hued gloom of the wide hall.

In the great banqueting-room a dinner of two covers was laid. The service was of agate and silver, the glasses twisted with milk-white lines. The table was lit by six tall candles painted with wreaths of pinks and forget-me-nots, and their light ran gleaming and faint over the white cloth.

"I am going to try on my wedding-dress," said Lady Serena. "Will you wait for me?"

"It is unlucky to wear your wedding-dress before your wedding-day," answered Lord James.

But she left the chamber without a word or a smile.

The room opened by wide windows on to the terrace at the back that sloped down to the river, and the sound of the water throbbing between its banks seemed to grow in volume and to speak threateningly to Lord James as he sat at the table with the glass and silver glittering before him, and the heart-shaped candle-flames casting a flickering glow over his sickly face.

It was the same river, and he knew it. As the last flush of light faded from the heavens he could see the moon, a strong pearl colour, rise above the trees, and a great sparkling reflection fell across the river, marking with lines of silver the turbulent eddies that chased one another down the stream.

After a while Lord James rose and walked softly to the window, and his eyes became wide and bright as he stroked his chin and stared at the river.

When he turned round again, Lucius Cranfield stood in the doorway looking at him.

A spasm of fear contracted Lord James's features; then he spoke evenly.

"Good-evening," he said.

"Good-evening," replied Lucius Cranfield, and he bowed. "I have brought back a parasol I have mended—a lady's parasol, purple, with an ivory rose on the handle."

Between them was an ill-lit space of room and the bright table bearing the candles. They looked at each other, and Lord James's face grew long and foxy.

"How much do I owe you, Mr. Cranfield?" he asked.

"A great deal," said the sign-painter, shaking his head. "Oh, a great deal!"

Smiling, he set the parasol against a chair. His eyes were no longer bloodshot nor his cheeks pallid. His hair was neatly dressed. He wore the same red suit, and between the shoulder-blades it had been slit and mended with stitchings of gold thread.

"How much?" repeated Lord James.

Lucius Cranfield laughed.

"I do not believe that you are alive at all," sneered the other, rubbing his hands together. "How did you get away from the rats?"

"Do you hear the river?" whispered the sign-painter. "It is the same river."

Lord James came towards the table.

"I will pay you to-morrow for your work," and he pointed to the mended parasol.

"That is no debt of yours," answered Lucius Cranfield. "I did it for the lady of the house, Serena Thornton."

"She is my betrothed," said Lord James. "And I will pay you to-morrow—"

"No . . . to-night."

And the sign-painter smiled and stepped nearer.

"You lost the crystal fish," murmured Lord James, biting his forefinger and glancing round the dark, lonely room.

"But some one else has found it."

The other gave a snarl of rage.

"No! It is at the bottom of the river!"

At that Lucius Cranfield leant forward and seized his enemy by the throat. Lord James shrieked, and they swayed together for a moment. But the sign-painter twisted the other's head round on his shoulders and dropped him, a heap of gay clothes, on the waxed floor.

Then he began to sing, and turned to the open window.

The river was quiet now, flowing peacefully in between its banks, and Lucius Cranfield stepped out on to the terrace and walked towards its waters shining in the moonlight.

Almost before the last echo of his footsteps had died away in the silent room, Lady Serena Thornton entered, holding her dress up from her shoes.

Her gown was white, all wreathed across the hoop with ropes of seed-pearls, and laced across the bodice with diamonds. In her high headdress floated two soft plumes fastened with clusters of pale roses. Round her neck hung Lord James's gift of amethysts.

She stood in the doorway, her painted lips parted, her dark blue eyes fixed on the body of her betrothed husband.

Presently she went up and looked at him; then she sat down on the chair by the table—sat down, breathing heavily—with her right hand on the smooth satin of her bodice, and slow, strange changes passing over her face. She glanced at the purple parasol, resting across the chair where Lord James should have sat, and then out at the distant river, that showed white as her bridal-dress where the moonlight caught its ripples.

She heard the far-off singing of the sign-painter, and she sighed, closing her eyes.

The six candles burnt steadily, casting a rim of dark shadow round the table and the dead man on the floor, and glittering in the embroidered flowers on his gaudy coat and in the jewels of the woman at the table.

The black clock on the mantelshelf struck ten. The sound was echoed by the chimes from the village church.

Lady Serena Thornton rose and went upstairs, her wide hoop brushing the balustrade either side, her high heels tapping on the polished wood.

She entered her room and lit a little silver lamp on the dressing-table.

The chamber looked out upon the back; the window was open, and she could still see the river and hear Lucius Cranfield singing.

Slowly she took the feathers, ribbons, and flowers out of her curls, and laid them on the tulipwood table. Then she shook down her hair from its wire frame and brushed the powder out of it. She had almost forgotten what colour it was—in reality a ruby golden-brown, like the tint of wallflowers.

She unlaced her bodice and flung aside her jewels. She stepped out of her hoop and took off her satin shoes and stood a moment in her emerald-green petticoat, staring at herself in the gilt oval mirror.

Then she washed her face free of paint and powder in her gold basin, and tied up her locks with a red ribbon. She cast off her long earrings, her bracelets, her rings, the necklace Lord James had given her. This slipped, like a glitter of purple water, through her fingers, and shone in a little heap of stars on the gleaming waxed floor.

She arrayed herself in a brown dress, plain and straight, and took the two fish from their velvet bag to hang them round her neck.

Again she looked at herself. Who would have known her? Not Lord James himself, could he have risen from the floor in the solitary room below, and come up the wide stairs to gaze at her. Her face was utterly changed, her carriage different.

She blew out the lamp. A faint trail of smoke stained the moonlight that filled the room. She listened and heard the river and the sign-painter singing. On her bosom the fishes throbbed and glowed, opal-coloured and luminous.

Leaving the room lightly, softly she descended through the dark to the dining-room.

The six flower-wreathed candles still burnt steadily among the glass and silver. She glanced at Lord James sorrowfully, and picked up the mended parasol.

As she did so the bells broke out in a volume of glad sound—the villagers practising yet again for her wedding on the morrow.

Lady Serena Thornton smiled, and as Lucius Cranfield had done, and almost in his steps, went down the long room and through the open window on to the terrace. Slowly she walked towards the river, which she could see moving restlessly under the moonlight. The bells were very loud, but through them came the words of his song—

"The clouds were tangled in the trees—
    They broke the boughs and spoiled the fruit;
The sleeper knows what the sleeper sees—
    You play spades, and I follow suit!

The clouds came down in drops of rain,
    And woke the grass to blooms of fire;
The sleeper tore his dream in twain,
    And sought for the cards in the bitter mire!"

The bells ceased suddenly. Lady Serena saw the dark figure of the sign-painter, standing at the edge of the water, his back to her.

"If I have won, 'tis little matter;
    If I have lost, 'tis nought at all;
The wind will chill and the sun will flatter,
    And the damp earth fill the mouth of all."

There was a boat before him, rocking on the argent water, and as the lady came up the sign-painter stooped over it. Then he turned and saw her.

"Good even," said Lady Serena. He took her hands and kissed her face. The sound of the river was heavily in their ears.

"I found your fish," she whispered.

He nodded, and they entered the boat. It was lined with violet silk and scented with spices.

"The villagers will have practised for nothing," said Lady Serena.

Lucius Cranfield loosened the rope that held the boat fast to a willow, and it began to drift down the stream towards the town.

"We are going to a house where a tree with white flowers knocks for admittance on the shutters," he said.

"I know," she answered; "I know."

She sat opposite to him, leaning back, and the light night wind blew apart her brown robe here and there on the gleam of the bright green petticoat beneath. Her yellow hair floated behind her, and the crystal fishes rose and fell with her breathing. Across her knees lay the purple parasol.

They looked at each other and smiled with parted lips. The boat sped swiftly under a high bank, treeless and full under the rays of the moon. Here, by a round stone, sat two figures playing cards.

Lucius Cranfield glanced up. The players turned white, grinning faces down towards the boat. They were the one-eyed gipsy and Lord James.

"Good-night," nodded the sign-painter. "I do not believe you are alive at all. Why, I can almost see through you! . . ."

"Do you know me?" mocked Lady Serena.

And the boat was swept away along the winding river.

Lord James listened to the sign-painter's song that floated up from the dark water.

"If I win, 'tis little matter;
   If I lose, 'tis nought at all;
The wind will chill and the sun will flatter,
   And the red earth stop the mouths of all."

"They will never get there," grinned Lord James. "I shall go down to-morrow and see the empty boat upside down, tossing outside the shuttered house."

"There is no to-morrow for such as you," leered the gipsy. "You had your neck broken an hour ago . . . presently we will go home . . . your deal . . ."

Lord James sighed, and a great cloud suddenly overspread the moon.

The gipsy began to sing in a harsh voice, and his eyes turned red in his head as he shuffled the cards.

"If I win, 'tis little matter;
   If I lose, 'tis nought at all;
The wind will chill and the sun will flatter,
   And the damp earth stop the mouths of all."

Far away down the river the boat flashed for the last time in the moonlight, then was lost to sight under the shadow of the overhanging trees.

LOVE IN ANOTHER DIMENSION . . .
ORDAINED BY BIRTH . . . RULED BY THE STARS

House of Scorpio

The Extraordinary Gothic Novel By
PAT WALLACE

The reign of ordinary passions is at an end! Six
orphaned sisters separated at birth have only a mysterious golden scorpion to connect them. Born under
different astrological signs, each sister meets her
predestined, "fatally attractive" lover and must defy
the very stars to win happiness.

The sisters are reunited at last as their tangled lives
are slowly woven together in a thrilling tale of love
. . . in another time and another place.

AVON ◆ 25601 $1.95

Now an Avon paperback on sale everywhere, or order direct
from the publisher. Address Avon Books, Mail Order Department, 250 West 55th St., New York, N.Y. 10019. Include 25¢
per copy for mailing; allow three weeks for delivery.

HS 11-75

AVON ◆ NEW LEADER IN
WITCHCRAFT AND THE OCCULT

THE ETERNAL MAN
Louis Pauwells and Jacques Bergier   16725 $1.50

EVIDENCE OF SATAN IN THE MODERN WORLD
Leon Cristiani   25122   1.50

FIFTY YEARS A MEDIUM
Estelle Roberts   07286   .95

IMPOSSIBLE POSSIBILITIES
Louis Pauwells and Jacques Bergier   15255   1.25

MOONCHILD
Aleister Crowley   08557   1.25

MORNING OF THE MAGICIANS
Louis Pauwells and Jacques Bergier   15768   1.50

THE SATANIC BIBLE
Anton Szandor LaVey   15669   1.25

THE SATANIC RITUALS
Anton Szandor LaVey   10629   1.25
